THE Marriage PACT

LINDA LAEL MILLER

THE Marriage PACT

DOUBLEDAY LARGE PRINT HOME LIBRARY EDITION

⬥HARLEQUIN® HQN™

COLUSA COUNTY FREE LIBRARY

This Large Print Edition, prepared especially for Doubleday Large Print Home Library, contains the complete, unabridged text of the original Publisher's Edition.

ISBN 978-1-62953-008-6

THE MARRIAGE PACT

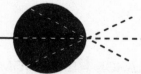

**This Large Print Book carries the
Seal of Approval of N.A.V.H.**

Dear Readers and Friends,

I'm excited to introduce you to an entirely new series of contemporary Western romances, The Brides of Bliss County.

Set in Wyoming in and around a small fictional town called Mustang Creek, the stories come directly from my heart.

The saga begins with **The Marriage Pact,** and the agreement between three close friends—Hadleigh, Melody and Becca (also known as Bex)—to work together to find a Mr. Right for themselves and each other. They're successful in their chosen careers, and that's fine with all of them, but they're also tired of being perennial bridesmaids; they want homes and families of their own, beginning with a husband—preferably perfect.

In **The Marriage Pact,** you'll read about cowboy/businessman Tripp Galloway, who has just sold a very successful charter-jet company and come home to the family ranch, along with his dog, Ridley, to help his widowed stepfather and maybe—just maybe—come to terms with his own past. Hadleigh Stevens, local quilt-shop owner and quilt designer, is a big part of that past, and not just because Tripp "rescued" her from marrying the wrong man a decade before—by carrying her bodily out of the church before the "I dos" could be said. Hadleigh's known her share of tragedy, losing both parents and then her beloved older brother, Will, who just happened to be Tripp's closest friend. He'd made a solemn promise to look after Will's kid sister, to step in and be her big brother.

Promises have consequences, though, don't they?

What happens when time and trouble have mellowed both Hadleigh and Tripp, and fate has brought them together again?

And what happens when Hadleigh decides to let go of her childhood crush on Tripp and get on with her life, just when Tripp is finally realizing she's all grown-up and he wants to be her partner, **not** her honorary big brother?

Read on, my friends…

With love,

For Buck and Goldie Taylor,
cherished friends and true Westerners,
with love.

PROLOGUE

**One Saturday in September,
Ten years ago...**

Both sides of the shady street were jammed with cars and trucks for what seemed like a mile in both directions, and time was running out—fast. So Tripp Galloway double-parked his stepdad's ancient truck alongside the bride and groom's waiting limo, shifted into Neutral, set the emergency brake and jumped out, leaving the engine running and the door gaping.

The limo driver, probably rented along with the car, was killing time on the sidewalk, cell phone pressed to one ear. **A clock-watcher,** Tripp decided distractedly. The chauffeur was obviously waiting for the shindig to end so he could collect his money and beat it. His jowly face was florid.

Seeing that Tripp meant to leave the rig unattended, the man broke off his ongoing conversation to protest, "Hey, buddy, you can't park there—"

Tripp went right past him without a word, through the open arbor-style gateway and up the flagstone walk.

The doors of Mustang Creek's small and venerable redbrick church, one of the oldest buildings in the county, were wide-open, despite the faint chill of the autumn afternoon, and the place was ominously quiet.

And that might—or might not—be a good sign.

Tripp didn't know all that much about wedding protocol, especially these days, when a lot of couples got hitched free-style, but if the thing was over—if he was too late to stop what amounted to a matrimonial train wreck—there would be rivers of triumphant organ music swelling out into that sunny afternoon. Wouldn't there?

On the other hand, the silence **could** mean that Hadleigh Stevens was just now saying, "I do." That the deed was done.

Tripp drew an anxious breath and hurried inside.

Three ushers occupied the tiny vestibule, watching the proceedings up by the altar and nervously adjusting their spiffy black bow ties. Hoping there wouldn't be a tussle, Tripp shouldered his way between them, bold as a brass bowling ball, and strode into the sanctuary.

Fortunately, no one tried to stop him.

This incident was bound to be hard enough on Hadleigh as it was, without a knock-down, drag-out brawl to ratchet up the drama a notch or two.

Not to mention, Tripp reflected grimly, that this was a church, not a cowboy bar.

He kept walking, only peripherally aware of the guests crowding the pews, packing the choir loft, lining the walls.

Clearly, this wedding was the main event of the season. Except in July, when the rodeo was on, there wasn't much to do in Mustang Creek, and it would have been plenty talked about, even without the impending interruption. Now, Tripp thought, the day would spawn legends.

Time slowed to a crawl, it seemed to him, as he moved steadily forward.

Hadleigh was up ahead, a vision in white, beautiful even facing in the other direction, her veil sparkling with tiny rhinestones, tumbling down her slender— and mostly bare—back, iridescent as a waterfall reflecting flashes of light. She and the bridegroom stood facing the minister, who spotted Tripp's approach before the happy couple did, of course. The old man raised his eyebrows, sighed heavily and closed the small book he'd been reading the ceremony from with a snap that echoed through the gathering like a bullet ricocheting off cold steel.

The guests, briefly dumbstruck, soon began to murmur among themselves.

Tripp prepared himself for a row but, once again, no one interfered.

Hadleigh, turning her head to follow the preacher's gaze, started when she saw Tripp, standing just a few feet away from her now, his boots splotched with the pink-and-white rose petals strewn along the aisle.

She didn't make a sound, not then at least, but even through the layers of chiffon comprising her veil, Tripp saw Hadleigh's luminous brown eyes widen in surprise. Over the course of the next few seconds, which passed with all the speed of a glacier carving out a new canyon, however, the bride's astonishment gave way to pure feminine fury.

She whirled, took a step toward him and nearly tripped on the hem of that over-the-top dress. This, of course, did nothing to improve her general outlook.

Always undaunted, a combat veteran and a man who flew commercial airliners for a living, Tripp realized his heart was hammering, and he felt heat climb up his neck, pulse behind his ears.

Say something, commanded a voice in his head—the voice of his dead best friend, Hadleigh's older brother, Will.

Tripp cleared his throat and asked benevolently, "Did I miss the part where the preacher asks if anybody here can give just cause why these two should not be joined together in holy matrimony?"

More gasps sounded behind him, followed by a lot of whispering and a few nervous chuckles, but, for the time being, these were the least of his concerns.

He merely looked straight at the preacher and waited for an answer to his question.

Hadleigh's face went apricot-pink behind that veil; her mouth opened and then closed again. It was as if her vocal chords had been tied up in a knot.

The reverend, a balding, rotund man named John Deever, who raised hogs when he wasn't preaching the Gospel, conducting weddings or teaching shop at Mustang Creek High School nine months out of the year, had been known to wear bib overalls under his stately ministerial robes during busy times so he could get right back to his farmwork without having to change his clothes.

"This," Deever announced, ponderous as a judge, "is highly irregular."

Tripp could have sworn he saw a brief

twinkle dance in the man's eyes, for all his outward show of disapproval.

Oakley Smyth, the bridegroom, finally turned around, looking faintly shocked to find himself where he was, in a church, surrounded by people, confronted with opposition. He resembled a man who'd been cruelly jolted out of a sound sleep —or a coma. As he registered Tripp's presence and what it meant, Oakley's eyes narrowed and a flush appeared on his smooth-shaven face.

"What the—" he muttered, then bit back the rest of whatever he'd been about to say.

"Because," Tripp went on, in that forceful way people use when they intend to override any argument, operating on the theory that they might all be standing there glowering at each other for the rest of the day if he didn't get things rolling, "it just so happens that I know a reason, and it's a damned good one."

Hadleigh, clenching her bridal bouquet in white-knuckled hands, closed the short distance between Tripp and herself in a few purposeful steps, cheeks glowing like neon, eyes flashing whiskey-colored outrage. **"What,"** she demanded, looking as though she'd gladly have swapped that delicate cluster of pink-and-white flowers for a loaded pistol, "do you think you're **doing,** Tripp Galloway?"

"I'm stopping this wedding," Tripp said, deciding Hadleigh's question must have been rhetorical, since the answer was so obvious.

A short silence throbbed between them.

"Why?" Hadleigh whispered, ending that silence, sounding stricken now as well as furious. At eighteen, she was a budding beauty, but not yet a full-grown woman, not in Tripp's estimation, anyway. No, she was still his late best friend's kid sister, the one he'd promised to protect, still too young and naive to know what was good for her, let alone guess that she'd been dancing on the razor's edge.

Instead of offering a reply, Tripp locked eyes with Smyth and asked, quietly and evenly, "Shall I tell Hadleigh why she shouldn't marry you, Oakley, or would you rather do that yourself?"

The groom hadn't moved, except for a few reflexive twitches here and there, but the look in his eyes would have scorched two layers of olive-drab paint off an army jeep.

In Oakley's place, Tripp reckoned, he would've done more than just glare—he'd have decked any man with the gall to barge in at the last possible second and wreck his wedding. Oh, yeah. He'd have thrown a punch, all right, church or no church.

An ironic insight for sure, considering what he was there to do, but, damn it all, it was the **principle** of the thing.

Oakley gulped visibly and shook his head once, very slowly.

The best man, standing at Oakley's right side, studied the ceiling as though he'd developed a sudden fascination with the rough-hewn rafters.

None of the ushers stepped in, nor did any of the guests, for that matter.

It was as if the entire group was standing on the outside of some giant impenetrable bubble, looking in at Hadleigh and the bridegroom and Tripp as if they were figures in a snow globe.

Hadleigh was still glaring at him, still trembling with the effort of subduing her anger, but tears stood in her eyes, too, and her full lower lip wobbled.

Don't cry, Tripp pleaded silently. **Anything but that.**

She was hurt and confused, and when Hadleigh was in pain, he was, too. It was a law of the universe.

"How could you?" she whispered, and the misery in her voice cracked open Tripp Galloway's heart like the shell on a walnut.

Tripp had intended to explain, but later, someplace quiet, without half of Bliss County there watching, so he just put out one hand and waited for Hadleigh to take it, the way she'd done so many times as a kid, when she was scared or uncertain and Will was elsewhere or too distracted to notice.

Instead of accepting Tripp's help, though, Hadleigh raised the bouquet, gripping it with both fists, and whacked him hard across the knuckles. The blow stung as if she'd wielded a bullwhip instead of a bunch of fragile flowers, rendering a low and somewhat affronted "Owww!" from Tripp.

"I'm not going anywhere with you," Hadleigh informed him once she'd calmed down a little, breathing hard, squaring her slender shoulders and jutting out her chin. "I came here to get married, and that's **exactly** what I'm going to do, because I love Oakley and he loves me, so I'll thank you to **get out of this church** before God goes all Old Testament and sights in on you with a lightning bolt!"

Tripp sighed, shaking his still-smarting hand in an attempt to restore the circulation. Clearly, everybody in the place— with the notable exception of the bride— understood that the party was over.

There wasn't going to be any wedding, not today, anyhow.

No reception, no tiered cake, no honeymoon.

Tripp tried to reason with Hadleigh, an admittedly ambitious endeavor under the circumstances, given that he was dead certain all she really wanted to do was kill him where he stood.

"Hadleigh," he began, "if you'll just—"

She took another swing at him with the bouquet, this time going for his face, putting so much energy behind it that she nearly threw herself off-balance and took a header. Tripp dodged the blow, hoisted her off the floor and slung her over his right shoulder, fireman-style.

"Well, **damn** if you aren't as contrary as you ever were," Tripp muttered. She was heavier than she looked, too, although pointing that out would definitely be a tactical error. Besides, he was swamped, all of a sudden, by great billows of silky white fabric and rhinestone-studded lace, so that he could barely see or even breathe.

And Hadleigh, a Wyoming cowgirl born and bred, struggled wildly all the while, yelling and banging away at Tripp's back with what remained of the bridal bouquet as he carried her down the aisle, treading on the bruised rose petals, striding past all the guests without looking to the left or right, on through the vestibule and then outside, into the crisp sunshine.

Still, nobody said a word, let alone made a move to intercede, even with Hadleigh ranting and raving that she was being **abducted,** damn it, and this was **wrong.** It was a **crime,** and she needed **help.** Why didn't somebody **do** something?

Tripp's strides were long as he headed toward the waiting truck, its oft-rebuilt engine chortling loudly, the dented, primer-spotted chassis fairly vibrating with the need for speed. The limo driver was still standing on the sidewalk, chain-smoking and blabbing into his cell phone, but when Tripp emerged from the redbrick church, lugging a squirming, squealing bride, he shut up and gaped.

By then, the bouquet must have finally fallen apart, because Hadleigh was slugging away at Tripp with her fists, evidently out to pound one or both of his kidneys into a bloody pulp.

Reaching the truck, at long last, Tripp allowed himself a sigh of relief and wrestled Hadleigh and her bride getup until he could yank open the passenger-side door and thrust her into the cab, then stuff the voluminous skirts of her wedding dress in after her and shut the door hard. He figured she'd try to make a break for it, but by the time she'd managed to burrow through all that frothy lace to get hold of the door handle, Tripp was in the driver's seat and they were rolling.

It seemed a safe enough bet that Hadleigh was half-again too smart to jump from a moving vehicle—though her taste in men, Tripp had to concede, belied her famously high IQ—and he took a firm grip on her left arm just in case he was giving her too much credit for brainpower.

She settled down a bit, although she was still generating enough steam to run an old-time locomotive up a steep incline.

"I can't **believe** you just did that!" she finally sputtered when he let go of her. By then, they were doing forty, so she wasn't likely to make a leap, but there was another problem. That damn wedding dress of hers practically filled the whole inside of the truck, creating a variety of hazards. Tripp was reminded of the time he and Will, young enough then that they were still waiting for their permanent front teeth to grow in, somehow got hold of a box of powdered laundry soap and dumped it in the big fountain in front of the courthouse over in Bliss River. In two shakes, the suds had been over their heads.

"Believe it," Tripp said flatly.

Hadleigh shoved the veil back, revealing a splotchy, mascara-streaked face and fiery eyes as she did her best to glare a scorching hole in Tripp's hide. One of her stick-on eyelashes had come loose, clinging to the middle of her eyelid like a bug to a windshield—and he laughed.

A mistake, of course—not that he could have kept a straight face if his life depended on it. He'd already pushed his luck about as far as it was likely to go, by his reckoning. Laughing at a woman this pissed off was downright foolhardy, but there it was.

If Will was looking on from heaven, or wherever good men wound up for the duration, Tripp hoped he was satisfied.

Waltzing with a mama bear would have been easier—and safer—than rescuing Hadleigh from a lifetime spent hog-tied to the likes of Oakley Smyth.

The air inside that truck was all but electrified. "You think this is **funny?**" Hadleigh snapped, folding her arms, which took some doing, with all that dress getting in her way.

Tripp choked back one last chortle. "Yeah," he admitted. "I do think it's funny. And I'm betting that someday, you'll think so, too."

"I could have you arrested!"

"Go ahead," Tripp said blithely. "Get Spence Hogan to toss me in the hoosegow. 'Course, I'll be out before you can say 'poker buddy.'" He paused, frowned thoughtfully. "But now that you mention it, I **would** like to ask my old pal Spence why you weren't taken into protective custody and held until you came to your senses and broke it off with Smyth." Another pause, a shake of his head. **"Smyth,"** he repeated disdainfully. "Just how pretentious does somebody have to be to spell an otherwise ordinary name with a **y?**"

"You think you know Oakley," Hadleigh protested hotly, "but you **don't.**"

"No," Tripp argued mildly, "**you** don't."

"We're in love! Or, at least, we **were** until **you** butted in! How am I supposed to **face** people after this, Tripp? What about all the planning and the money Gram and I spent on this dress, plus the flowers and the cake and the bridesmaids' gowns for Bex and Melody? On top of all that, there's a **mountain** of presents in our dining room, all of which will have to be returned—"

She fell silent, and Tripp let things quiet down for a few minutes before he said, "You're in love with love, Hadleigh. That's all. And, oh yeah, has it occurred to you yet that a man who loves a woman—**really** loves her—would at least speak up, if not fight to keep her from being hauled out of church on their wedding day?"

That reasoning deflated Hadleigh a little, and Tripp felt a stab of regret. **The truth hurts.** No wonder that saying had been around long enough to turn trite.

"Oakley's a gentleman," she finally replied, with a disdainful sniff. "Not a rough-and-tumble **cowboy** who thinks he can settle anything with his fists!"

"You have something against cowboys?" Tripp drawled the question.

Her cheeks flared again. "Shut up, Tripp. Just **shut up.**"

Discretion had never been one of Tripp's great strengths. "And while we're at it, why in hell would you glue fake lashes on your eyelids like that?" he asked, with matter-of-fact ease and genuine curiosity. "There's nothing wrong with the eyelashes you were born with, far as I can tell."

Hadleigh gave a strangled squeal of frustration. "Are you through?" she inquired acidly.

So much for reasonable adult conversation.

Normally, Tripp would have insisted that Hadleigh put on her seat belt, since he'd just noticed she wasn't wearing one, but he was pretty sure she wouldn't be able to **find** it in that burgeoning cloud of virginal white lace.

Virginal.

Was Hadleigh still innocent? Or had Oakley Smyth—or some other smarmball yahoo—sweet-talked her into his bed?

The thought galled Tripp through and through, even though Hadleigh's sex life was purely none of his damn business. Granted, eighteen was young, but it wasn't that young. Lots of women her age were twisting the sheets with some guy, whether they were married to him or not.

Tripp decided not to pursue that train of thought, aloud **or** in the privacy of his own mind, since it would be the equivalent of lighting a match to a fuse.

He'd concentrate on his driving instead.

So they cruised along the quiet main street of Mustang Creek, past the post office and the grocery store and the old movie house, the latter having been boarded up two or three recessions back, in incendiary silence.

Gradually, Tripp relaxed a bit, smiled to himself, remembering days of old, when Hadleigh was a gawky preteen, all scraped knees and bony elbows and piano-key teeth, freckle-faced and wide-eyed, full of questions, tagging along after him and Will and some of their other friends whenever they allowed it. She'd changed a lot since then, of course, but she still had a way to go before she had any business getting herself tied down to one man for the rest of her life.

What about college, damn it? Hadleigh was smart as hell; her SAT scores were off the charts, and she'd been offered full-ride scholarships to some of the best schools in the country. Besides, didn't she want to see at least **some** of the world beyond Wyoming, Montana and Colorado? Try a few different jobs on for size, figure out what she really wanted or simply have a place of her own for a while?

A horrible thought struck Tripp then, a reason she might have been in a hurry to land a husband and, like a damn fool, he blurted it right out instead of keeping it to himself like he should have. "Hadleigh—are you pregnant?"

She stiffened as if he'd slapped her, frozen in the process of ripping off her faux eyelashes. "Of **course** not," she said. "Oakley and I do—**did**—plan on having children, but not right away." Once again, her eyes swam with tears of indignation.

No wonder she was ticked off and disappointed. After all, this should have been the best day of her life so far—and maybe it was, but at the moment, it had to feel like one of the **worst.** Tripp was half-sick with relief at her answer, but he had regrouped enough to hide any further reaction to the possibility that Hadleigh, normally sweet, sensitive and predominantly reasonable Hadleigh, might have been carrying another man's child.

Especially when that man was likely to break her heart before the honeymoon was even over.

And Hadleigh was unique. The kind of woman who ought to be loved full-out, even cherished, and certainly protected, along with any baby she might have.

"If Oakley loves you," he said, in a gentle rasp, "he'll stick around. He'll **wait,** Hadleigh, until you're ready to be a wife."

Hadleigh looked away, and Tripp saw

that she was crying again and didn't want him to know it. Something clenched the pit of his stomach.

"Tell. Me. Why." She said each word distinctly and very slowly.

Tripp hadn't thought much further than getting Hadleigh out of that church before she became Oakley Smyth's property and thereby wrecked her life, but now that it was all over but the shoutin', he began to consider his options.

Such as they were.

He couldn't take Hadleigh home to the little house she shared with her grand-mother, not yet, anyway, because Alice Stevens was most likely still back at the redbrick church, trying to make the best of a tough situation and maybe put a lid on the inevitable gossip.

God knew, there would be plenty of juicy talk as things stood, and Tripp wasn't inclined to compound the problem by spending time alone with Hadleigh behind closed doors, not even for the few minutes it would take Alice to get home from the church.

Folks might assume that if he'd gone to such lengths to stop Hadleigh from marrying somebody else, especially in such a high-profile way, and then taken her somewhere private, he could be doing more than just drying her tears.

They had to have a difficult conversation, he and Hadleigh, and soon, but any old place wasn't going to do. His stepdad's ranch wouldn't fit the bill, either, since it was several miles out of town and chances were that Jim wouldn't be hanging around home at this hour, anyway. While there was daylight, a thing Jim viewed as a valuable commodity and spent carefully, like his money, he'd be out on the range somewhere, mending rusted fences or rounding up the few scrawny cattle that had survived the previous winter.

"You," Hadleigh seethed, "are **not** going to blow this off, Tripp Galloway. You're not going to act as if nothing happened, because you just nuked the wedding of my dreams and I'm not about to forgive **or** forget!"

Tripp didn't take Hadleigh's threat as an

empty one, and a forlorn feeling settled over him. If this was the price he had to pay for doing what he flat-out knew was right, fine, but that didn't mean it was going to be easy.

Then he spotted Bad Billy's Burger Palace and Drive-Thru up ahead, and decided it would have to do as the site of further discussion. With luck, only the staff and a few tourists would be around— no curious mob. And the locals could state unequivocally, ever afterward, that there hadn't been any monkey-business going on between Tripp and the bride he'd stolen right out from under Oakley Smyth's aristocratic nose. Like as not, everybody else with even a remote interest in the recent spectacle was still back at the scene of the crime, a conglomerate of busybodies clucking their tongues and asking each other what this world was coming to, acting as if they hadn't enjoyed the whole circus from start to finish.

"I hear you," Tripp said wearily, in his own good time, signaling for the turn. Come to think of it, he **was** a little hungry, since he hadn't had a chance to grab either breakfast or lunch before fighting his way along California's notorious 405 freeway to the hangar where he kept his thirdhand Cessna and scrambling for Wyoming like a one-man bombing raid. Alas, as it turned out, air traffic over L.A. had been almost as bad as the bottlenecks on the highway below.

By the time he'd finally landed at the airstrip outside Bliss River, thirty-five miles from Mustang Creek, Tripp was beginning to question his own sanity.

Jim's rattletrap of a truck was waiting, per Tripp's harried request by phone, with a full gas tank, keys in the ignition and a note scrawled on the back of a page from an old feed store calendar—April 1994, to be precise.

Couldn't hang around to wait for you, Jim had written in his curiously elegant handwriting. **Got a couple of sick calves on the place, so I had Charlie—he's the new hired man—follow me over here to drop off the rig and give me a lift straight back home. See you later**

at the ranch. P.S. Be sure to break the news to Hadleigh real gentle, now. She's going to be mighty hurt and mad as a wildcat with all four paws caught in a vat of molasses.

With that sage advice running through his mind, Tripp had raced over twisting highways and dirt-road shortcuts with his foot practically jammed into the carburetor of that old truck, desperate to get to the church before the preacher made it official with the customary words.

I now pronounce you husband and wife.

They were well past the danger point, but, in spite of that, Tripp shuddered at the thought of Hadleigh as Mrs. Oakley Smyth.

The marriage could have been annulled, of course, but only if the wedding night didn't happen first. Even then, Hadleigh would have needed some serious convincing, and there'd still be a lot of legal wrangling once she'd seen the light. In the interim, Oakley might just be able to charm her down the aisle all over again.

Squinting through the dust-coated windshield, Hadleigh blinked, her expression one of baffled disbelief. "Bad Billy's?" she asked, as Tripp swung the truck into the lot. "What are we doing here?"

"I'm starved," Tripp replied affably, gliding into a parking spot near the entrance. The lot was nearly empty, a good sign. "And I believe you wanted a few answers?"

"I am wearing a wedding dress," Hadleigh pointed out, pushing the words out between her perfect white teeth. Not so long ago, Tripp mused nostalgically, she'd been a "metal-mouth," as Will used to put it, reluctant to smile, lisping through so much steel grillwork that she could have moonlighted as a blade on a snow plow.

"So I noticed." Tripp shut off the engine, setting the brake.

"Can't you just take me home?" Hadleigh's voice was small now; her batteries were running down. A temporary condition, for his money. In another minute, unless Tripp missed his guess, she'd be trying to claw his eyeballs out of their sockets.

"Think of your reputation," he counseled benevolently. "How would it look if we were alone at your place after what happened? What would people say?"

"As if you cared what anybody says," Hadleigh said, rolling her eyes as she spoke. "Anyway, I'm trying **not** to think of my reputation," she lamented. "Since it's been thoroughly trashed."

Tripp grinned, got out of the truck, came around to Hadleigh's side and opened the door while she was still searching, he supposed, for the lock button, probably planning to shut him out. In her state of mind, it might not occur to her that he could use his key to get in.

"Do you want to walk," he asked her with exaggerated politeness and a slight bow, "or shall I carry you?"

Hadleigh sort of spilled out of the cab and onto the running board, in a shifting, glimmering cloud of fuss and fabric, and stepped awkwardly to the ground, refusing to let Tripp assist her in any way. The glittering hem of her resplendent gown dragged in the unraked gravel surrounding Bad Billy's place, swishing among cigarette butts and discarded gum wrappers and drinking straws squashed flat.

"Don't you dare **touch** me," she commanded loftily, every part of her bristling visibly. That said, Hadleigh swept regally past Tripp, like a queen about to make a grand entrance at court—or go to the guillotine with the dignity of the righteously innocent. Her veil dangled down her back, caught precariously on one of the hairpins threatening to slip and send her glorious brown hair tumbling from its once-graceful chignon.

"I wouldn't think of it," Tripp said with another grin. "Touch you, I mean."

He quickened his pace to get ahead of Hadleigh, who was covering a lot of ground with every stride, opened the heavy glass door and held it until she glided through.

Hadleigh gave him a poisonous look over one shoulder, then walked straight past the please-wait-to-be-seated sign with her shoulders back and her head held high.

As Tripp had hoped, there were only a few waitresses and carhops on the scene, along with the fry cook and some guy plunked on a stool at the far end of the counter with a cup of coffee and a slice of cherry pie in front of him.

Tripp's stomach rumbled.

Hadleigh, meanwhile, proceeded majestically toward the nearest booth and slid onto the vinyl seat, making a comical effort to contain her surging skirts and whatever was underneath them as she did so. Her face was pale now, a mask of quiet decorum, and Tripp felt yet another pang of sympathy for her. Or was it regret?

A little of both, probably.

He took the seat opposite hers.

A waitress—her name tag read Ginny—sashayed over to their table, wide-eyed. Folks might wear a getup like Hadleigh's in greasy spoons out in L.A., or down in Vegas, but it just didn't happen in Mustang Creek, Wyoming.

Not until today, anyhow.

"What'll it be?" the fiftyish woman asked, as calmly as if she served food to women in full bridal regalia every day of the week. "The special's a meatloaf sandwich, salad on the side, your choice of dressing."

Half expecting Hadleigh to announce that she'd been kidnapped and demand that the police be called immediately, Tripp was a touch surprised when, instead, she said decisively, "I'll have a cheeseburger, medium rare, and a chocolate shake, please. With whipped cream."

"I'll try the special," Tripp said, somewhat hoarsely, when it was his turn to order up some grub. "Blue cheese dressing on the salad."

Ginny—she didn't look familiar, but then he'd been away from Mustang Creek for a long time—made careful notes on her order pad and hurried away.

"I haven't had a milk shake in six weeks," Hadleigh confided, rather defensively, Tripp thought, as though she'd expected him to criticize her choice. "There's no room inside this blasted dress for a single extra **ounce,** even after months of exercising like a crazy woman and living on lettuce leaves and water."

Tripp stifled a grin. "I reckon you can afford to take a chance," he said. She looked fine to him, better than fine, actually, given the way that dress hugged her curves with sinful perfection.

She made a face at him. "Thanks so much," she answered, her tone as sour as her expression.

He chuckled. "Well, now, why not look on the bright side? Since the wedding's off, you can pig out all you want." He paused. "Long as you don't bust a seam before you get home, it's all good."

She narrowed her expressive gold-flecked eyes. Even with her face in need of scrubbing, she was beautiful, in an unformed kind of way.

"You do realize," she purred tartly, "that my **entire** life is completely ruined, and it's all your fault?"

"You're eighteen, Hadleigh," Tripp reminded her. "Your 'entire life' hasn't actually started yet."

"That's what **you** think," she retorted.

"Besides, I'm mature for my age."

"The hell you are," Tripp countered.

"In your opinion, maybe," she said. "Anyway, in case you've forgotten, it's perfectly legal for a woman to get married at eighteen." A pause, coupled with a scowl, and even that looked good on her. "And if Gram doesn't object, why should you?"

He leaned in a little. "Your grandmother probably **does** object—she's just not strong enough to carry you bodily out of the church. And don't try to tell me she didn't talk herself blue in the face trying to convince you to wait awhile before you got hitched, sweetie pie, because I know Alice Stevens too well to believe that for a nanosecond. You were too hardheaded to listen to her, that's all."

Hadleigh blushed again, averting her eyes—obviously, Alice **had** disapproved of the match—then sliced her gaze straight back to Tripp's face, sharp enough to draw blood. "Was it Gram? I mean, did she ask you to come back here and...and do what you did?"

"No," he said. "I follow the local news

online. That's how I found out you were getting married. Your grandmother had nothing to do with it."

Hadleigh ruminated for a few minutes, then colored again and said accusingly, "You never liked Oakley. Neither did my brother. And I can't imagine why, because he's really very sweet."

It was true that neither Tripp nor Will had wanted to hang around with Oakley, who had been in their class all through school and was therefore a full seven years older than Hadleigh, but it was also beside the point.

This wasn't about his low opinion of Oakley, who had been a slimeball and an all-around sneaky, bullying son of a bitch from kindergarten right on through senior year. It was about a promise Tripp had made to Will, several years ago, as his friend lay dying in a field hospital in Afghanistan. Most of all, it was about the thorough background check Tripp had commissioned, even after knowing Smyth for most of his life, on a hunch that there was more to the story.

And sure as hell, there was.

So here he was, back in the old hometown, sitting across a burger-joint table from the bride he'd kidnapped less than thirty minutes before.

Their food arrived, and the waitress scuttled away again, after giving them both a quick and searching once-over, but Hadleigh didn't touch her burger, and Tripp left his meatloaf sandwich on his plate.

Quietly, he told Hadleigh about the pole dancer up in Laramie, a woman named Callie Barstow, and how Oakley had been living with her, off and on, for over five years—right up to last weekend, actually. Furthermore, they had kids, a four-year-old boy and a girl of six months, although the children went by Callie's last name, not Oakley's, and the Smyth clan either didn't know they existed or figured on ignoring them until they went away.

According to the detective's report, Callie was beginning to chafe under all the secrecy; she wanted some respect, a significant degree of financial assistance and for her children to be acknowledged as rightful heirs to the Smyth fortune. Oakley had evidently balked, not only at marriage, but at making the introductions to Mom and Dad, as well. The upshot was that Callie had been complaining to friends and coworkers for nearly a year that she was fed up with the whole situation. If Oakley wouldn't tell his parents about their grandchildren, **she** would.

Oakley, who wanted to forestall this embarrassing confrontation, and yet knowing he wouldn't be able to prevent it indefinitely, had made a big production of breaking things off with Callie. He'd continued to support his children—a point in his favor, Tripp had to admit, however grudgingly—and then gone after Hadleigh in earnest. Evidently, he'd hoped to take the sting out of Callie's inevitable revelation by beating her to the proverbial punch, marrying a woman the folks would find socially acceptable.

Though poor in comparison to the Smyths, the Stevens family was practically part of the landscape, they'd been around so long, and the name was an honored one in this part of the state and else-where. Hadleigh and Will's ancestors had been among the first pioneers to settle in the area, back in the 1850s, well before the rush of land-hungry immigrants that followed the Civil War. In places like Mustang Creek, that kind of longevity mattered.

All of this might have been okay—everybody had a past, after all—but for the fact that Oakley was still sleeping with Callie on a regular basis.

Watching Hadleigh absorb it all was harder than anything Tripp had ever had to endure, except for the all-time lows of losing his mother and then, just a few years later, keeping a hopeless vigil beside his best friend's deathbed in a strange and unwelcoming place incom-prehensibly far from home.

Some people, a **lot** of people, would have demanded proof, pictures, docu-mentation, some kind of evidence that everything Tripp was telling her was true, but Hadleigh simply listened, believing, her illusions crumbling visibly, lying fractured in her brown eyes.

The worst was yet to come, though, because Hadleigh asked Tripp to take her back to L.A. with him when he left town, and he had to give her an answer he knew would hurt almost as much as the broken fairy tale.

"I can't do that, Hadleigh," he said evenly. "My wife wouldn't understand."

CHAPTER ONE

Present-day Mustang Creek, Wyoming
Mid-September

"Well, dog," Tripp Galloway said, addressing his sidekick, a cross-eyed black Lab he'd bought as a pup out of the back of a beat-up pickup alongside a Seattle highway the year before, "we're almost home."

Ridley glanced over at him and yawned expansively.

Tripp sighed. "Truth is, I'm not all that excited about it, either," he confided.

Ridley gave a sympathetic whimper, then turned away to press his muzzle against the well-smudged passenger-side window—his way of saying he'd like to stick his head out, if it was all the same to Tripp, and let his ears flap in the wind like a pair of furry flags.

Tripp chuckled and hit the button on his armrest to open Ridley's window half-way, and the inevitable roar filled the extended cab of the truck. The dog was in hog heaven, while his master wondered, not for the first time, how the hell the critter could breathe with all that air coming at him.

Tripp sighed again. Another of life's little mysteries, he thought.

He could see the ragged outskirts of Mustang Creek just ahead—a convenience store/gas station here and there, a few lone trailers rusting in weedy lots, their best days far behind them, and more storage units than any community ought to need, especially one the size of his hometown.

It was a sign of the times, Tripp supposed, a mite glumly, that people had so damn much **stuff** that their houses and garages were overflowing. Instead of taking a good long look at themselves and figuring out what kind of interior hole they were trying to fill, they bought **more** stuff and rented a place to stash the excess. At this rate, the whole planet would be clogged with boxes and bins full of forgotten belongings in no time at all.

He shook his head, resigned. He was a wealthy man, but he believed in owning **one** of most things, from watches and pairs of boots to houses and cars. He did make certain exceptions, of course—dogs, horses and cattle, to name a few, but, then, of course, animals weren't **things.**

Tripp shifted his attention back to coming home. He'd been there inter-mittently, over the years, returning for the odd Thanksgiving or Christmas holiday, the usual funerals and weddings—one of them particularly memorable—and a class reunion or two at the high school. It had been a long time, though, since he'd been a resident.

In the off-season, Mustang Creek was a sleepy little burg nestled in a wide valley, with mountains towering on all sides, but in the summer, when folks came through in campers and minivans on family vaca-tions, taking in the Grand Tetons as they made their way either to or from Yellowstone, things livened up considerably. The second big season, of course, was winter, when visitors from all over the world came to ski, enjoy some of the most magnificent scenery to be found anywhere and, to the irritated relief of the locals, spend plenty of money.

As it happened, he and Ridley were arriving during the brief lull between the sizable influxes of outsiders, that being September, October and part of November, and Tripp was looking forward to living quietly on his stepdad's ranch for a while, doing **real** work of the hard physical variety. After several years spent running his small but profitable charter-jet service out of Seattle—ironically, he'd put in most of his hours behind a desk instead of in the cockpit, where he would have preferred to be—Tripp hankered for the sweat-soaked, sore-muscle satisfaction that came with putting in a long day on the range.

He'd made some heavy-duty changes in his life, most of them recent, selling his company and all six jets, leasing out his penthouse condo with its breathtaking view of Elliott Bay and points beyond, including the snow-covered Olympic mountain range.

He didn't miss the city traffic, the honking horns and other noise, or jostling through crowds everywhere he went.

Oh, yeah. Tripp Galloway was ready for a little un-urban renewal.

More than ready.

There were some things in his past he needed to come to terms with, now that he'd shifted gears and left his fast-track life, with its pie-charts and spreadsheets, three-piece suits and meetings, not to mention the constant barrage of texts, emails and telephone calls and the decisions that had to be made

Now. Or better yet, yesterday.

Out here, in the open country, he wouldn't be able to dodge the stuff that prodded at the underside of his conscious mind 24/7. Losing his mom when he was just sixteen, for instance. Sitting by helplessly while his best friend died, thousands of miles from home. And then there was his short-term marriage, over for some eight years now—he and Danielle were better off without each other, no doubt about it, but the divorce had hurt, and hurt badly, just the same.

He'd dated a lot of women since then, but he'd always been careful not to get too involved. Once the lady in question started bringing up topics like kids and houses—and leaving bridal magazines around, with pages showing spectacular wedding gowns or knock-out engagement rings—he was out of there, and quick. It wasn't that Tripp didn't **want** a home and family. He did.

He'd been led to believe that Danielle did, too.

Wrong.

When they'd finally called it quits over that disagreement and numerous others, it wasn't Danielle's departure that grieved him for months, even years, afterward, it was the death of the dream. The failure.

Tripp banished his dejection—no sense getting sucked into the past if he could avoid it—just as he and the dog rolled on, into the heart of town. By then, Ridley had pulled his head back inside the truck and was checking out their surroundings, tongue lolling.

Mustang Creek proper was something to see, all right. The main street was outfitted to look like an Old West town, with wooden facades on all the buildings, board sidewalks and hitching posts and even horse troughs in front of a few of the businesses. While a number of the local establishments had saloonlike names—the Rusty Bucket, the Diamond Spur and so on—there was only one genuine bar among the lot of them, the Moose Jaw Tavern. The Bucket housed an insurance agency, and the Spur was a dentist's office.

Tripp supposed the whole setup was pretty tacky, but the fact was, he sort of liked it. Sometimes, at odd moments, it gave him the uncharacteristically fanciful feeling that he'd slipped through a time warp and ended up in the 1800s, where life was simpler, if less convenient.

Once they'd left the main street behind, the town began to look a little more modern, if the 1950s could be called modern. Here, there were tidy shingled houses with painted porches and picket-fenced yards bursting with the last and heartiest flowers of summer. The sidewalks were buckled in places, mostly by tree roots, and dogs wandered loose, clean and well fed, safe because they belonged, because everybody knew them by name and finding their way home was easy.

Ridley made a whining sound, probably born of envy, as they passed yet another meandering canine.

Tripp chuckled and reached over to pat the Lab's glossy ruff. "Easy, now," he said. "Once we get to the ranch, you'll have more freedom than you'll know what to do with."

Ridley rested his muzzle on the dashboard, rolled his eyes balefully in Tripp's direction and sighed heavily, as if to say, **Promises, promises.**

And then, just like that, there it was, the redbrick church, as unchanged as the rest of the town. Looking at the place, remembering how he'd crashed Hadleigh Stevens's wedding, called a halt to the proceedings and then carried her out of there like a sack of grain made his stomach twitch.

It wasn't that Tripp regretted what he'd done; time had proven him right. That pecker-head she'd been about to marry, Oakley Smyth, was on his third divorce at last report, due to a persistent gambling habit and an aversion to monogamy. Moreover, his trust fund had seized up like a tractor left out in the weather to rust, courtesy of a clause in his parents' wills that allowed for any adjustments the executrix might deem advisable, pinching the cash flow from a torrent to a trickle.

These days, evidently, it sucked to be Oakley.

And that was fine with Tripp. What **wasn't** fine, then or now, was seeing Hadleigh hurt so badly, knowing he'd per-sonally broken her heart, however good his intentions might have been. Knowing she'd never found what she really wanted, what she'd wanted from the time she was a little girl: a home and family, the traditional kind comprising a husband, a wife, 2.5 children and some pets.

A light, dust-settling drizzle began just then, reflecting his mood—the weather could change quickly in Wyoming—as they were passing the town limits, only ten miles or so from the ranch, and Tripp eased his foot down on the gas pedal, eager to get there.

As the rig picked up speed, Ridley let it be known that he'd appreciate another opportunity to stick his head out into the wind, rain or no rain.

Rain.

Well, Hadleigh Stevens thought philosophically, the farmers and ranchers would certainly appreciate it, even if she didn't.

Such weather made some people feel downright cozy; they'd brew some tea and light a cheery blaze in the fireplace and swap out their shoes for comfortable slippers. But it always saddened Hadleigh a little when the sky clouded over and the storm began, be it drizzle or downpour.

It had been raining that long-ago afternoon when her grandmother had shown up at school, her face creased with grief, to collect Hadleigh, saying not a word. They'd gone on, in Gram's old station wagon, to pick up Will. He was waiting out in front of the junior high building, pale and seemingly heedless of the downpour. Being seven years older than Hadleigh, he'd known what she hadn't—that both their parents had died in a car crash just hours before, outside Laramie.

It rained the day of their mom and dad's joint funeral and again a few years later, when Hadleigh and her grandmother got word that Will had died as a result of wounds received during a roadside bombing in Afghanistan.

And when Gram had passed away, after a long illness, the skies had been gray and umbrellas had sprouted everywhere, like colorful mushrooms.

Today, Hadleigh had tried to shake off the mood by her usual method—keeping busy.

She'd closed Patches, the quilting shop she'd inherited from her grandmother, at noon; her two closest friends were coming over that evening, on serious business. The modest house was neat and tidy. She'd vacuumed and dusted and polished for an hour after lunch, but there was still plenty to do, like have a shower, do something with her hair and bake a cake for dessert.

She was taking one last narrow-eyed look around the living room, making sure everything was as it should be, when she heard the familiar whimper outside on the porch, followed by persistent scratching at the screen door.

Muggles was back.

Hadleigh hurried to open up, and her heart went out to the soggy golden retriever sitting forlornly on her welcome mat, brown eyes luminous and hopeful and apologetically miserable, all at once.

"Hey, Mugs," Hadleigh said with a welcoming smile. She unlatched the screen door and stepped back to admit the neighbor's dog. "What's up?"

Muggles crossed the threshold slowly, stood dripping on the colorful hooked rug in the small foyer, and gazed up at Hadleigh again, bereft.

"It's okay," Hadleigh assured her visitor, bending to pat the critter's head. "You just sit tight, and I'll get you a nice, fluffy towel. Then you can have something to eat and curl up in front of the fire."

Obediently, Muggles dropped onto her haunches, rainwater puddling all around her.

Hadleigh rushed into the downstairs bathroom—Gram had always called it "the powder room"—and snatched a blue towel off the rack between the sink and the toilet.

After returning to the foyer, she crouched to bundle Muggles in the towel, draping it around those shivering shoulders, drying the animal's grubby coat as gently as she could.

"Now for some food," she said when Muggles was as clean as could be expected, without an actual tub bath or a thorough hosing-down. "Follow me."

Muggles wagged her plumy tail once and rose from the rug.

The poor thing smelled like—well, a wet dog—and clumps of mud still clung to her fur, but it didn't occur to Hadleigh to fret about her clean carpets and just-washed floors.

Reaching the kitchen, which was pleasantly outdated like the rest of the house, Hadleigh made her way to the pantry and found the plastic bowls she'd bought especially for Muggles, who'd been a frequent visitor over the three months since her doting mistress, Eula Rollins, had passed away. Eula's husband, Earl, was elderly, grieving the loss of the wife he'd adored, and in frail health besides. While Earl certainly wasn't an unkind person, he understandably tended to forget certain things—like letting the dog back inside after she'd gone out.

That was why Hadleigh kept a fifty-pound sack of kibble on the screened-in back porch and a stash of old blankets in the hall closet, for those times when

Muggles needed water, a meal and a place to crash.

At the sink, she filled one of the bowls with water and set it down nearby. While Muggles drank thirstily, Hadleigh zipped out onto the porch to scoop up a generous portion of kibble.

As Muggles munched away on her supper, Hadleigh fetched the blankets from the closet in the hall and arranged them carefully in front of the pellet stove in the corner of the kitchen. The moment she'd eaten her fill, the animal ambled wearily over to the improvised dog bed, circled a few times and lay down to sleep.

Hadleigh sighed. Like most of the other women in the neighborhood, she'd taken her turn looking in on Earl, bringing over a casserole now and then or a freshly baked pie, picking up his medicine at the pharmacy, carrying in his newspaper and his mail. Before each visit, she'd made up her mind to speak to the old man about Muggles, very gently of course, but once she'd crossed the street and knocked on the familiar door and he'd let her in, his loneliness and despair so poignantly evident that she felt bruised herself, she always seemed to lose whatever momentum she'd managed to drum up.

Another time, she'd tell herself guiltily. **I'll make my pitch to adopt Muggles tomorrow or the next day. Earl** loves **this dog. And she's all he has left of Eula, besides a lot of bittersweet memories, this old house and its overabundance of knickknacks.**

Well, she thought now with another sigh, the rain beating down hard on the roof over her head, **maybe "another time" has finally come.** However much she sympathized with Earl, and that was a great deal, since she'd grown up knowing him and Eula, somebody had to step up and **do** something about the situation. Muggles couldn't speak for herself, after all. So Hadleigh was stuck.

Decision made, Hadleigh took her hooded jacket from the row of pegs on the back porch—she had to rummage for it, since Gram's coats were still hanging there, along with a tattered denim jacket that had belonged to her dad and then to Will.

Her throat thickened, and she touched one of the sleeves, worn soft at the elbows and frayed at the cuffs. For a moment, she allowed herself to remember both men, and then, because she had a clearer picture of Will, she recalled the sound of his laugh, the way he always slammed the screen door coming in or going out, accompanied by Gram's good-natured fussing.

Like many kid sisters, Hadleigh had idolized her big brother. She'd accepted his loss, she supposed, but she still wasn't reconciled to the unfairness of it. He'd been so young when he was killed, full of promise and energy and idealism, and he'd never gotten the chance to chase his own dreams.

For several years, the scent of Will's aftershave had clung to the fabric of that jacket, along with a tinge of wood-smoke, but now the garment had a dank, rainy-day smell, faintly musty, like an old sleeping bag somebody had rolled up, put away in an attic or a basement and forgotten.

Get a grip, Hadleigh told herself when sadness threatened to overwhelm her. **Think about** right now, **because that's what matters.**

Resolutely, she raised the hood of her jacket, tugged the drawstrings tight around her face and marched out into the rain.

Hands jammed into her pockets, head lowered slightly against the continuing downpour, Hadleigh followed the concrete walkway that ran alongside the house, past the flower beds and the familiar windows, silently going over the things she might say to Earl when he opened his door—and discarding each one in turn.

Everything sounded so...patronizing. How could she tell this good man that he was too old and too sick to take proper care of his own dog? Earl Rollins had worked hard all his life, been active in his church and in the rest of the community, and he'd already lost not only his professional identity and the ordinary freedoms younger people took for granted, such as a driver's license. He'd lost Eula, his soul mate, too.

Still, there was Muggles, a living, breathing creature who needed food, shelter and love.

Torn between responsibility and sentiment, Hadleigh forged on, reached her front yard and came to a sudden, startled stop in the soggy grass.

An ambulance was just pulling into the Rollinses' driveway, lights flashing.

Hadleigh peered both ways and then splashed across the street, her heart wedging itself in her throat.

Another neighbor, Mrs. Culpepper, stood in Earl's doorway, gesturing anxiously for the paramedics to hurry.

They parked the ambulance, circled to the back of the vehicle and opened the doors to pull out a collapsible gurney.

"Quickly," Mrs. Culpepper pleaded.

Hadleigh must have read the woman's lips, because the pounding rain, crackling like fire on roofs and sidewalks and asphalt, made it impossible to hear.

The EMTs moved past Mrs. Culpepper swiftly, disappearing inside the house.

Hadleigh hurried over to the porch. She didn't want to get in the way, but she needed to know what was happening.

Mrs. Culpepper, after directing the paramedics to the kitchen in a shrill and tremulous voice, turned to meet Hadleigh's gaze.

"This is terrible," the older woman moaned.

Hadleigh felt an unbecoming—her grandmother's word, **unbecoming**—rush of impatience, which she stifled quickly. Mrs. Culpepper, though long retired, had been her first-grade teacher and, like Earl and Eula, she was as much a part of Mustang Creek, Wyoming, as the landscape.

So Hadleigh waited politely for more information.

"I came over to check on Earl," Mrs. Culpepper said, after some swallowing and fluttering of one hand, as though fanning herself on a hot day. "I realized I hadn't seen hide nor hair of him since

Tuesday. Lucky thing he never locks his doors. Eula didn't either, even back in the day, when Earl was on the road so much because of his work. Anyhow, when nobody answered my knock—I called out a couple of times, too—I let myself in and there he was, just lying there on the kitchen floor, his eyes wide-open, staring at me. I could see what a struggle it was for him to speak…" She paused to draw a wavery breath. "I called nine-one-one right away, and then I knelt beside poor Earl and bent down, trying to hear what he was saying."

Hadleigh rested a hand on Mrs. Culpepper's bird-boned shoulder. "Maybe you should sit down," she said, worried by the papery pallor in the lady's face and the tremor in her voice.

But Mrs. Culpepper shook her head. "No, no," she protested distractedly. "I'm fine, dear." Another indrawn breath, this one raspy and shallow. "When I finally managed to make out what Earl was trying to tell me, this old heart of mine just cracked right down the middle. Sick as he

is, that man was fretting over the dog.
Wanted to know who'd take care of it."

Hadleigh's eyes welled with tears—
she'd been right; Earl did love Muggles.
But before she could formulate a reply,
she saw the paramedics emerging from
the kitchen, the gurney between them,
Earl lying shrunken and gray under a
hospital blanket, eyes closed.

Hadleigh stepped into the tiny foyer
then, easing Mrs. Culpepper to one side,
so the EMTs could pass, then hurrying
to catch up. Stepping alongside the
gurney, she managed to grasp one of
Earl's hands.

His flesh felt cold and dry against her
palm and fingers.

"Don't worry," she said, raising her
voice, the rain pelting down on all of them.
"Do you hear me, Earl? **Don't worry** about
Muggles. She's at my house right now,
and I promise I'll look after her for as long
as necessary!"

Remarkably, Earl opened his eyes,
blinking in the rain. He smiled, ever so
tentatively, and his lips formed the words,

"Thank you."

"Step aside, please, ma'am," one of the paramedics ordered, his tone and manner brisk but still polite.

Hadleigh moved out of the way and stood in the wet grass of Earl's front lawn, watching as the EMTs deftly folded the gurney's legs, then slid the patient inside. One of the men climbed in beside Earl, while the other secured the ambulance doors and then jogged around to get behind the wheel.

Seconds later, the vehicle sped away.

Dazed, Hadleigh nonetheless had the presence of mind to cross the street again, back her dilapidated, wood-paneled station wagon out of the garage and drive Mrs. Culpepper home. She lived close by, just around the block, as she pointed out, but the rain wasn't letting up and one neighbor headed for the hospital was, Hadleigh felt, quite enough.

Once she'd delivered Mrs. Culpepper to her door, Hadleigh dashed back to the car and headed for her own place.

As she drove, she thought about Will,

and how proud he'd been of that ancient station wagon. He'd insisted it was a classic and planned to restore it to its original glory as soon as he'd finished his hitch in the air force and came home to Mustang Creek.

In the end, he'd come home, all right—in a flag-draped coffin, with a bleak-eyed Tripp Galloway and two other uniformed soldiers serving as escorts.

Tripp Galloway.

Just **thinking** about the man still raised her hackles, but on this dreary, gray-skied afternoon, even the rush of acidic irritation came as a welcome distraction.

Tripp certainly hadn't planned on dropping by to see Hadleigh, not consciously, at least, but here he was, parked in front of that house where he'd spent so much time as a kid, hanging out with Will. He found himself smiling as he recalled those halcyon days, shooting hoops in the driveway, playing beat-up guitars in the garage, blithely convinced that their ragtag crew of potential rednecks was destined to be the next chart-busting grunge band.

He'd always been welcome here, back then. Always.

Alice had simply smiled and set another place at the supper table when he came home with Will after basketball, baseball or football practice, depending on the time of year. She'd make up the extra bed in Will's room if Tripp lingered long enough after the meal, which he often did, helping with the follow-up chores. He'd clear the table, carry out the trash, help either Will or Hadleigh, whoever's turn it was, wash and dry the dishes. Then, after his mom had died, when he was sixteen, Alice had taken it upon herself to oversee his homework and sometimes even wash his clothes.

That was Alice, God rest her generous soul.

Now, **Hadleigh** was in charge, and from her perspective, he'd be about as welcome under her roof as a flea infestation.

Ridley gave a low growl, not hostile, but a mite on the desperate side.

Great, Tripp thought, recognizing the dog communique for what it was, a plea to be let out before he disgraced himself. He'd lift a leg against the pole supporting Hadleigh's mailbox or crap on her lawn for sure. Or both.

With a sigh, Tripp got out of the truck, shoulders hunched against the continuous rain, walked around to the other side and opened the door so Ridley could jump down. He snapped the leash onto the Lab's collar, tore a poop bag from the roll he kept under the passenger seat and started purposefully down the sidewalk, his trajectory away from Hadleigh's mailbox and the trellis arching at the entrance to her front yard.

Ridley, usually a cooperative sort, balked, hunkering down and refusing to budge.

"Shit," Tripp muttered.

Ridley immediately complied.

And that, thanks to Murphy's Law, was the precise moment Hadleigh pulled into her driveway, at the wheel of the station wagon that had once been Will's proudest possession. Even with the windshield awash with rain and the wipers going back and forth at warp speed, Tripp had a clear view of her face.

She looked surprised, then confused, then affronted.

Tripp bent to deploy the poop bag. Fortunately, garbage day must have been imminent, because there were trash containers in front of every house.

He tossed the bag into one of them and braced himself when he heard the heavy door of the station wagon slam, doing his best to work up a grin as he turned around to face Hadleigh, who was already headed in his direction.

The grin was flimsy, and it didn't hold.

Hadleigh favored the dog with a heart-warming smile and a pat on the head, but when she looked up at Tripp, the smile immediately morphed into a frown.

It was a safe bet she wasn't fixing to pat **him** on the head.

"What are you doing here?" she demanded tersely. Her fists were bunched in the pockets of her jacket, and she'd pulled the strings of her hood so tight around her face that she reminded him of a little kid all trussed up in a snowsuit for a cold winter day.

Tripp considered the question. In light of the fact that he'd gotten almost to the ranch and then doubled back, it was worth answering.

What **was** he doing there?

Damned if he knew.

Ridley wagged his tail, glanced quizzically up at Tripp, then turned a fond gaze on Hadleigh.

Tripp scrambled for a reply. "Getting wet?" he suggested.

CHAPTER TWO

Was Tripp Galloway real—or was he a figment of her frazzled imagination?

Hadleigh bit her lower lip, shifted her weight slightly, wondering why she didn't just turn her back on him and walk away. Instead, she seemed stuck there, as surely as if the soles of her shoes were glued to the very ordinary sidewalk in front of her equally ordinary house. There was a strange sense of dissociation, too, as though she'd left her body at some point, sprung back suddenly and landed a smidgen to one side of herself, like her own ghost.

The relentless rain continued, drenching her, drenching the man and the dog.

Both Tripp and the animal seemed oblivious to the weather, and both of them were staring at her. The dog acted cheerfully expectant, while its master looked almost as disconcerted as Hadleigh felt.

In the next instant, another dizzying change occurred, bringing her back to herself with a jolt not unlike the slamming of a steel door.

Patches of warmth pulsed in Hadleigh's cheeks—it would be bad enough if it turned out she was teetering on the precipice of a breakdown, but having Tripp there to witness it? Unthinkable.

Her only recourse, she concluded, was to get mad.

And what **was** he doing here, anyway?

Hadn't the man already done enough to mess up her life? And never mind that he'd arguably rescued her from a potentially miserable situation by stopping her from marrying Oakley on that long-ago September day, because, damn it, that was beside the point!

Just about anybody else would have had the common decency to butt out, let her make her own mistakes and learn from them.

But not Tripp Galloway. Oh, no. From his officious and arrogant point of view, she'd been too young back then, too fragile, too naive—okay, too **dumb**—to make decisions, right **or** wrong, without his interference.

As though he might be reading her mind, a grin lifted one corner of Tripp's mouth, and he gripped Hadleigh's elbow gently. "Can we go inside?" he asked reasonably, tilting his head in the direction of the house. "Maybe you and I don't have the sense to come in out of the rain, but poor Ridley here probably does. He's just not in a position to say so, that's all."

Hadleigh felt a stab of sympathy—not for Tripp, but for the dog.

She wrenched her elbow free from Tripp's grasp but gave a brisk nod of assent before moving toward the house. They trooped along the front walk, single file, Hadleigh in the lead, head lowered, shoulders hunched against the rain. Ridley was right behind her, Tripp bringing up the rear.

As she hurried along, Hadleigh silently

willed herself to turn on one heel, stand there like a stone wall and flat-out tell the man to get gone and stay that way.

It didn't happen.

She was behaving irresponsibly, even recklessly, allowing Tripp into her house— into her **life.** Where were her personal boundaries?

The whole situation reminded her more than a little of Gram's favorite cautionary tale, that timeworn fable of a gullible frog hitching a ride across a wide river on a scorpion's back, only to sustain a fatal sting in the middle of the waterway.

Why did you do it? the feckless toad had cried, knowing they'd both drown, ostensibly because the scorpion could not survive without its stinger, a factor Hadleigh had never completely understood—but the answer made a grim sort of sense. **Because I'm a scorpion. It's my nature to sting.**

Tripp might not be a scorpion, but he could wound her, all right. Like nobody else could, in fact.

Still disgruntled, standing on the welcome mat now, and therefore out of time, Hadleigh curved a hand around the cold metal doorknob and glanced back over one shoulder, hoping her visitor would conveniently have second thoughts about the visit and leave—just load his dog and himself into his truck and drive away.

As if. Nothing about Tripp Galloway was now or ever had been "convenient," not for Hadleigh, anyhow.

He was way too close, and he was watching her with a sort of forlorn amusement in his eyes. They looked nearly turquoise in the rain-filtered light. His hair dripped and water beaded his unfairly long eyelashes and there was something disturbingly, deliciously **intimate** about his proximity. They might have been naked, both of them, standing face-to-face in a narrow shower stall, instead of fully clothed on her front porch.

Ridley broke the silence, suddenly shaking himself off exuberantly, baptizing both Tripp and Hadleigh in sprays of dog-scented rainwater.

There was a taut moment and then,

entirely against her will, Hadleigh laughed.

Tripp's eyes lit up at the sound, and he uttered a raspy chuckle.

Damn, even his **laugh** was sexy.

Thinking of the ill-fated frog again, Hadleigh turned away quickly, rattling the knob. The door jammed, since the wood was old and tended to swell in damp weather, and she was about to give it a hard shove with her shoulder when Tripp calmly reached past her, splayed a hand against the panel and pushed.

"This place needs some work," he observed quietly.

Of course, the door flew open immediately, creaking on its hinges, and Muggles, who must have been waiting with her nose pressed to the crack, scrabbled backward, nails clicking on the wooden floor, to get out of the way.

Hadleigh felt a little swell of joy, despite the fact that she wasn't over watching poor Earl being shoved into the back of an ambulance and rushed to the hospital. And now, without warning, here was Tripp.

Of all people.

Still, she had **one** reason for celebration: Muggles would be staying with her from now on, with Earl's blessing.

"She's harmless," Hadleigh said, for whose benefit she didn't know, when Tripp's dog and the retriever met on the threshold, nose to nose, conducting a silent standoff.

Ridley gave in first, wagging his tail and drawing back the corners of his mouth in a doggy grin. His whole manner seemed to say, **Charmed, I'm sure.**

"This guy's pretty timid himself," Tripp replied, making no move to unsnap the leash.

A few tense moments passed—at least, Hadleigh felt tense—and then Muggles apparently lost interest, because she turned and meandered into the living room to settle on the rug in front of the unlit fireplace.

Relieved that a dogfight hadn't broken out but otherwise as unsettled as before, Hadleigh led Tripp through the small dining room and into the tidy kitchen beyond, although she knew he could have found his way on his own, blindfolded. After all, he'd spent almost as much time in this house, growing up, as in his own. He and Will had been all but inseparable in those days.

Hadleigh took off her hoodie as they entered the heart of the house, where countless meals had been shared, where flesh-and-blood human beings had laughed and cried, celebrated and mourned, swapped dreams and secrets and silly jokes.

Heedlessly, in contrast to her usual freakish neatness, she tossed the sodden garment through the laundry-room doorway and moved automatically toward the coffeemaker. It was what country and small-town people did when someone dropped in—whether that someone was welcome or not. They offered a seat at the table, a cup of hot, fresh coffee, especially in bad weather, and, usually, food.

Since this busywork afforded Hadleigh a few desperately needed minutes to recover from the lingering shock of seeing Tripp Galloway again, she took full advantage of it. Of all the things she might have expected to happen that day, or any other for that matter, an up-close-and-personal encounter with her girlhood hero, teenage heartthrob and erstwhile nemesis wouldn't have been anywhere on the radar.

The decision to come home must have been a sudden one on Tripp's part. If he'd mentioned his plans to anyone, the news would have spread through Mustang Creek like a wildfire. She'd have heard about it, surely.

Or not.

"Sit down," she said. This, too, was automatic, like the offer to serve coffee. Inside, she was still thinking about the scorpion and the toad.

Dumb-ass toad.

She heard a familiar scraping sound as Tripp pulled back a chair at the table.

Ridley ambled over to Muggles's bowl and lapped up some water, and that made Hadleigh smile. **Make yourself at home, dog,** she thought fondly. She might have issues with Tripp—hell, she had a lot of them—but she'd never met a dog she didn't like.

The silence in the kitchen was leaden.

While the coffee brewed, Hadleigh went to the hallway and grabbed a couple of neatly folded towels from the linen closet. After returning to the kitchen, she handed them to Tripp, one for him and one for the dog. Or, more accurately, she **shoved** them at him.

"Thanks," Tripp murmured, with a twinkle in his eyes and a quiver of amusement on his lips.

Hadleigh didn't bother with the customary "You're welcome"; it would have been insincere and, anyway, she didn't trust her voice.

A moment later, she rushed off again, this time making for her bedroom. Shivering with rain chill, she shut the door and hastily peeled off her wet clothes, replacing everything from her bra and panties outward before returning to the kitchen in dry jeans and a sweatshirt, thick socks and sneakers.

Tripp was standing at the counter, his back to the room, pouring coffee into two mugs. He'd dried his dark blond hair with the towel she'd given him earlier, leaving it attractively rumpled, but his shirt still clung, transparent, to the broad expanse of his shoulders, and his jeans were soaked through.

Hadleigh paused in the doorway, not speaking, indulging, against her better judgment, in that rare, brief opportunity to take in his lean but powerful lines. Without trying to be subtle.

Damn, she thought, with a shake of her head. The man looked almost as good from the back as he did from the front—and where was the justice in that?

His still-damp hair curled fetchingly at his collar and she caught the familiar clean-laundry scent of his skin, even from a distance of several yards.

Hadleigh found it hard to swallow as the seconds ticked by, each one dissolving another fragile layer of the broken dreams and pretended apathy that had blanketed her heart, covering the cracks and fissures for so long.

Hadleigh felt stricken, not merely

vulnerable, but **exposed,** like a still-featherless chick, hatched too soon, up to its ankles in shards of eggshell.

She stifled a sigh, frustrated with herself, and brushed one hand across her forehead.

She was losing it, all right. She was **definitely** losing it.

Blithely unaware, it seemed, that he was upending Hadleigh's entire world all over again, the world she'd spent years gluing back together, after searching and sifting through the wreckage for all the pieces, Tripp set the coffee carafe on its burner, picked up a mug in each hand and turned around.

Hadleigh's breath caught. Just when she thought nothing could surprise her, that she might regain her equanimity at some point, the ground shifted beneath her feet.

Her brain kicked into gear, cataloging everything about Tripp as though this were their first meeting, all in the length of a nanosecond. He was at once a stranger and someone she'd loved through a dozen lifetimes. At least that was how it felt.

Enough, she told herself silently. **Get a grip. This isn't like you.** And that was true—except when she designed quilts or window displays for her shop, allowing whimsy to take over, Hadleigh Stevens simply wasn't the fanciful type.

And it wasn't as if she'd never laid eyes on this insufferably handsome yahoo, nor had she forgotten, for one second, what he looked like.

She'd grown up with Tripp and had caught glimpses of him a few times over the years since that fateful day when he'd crashed her fairy-tale wedding like a barnstormer, but there had always been a carefully maintained distance between them.

He'd returned to Mustang Creek now and then, to attend weddings and funerals, including Alice's memorial service two years before, but even then he'd been careful not to get too close. And while Tripp had come home for occasional visits with his stepfather, too, usually over the winter holidays, he'd never stayed long.

Never tried to contact her.

So what was different about today?

Hadleigh figured she wouldn't like the answer to that question, not that she was likely to get one, but, at the same time, she was desperate to know why he was **there,** in her house.

Tripp paused, still holding the steaming mugs, and sighed. Apparently reading both her expression and her mind, he said huskily, "I can't rightly say why I'm here, if that's what you're about to ask."

Without a word, Hadleigh walked to the table and sat down in her usual chair, figuring that Tripp would remain standing as long as she stayed on her feet, and she was beginning to feel wobbly-kneed.

Sure enough, once she was seated, he crossed to the table, set one of the mugs in front of her, and took a seat opposite hers. By then, Ridley, fur comically askew from a vigorous toweling several minutes before, promptly curled up at his master's feet, yawned broadly and closed his eyes to catch a nap.

Tripp cleared his throat, stared down

into his coffee for a few minutes and then raised his eyes to meet Hadleigh's gaze. A sad smile curved his mouth. "It feels strange—being here in this house again, I mean—after all these years."

Hadleigh swallowed. She was definitely overreacting to everything the man said or did, but she couldn't seem to help it. For good or ill, she'd **always** overreacted to Tripp, her brother's best friend, her first serious crush.

"Strange?" She croaked the word.

Tripp raised and lowered one of his strong shoulders in a shrug. "With Will gone and everything," he explained quietly, awkwardly, his voice still gruff.

Tears threatened—as often happened when her late brother was mentioned, even though Will had been dead for over a decade—but Hadleigh forced them back. She nodded once, abruptly, before cupping her hands around the mug to warm her fingers, although she didn't take a sip. "Yes," she agreed softly.

Then, and it was about time, her natural practicality began to reassert itself. Her closest friends, Melody Nolan and Becca "Bex" Stuart, would be arriving soon for the powwow the three of them had been planning for a week, and, for a variety of reasons, Hadleigh wanted Tripp gone before they showed up.

The three of them, Melody, Bex and Hadleigh, had serious business to attend to, after all. Strategies to map out. Goals to set.

And it was none of Tripp's business what those goals involved.

Conversely, though, Hadleigh found she wanted her visitor to stay as much as she wanted him to get the heck out of there, pronto, and never, ever return. This despite the fact that he seemed to suck all the oxygen out of the room, creating a deep-space vacuum that just might incinerate her.

She gulped back another sigh. The heat and substance Tripp exuded both attracted Hadleigh and scared her so badly she wanted to run in the opposite direction. He could be tender, she knew, particularly with small children, old folks and animals, but he was cowboy-tough, too, right to his molten core. Totally, proudly, uncompromisingly masculine, he was completely at ease in his own skin, solidly centered in his heart and his brain as well as his body. He had a sly sense of humor, a mischievous streak as wild and wide as the Snake River and a capacity for stone-cold, cussed stubbornness that could render him out-and-out **impossible.**

Once Tripp made up his mind about something—or someone—he was as immovable as the Grand Tetons themselves.

Well, Hadleigh reminded herself, she could be bullheaded, too.

This was **her** house, and she certainly hadn't asked Tripp to drop in to drink her coffee, dry himself and his dog with her clean towels and calmly proceed to topple the very structure of her life, like some modern-day Samson leveling a temple.

She had to take hold now, rein in her crazy emotions, or she'd be swept away for sure.

So she folded her arms and sat back in her chair, eyebrows raised, pointedly awaiting an explanation. If Tripp truly didn't know why he was there, she reasoned peevishly, he'd better get busy figuring it out, because the proverbial ball was in his court.

Tripp shifted uncomfortably in his chair. Then he cleared his throat again, but when he opened his mouth to speak, no words came out.

Hadleigh didn't move, yet she realized that every tense line of her body gave voice to the silent question "Well?"

He made another attempt—Tripp was constitutionally incapable of giving up on anything he set out to do—and his voice sounded rusty, even a little raw, as though what he said next had been scraped out of him. "I figure it's time we came to terms with the past, that's all," he told her. "Your brother was my best friend. I've known you since you were knee-high to a duck—" He paused, drew a breath and then forged on, his neck reddening slightly as he spoke, his expression grimly earnest. He was groping his way through this conversation; it wasn't something he'd planned. Or that was her impression, at least. "It's **wrong,** Hadleigh," he went on gruffly. "Our being on the outs for so long, I mean, always avoiding each other, like…like we're enemies or something."

"We **are** enemies," Hadleigh reminded him sweetly.

He glowered at her, shaking his head. "It doesn't have to be that way, and you damn well know it."

"You're asking me to forgive you?" Hadleigh inquired in an airy tone calculated to annoy him. Maybe it wasn't the most grown-up thing to do, but after what he'd put her through ten years ago, he could just deal with it. And if Tripp Galloway had to squirm a little, that was fine by her.

It was **so** his turn.

Tripp's jaws locked briefly, and blue fire blazed in his eyes. He raked one hand through his hair, mussing it even more, and glared at her in pure exasperation.

Obviously, he was stuck for an answer.

Good for him.

Once he'd regained a modicum of control, though, Tripp half growled, "You want me to **apologize** for keeping you from marrying Oakley Smyth? Hell will freeze over first." He actually dared to shake an index finger at Hadleigh, and, if she'd been closer, she'd have bitten it off at the knuckle. "Fact is, lady, I'd do the same thing all over again if I had to."

Hadleigh snapped then. She shoved back her chair to stand and would have tipped over the table—like a cheated gambler in an old Western movie, sending their cups crashing to the floor—if it hadn't been for the dog lying close to Tripp. No sense scaring the poor creature out of its wits if she hadn't already.

Great. Now, on top of everything else, she felt guilty, too.

"You have a real nerve, saying that!" she said, struggling to keep her voice down. **"How dare you?"**

Tripp stood, too, with an easy grace that, contrasted with Hadleigh's response, made her wish she hadn't reacted to his words. To him.

His gaze was level, steady, as he replied, "I did what I knew was right. And I'll be damned if I'll say sorry for that, now or ever."

Hadleigh willed herself not to shake, not to shout. Not to fling herself at Tripp with her fists knotted.

"I think you should go now," she said, her tone so calm and so foreign that it might not have been her speaking at all, but someone else.

Someone who hadn't been hopelessly in love with Tripp Galloway since puberty.

He was facing her now, looking into her eyes, seeing way too much. "Nothing's settled between us, Hadleigh," he informed her evenly. "Not by a long shot."

Time seemed to freeze.

Tripp's mouth moved perilously close to hers, and her lips tingled with anticipation. For one fabulously dreadful, shameful moment, Hadleigh actually thought he might kiss her. **Wanted** him to kiss her.

Instead, to her great relief and even greater disappointment, he stepped away, spoke mildly to the dog, then turned and simply walked off, making his way through the archway that led into the dining room and to the front door.

Good riddance, Hadleigh told herself, putting a finger to her lower lip to stop it from wobbling.

The dog followed, of course, though he paused once to look back at Hadleigh in what might have been resignation. Then he, too, was gone.

Hadleigh didn't move a muscle until she heard the front door close in the near distance, not with a slam but not with a faint click, either, just a firm and decisive snap.

She should be **glad** Tripp had left, considering she hadn't wanted him there in the first place.

So why wasn't she?

For a while, Hadleigh stood rooted to the kitchen floor, overwhelmed by all sorts of conflicting emotions—dull fury mingled with a strange, thrill-ride excitement, dread with an equal measure of relief, happiness all tangled up with sorrow.

Talk about confusing.

But, then, when had her feelings about Tripp been anything **but** confusing?

Back in his truck, the fancy silver extended-cab rig he'd bought in Seattle a year or so before in a fit of homesickness, Tripp started the engine with the push of a button and gunned the motor once, just to hear the satisfying roar. The rain had finally let up, turning from a torrent to a misty drizzle, and the sun was already muscling its way through slowly parting clouds.

Despite his lingering agitation, the clearing sky lifted Tripp's spirits.

Ridley sat alert in the passenger seat, watching Tripp intently, head tilted to one side as if awaiting an update.

After a quick, sidelong glance in the direction of Hadleigh's house, Tripp shifted gears and commented, "It's going to take a while to get back into the lady's good graces." He chuckled. "I always did like a challenge."

Ridley just looked at him, comically puzzled.

Grinning, Tripp checked his mirrors and, since the coast was clear, pulled away from the curb, rear tires flinging up sheets of muddy water as they spun and then grabbed the pavement with a noisy lurch.

The rain had stopped entirely by the time they passed the town limits, giving everything a just-washed sparkle. The clouds had stretched themselves thin and then disappeared, and dazzling shafts of sunlight spilled between the crimson and gold-leafed trees amid broad pastures along both sides of the road, creating an almost sacred glow.

Even Ridley seemed a little stunned by the scenery.

Tripp, meanwhile, whistled softly as he drove, admiring their surroundings anew, even though he'd traveled that road a zillion times before.

On either side, cattle, Black Angus and Herefords mostly, grazed on wind-bent grass sprinkled with diamonds of rain-water, as did horses of just about every breed. Farther on, they passed whole herds of bison, lumbering and deceptively passive behind sturdy fences.

The sky arching over all of it, pierced at the horizon by the rugged peaks of the

Grand Tetons, was blue enough to crack a man's heart right down the middle.

Home.

He'd had some misgivings about coming back here to stay—and Hadleigh's reception couldn't have been described as encouraging in any way, shape or form—but now, breathing in this place, like air, taking in the rugged terrain soul-deep, he knew he'd made the right decision.

Whether the going was easy or hard, this was where he belonged.

This, not the big city, was where he was most truly himself, where he was genuinely free.

The closer he got to the ranch, the more certain he was.

The home place, not so creatively called the Galloway Ranch, consisted of four hundred acres tucked away in one of the valleys folded into the otherwise craggy high country. They could take a newcomer by surprise, these flat, green expanses of rangeland, appearing out of nowhere at the rounding of a bend or the cresting of a hill.

The same old rural mailbox, rusted but sturdy, stenciled with the family name in weather-faded letters, stood like part of the landscape at the base of the drive, as it had for as long as Tripp could remember, listing slightly to the left.

"Fasten your seat belt," he told Ridley as they crossed the cattle guard. "It'll be a bumpy ride up to the house."

The driveway, too fancy a name for what amounted to a glorified cow path, was fringed here and there with towering poplars, planted back in homestead days to serve as windbreaks. As rutted as ever, the dirt road was almost a mile long, twisting around boulders and a scattering of ancient pines, crossing the same creek twice, plunging into shallow gullies and then rising again.

Ridley seemed unfazed by all the jostling; he looked eagerly out at the sprawling rangeland all around them, haunches quivering with anticipation whenever a rabbit or a flock of quail skittered across up ahead.

The barn, big and red and much in need

of a paint job, came into view first, then the log house, with its wraparound porch and gray shingled roof.

The front door opened and Jim stepped out, not quite as tall as the last time Tripp had seen him, significantly thinner and a little stooped in the shoulders.

And his hair, though still thick, had gone almost white.

For all that, a broad smile brightened Jim's weathered face. He stayed where he was, instead of striding out to meet Tripp the way he always had before, leaning against one of the thick pillars that supported the porch roof and raising one hand in greeting.

Tripp's heart squeezed at the sight of the only father he'd ever known, the man who hadn't just raised somebody else's son as his own, but had loved that boy's mother with the kind of quiet, steadfast devotion most women probably only read about in books or saw in movies.

Jim had never been a rich man, but he couldn't have been called poor, either. He worked long and hard, raising some of the finest cattle and horses in Bliss County, and he'd provided well for his wife and son. In good weather, he'd found time to take Tripp fishing and camping, taught him to ride and rope, shoot and drive the tractor. During the harsh Wyoming winters, when the land lay virtually bared to the bitter winds and snow gathered in drifts so high the fences were just shallow gray lines etched into glistening white, Jim had been the one to roll, uncomplaining, from a warm bed, haul on socks and boots and cross over icy floors to relight the temperamental old furnace in the basement, then come back up to the kitchen to start the coffee brewing and light the fire in the potbellied stove.

He'd always managed to get the truck running, no matter how low the temperature might have plunged during the night, good-humored even as fresh snow weighted the brim of his hat and slipped under the collar of his sheepskin-lined coat, so chilly it burned against bed-warmed flesh.

Some men **talked** a good game, when

it came to things like love and integrity, hard work and persistence, common decency and courage in the face of all kinds of adversity. Jim Galloway, never one to "run off at the mouth," as he put it, quietly **lived** all those stellar qualities and then some.

Now, studying his dad from behind the windshield of that fancy truck, Tripp gulped hard, figuring he'd better get a grip here if he didn't want to make a damn fool of himself. Resolved, he shut off the engine, shoved open the driver's-side door and got out. Ridley didn't stand on ceremony; he scrambled across the gearshift and the cushy leather seat and leaped to the ground, where he proceeded to bound around in happy circles.

Jim chuckled at the dog's antics, then fixed his gaze on Tripp's face, turning solemn. Beyond a slight shift of his weight, he didn't move, but remained where he was, with one shoulder braced against that pole on the porch. He seemed to lean in, as though he wasn't sure he could stand on his own.

Grim certainty clenched the pit of Tripp's stomach as he opened the front gate and approached. When they'd spoken over the phone a few days before, Jim had admitted he needed help but not much more than that. Now, in this moment, Tripp knew he'd been right to worry.

Something was wrong. **Really** wrong.

Ridley, having followed Tripp through the gate, commenced galloping in circles again, celebrating this new liberty.

Tripp kept the grin plastered to his mouth as he reached the porch steps, climbed them, ready to offer the customary hand-shake.

Instead, Jim put an arm around Tripp and held him close for a long moment before recovering enough to summon up another smile—probably no more genuine than Tripp's—and to clear his throat. Jim's pale blue eyes were watery when he clasped Tripp's shoulder, held him away a little and muttered. "Let me look at you, boy."

Tripp couldn't sustain the fake grin any longer; it had already hardened into a grimace, so he let it fall away, like a handful of pebbles clattering down the face of a cliff. "What's the story, Dad?" he demanded quietly. "And don't give me any of that John Wayne, man-of-few-words bullshit, either. **Tell me what's wrong.**"

Jim sighed and pushed away from the pole to stand up straight. He swayed almost imperceptibly, and his hold on Tripp's shoulder briefly tightened.

"I reckon you have a right to know," he allowed after a long time spent pondering. He gestured toward the gaping front door. "But we're letting the flies in, standing out here like this, and, besides, I'd just as soon have this conversation inside the house, with a cup of hot coffee in front of me—if it's all the same to you."

Tripp nodded tersely, willing to accept that much of a delay and no more, and wisely but barely refrained from taking hold of Jim's arm and ushering him over the threshold.

Pausing just inside, he whistled for Ridley, who ignored him completely, busy checking out one of the flower beds now.

"Let the poor critter be," Jim said in a

kindly rasp. "He needs to breathe some fresh air and stretch his legs a bit."

Tripp hesitated, walking close behind his stepfather, ready to catch him if he stumbled. "But he could run off or something..."

Jim, shuffling across the worn plank floors of the living room now, didn't look back. "He'll be **fine,**" he replied. He gave another scratchy chuckle. "This isn't the big city, son. If he runs off, he'll come back. Anyhow, there's not much traffic on the county road, let alone way out here, so it's not as if he's fixing to get himself run over by a garbage truck or one of those taxicabs."

In spite of what he'd guessed, and the dread of all he still didn't know, Tripp laughed, a short, hoarse bark of a sound. "No, sir," he countered. "This country's as safe as a Sunday-school picnic—if you don't mind a few wolves, coyotes, rattlesnakes and grizzly bears."

Jim shook his head, passing through the archway and into the dining room. "Been too long since you set foot on plain ol' dirt," he observed drily. "Living in Seattle all those years, surrounded by nothing but concrete and asphalt, why, it's done something to your brain. Made a worrywart out of you."

Tripp smiled—this time for real. To Jim's way of thinking, any community with a population over ten thousand was too big for its own good.

Therefore, he didn't bother to make a case for Seattle. Jim would only sigh and shake his head again. What Tripp did say was, "The point is, I'm back to stay."

Jim paused in the open doorway to the kitchen, gripped the framework with one hand to steady himself, take a moment's rest. "It's about damn time, too," he grumbled good-naturedly, squaring his bony shoulders and then, with a little too much effort, moving forward again.

Tripp was relieved when his stepfather finally made it to the kitchen, crossed to the table and pulled out a chair to sit down.

"I'll get you that coffee," Tripp said lightly. "In the meantime, start talking."

CHAPTER THREE

Jim took a while to catch his breath. He was pale under that perennial outdoorsman's suntan of his, and he closed his eyes for a second, summoning strength. When he opened them again, he looked at Tripp with a kind of weary directness.

"I've been sick," he finally confided. "That's the long and the short of it."

Tripp, in the process of filling the carafe from the coffeemaker at the sink, froze; his throat went tight as a cinch strap that'd been yanked hard around a horse's belly and buckled to the last notch. "What kind of 'sick'?" he asked when he was halfway certain he could speak without stumbling over every word.

His biological father, who'd died after a routine appendectomy when Tripp was still a newborn, was an unknown quantity, a story his mother told, an unfamiliar image in old snapshots.

Jim Galloway was his dad.

Jim sighed once more. "Not the dyin' kind, so don't go writing up my obituary and looking for places to scatter the ashes," he said in his slow and thoughtful way. "I'll be around awhile, most likely."

Tripp's jawbones locked at the hinges. "Most likely? What the hell is **that** supposed to mean?"

Jim, watching Tripp with a mixture of compassion and amusement in his eyes, dredged up a raw chuckle that sounded like it must have hurt some on its way out.

"Everybody has to die sometime, son," he said hoarsely. "No sense getting all knotted up over something that can't be helped."

Tripp leaned back against the counter while he waited for the coffee to brew, folding his arms. He probably appeared calm, but he sure as hell wasn't. "How long has this been going on?"

His voice, like his manner, was deceptively mild.

Jim likely wasn't fooled, but it was hard to tell with him. He tended to play his cards close to the vest—everybody's business was **nobody's** business; that was his credo. In other words, he operated on a need-to-know basis, and there was plenty he didn't think anyone needed to know.

After a beat or two, he smiled again, but he still took his time answering. "I've known for just shy of a year," he finally admitted and, sparse as the reply was, it was plain to Tripp that his dad didn't like giving up even that much.

Stunned that Jim—even Jim—could have kept something so important to himself for so long, Tripp had opened his mouth to raise more hell when the old man cut him off with a dismissive wave of one hand.

"Some things are—well, private," he said.

Behind Tripp, the ancient coffeemaker, pulling its weight since pre-Y2K days, chortled and thumped and steamed on the counter, like a small volcano about to blow.

"Private?" Tripp repeated, disbelieving.

Jim kept his gaze averted. A ruddy flush climbed his neck. "I'll be all right," he insisted, so quietly Tripp had to strain to hear him. "And I'd sure appreciate it if you'd stop repeating practically every-thing I say."

Tripp shoved away from the counter and the noisy coffee machine, scraped back a chair across the table from Jim and sank onto the hard wooden seat. "Well, now," he replied tersely and with a fair amount of irony. "Whatever disease it was that damn near killed you, and probably still could, is **private.** Why didn't you just say so in the first place?"

Jim met Tripp's eyes with stubborn reluctance. "I could do with a mite less attitude, if it's all the same to you," he grumbled in response. A muscle worked in one side of his jaw, as though he was chewing on a chunk of rawhide, then he went on. "The worst is over, son. I've done everything the doctors said I ought to, and I'm on the mend now. I just seem to tucker out a little sooner than I used to, that's all."

Tripp stared at his dad, imagining some of the things the man might have endured alone, depending entirely on his own stoicism, his damnable pride. In those moments, Tripp didn't know if he wanted to put a fist through the nearest wall or bust out bawling like a little kid.

In the end, he did neither; he simply waited for the rest of the story.

Meanwhile, Jim's neck went from red to a purplish-crimson. "Turned out to be my prostate that was causing all the trouble," he finally said. The words might have been dragged out of him the way he held on to each one of them like a grudge that went back for generations.

Tripp took a few moments to absorb the hard-won answer, exhausted by the effort of getting it. "I'll be damned," he ground out, once the information had begun to penetrate, "if it wouldn't have been easier to drive half a dozen mules out of a knee-deep mudhole than get an answer out of you."

With that, his vocal chords seized up again, and the breath rushed out of him, as though he'd been thrown from a horse, landed on hard-packed dirt and gotten his throat stepped on in the bargain.

On the one hand, he knew his dad hadn't gotten sick on purpose. On the other, he felt ambushed, cornered, kept in the dark. Combined, those emotions stung through his blood like venom.

Tripp had been in this place twice before—the first time when his mother had died suddenly, and then again, strangely chilled even in the stifling heat of a foreign field-hospital, watching help-lessly while the closest friend he'd ever had, or ever expected to have, breathed his last.

For once, it was Jim who got the conversation going again.

"Coffee's ready," he said amiably. From his tone, a person would have thought they'd been talking about something ordinary, like that year's hay crop or local politics.

"Screw the coffee," Tripp replied, jolted

all over again. He sucked in a breath and leaned forward in his chair. "What the hell, Dad?" he demanded in a raspy whisper. "All of a sudden, you're as delicate as somebody's spinster aunt, so hung up on **modesty**—or whatever—that you're embarrassed to mention your **prostate?**"

Jim said nothing, the bullheaded old coot.

Equally stubborn, Tripp pressed the issue. "It's not as if I didn't know you **had** one. And guess what? So do I."

Since the remark was rhetorical, and since he was Jim, Tripp's dad didn't comment right away, although he still looked sadly exasperated. He shoved a hand through his shock of gray-white hair and, at last, made an effort to explain.

"I didn't figure on it taking so long to get my strength back, that's all," he confessed. "I wouldn't have said a word about it, being sick, I mean, if I could have managed the ranch on my own." A sheen of moisture glistened in his eyes, and his Adam's apple bobbed as he swallowed hard. "As it turned out, I couldn't. Too many things were slipping around here, too fast." Jim paused again, colored again, this time in shades of defiance. "Just the same, I knew damn well I wasn't going to die, knew it from the first. I won't say there weren't some tough days, and some hard nights, too, because there were, but I've been through worse—a **lot** worse." He stopped once more, regrouping. "Like losing your mother. Ellie was my North Star. You know that."

Tripp felt a familiar stab of sorrow, because Ellie Galloway, his mom, had been true north on **his** inner compass, too. Even after all this time, there were still moments when he couldn't believe she was gone.

He didn't trust himself to speak, so he just scowled. Jim wasn't off the hook, and Tripp wanted him to know it.

Jim made an impatient sound low in his throat. "What was I supposed to do, Tripp? Tell me that. Should I have asked you to come home the minute all of this started, so we could **both** be miserable?"

Not in the least mollified, even though

he knew he would probably have done pretty much the same thing in Jim's place, Tripp didn't answer. He stalked over to the coffee machine, sloshed some java into a chipped mug and then set the stuff in front of his dad with a solid thump of crockery meeting tabletop.

He didn't return to his chair.

Jim took a sip of coffee, savored it for a moment or two and said, "Thanks." Another sip followed, and another. Eventually, though, he continued, "I guess I could have spoken up a little sooner."

Tripp, standing at the long row of windows now, his back to Jim, watched Ridley gamboling around the side yard, evidently chasing a bug. "You think?" he snapped.

The coffee, strong and black the way he liked it, must have rallied Jim considerably, because he sounded almost like his old self when he replied lightly, "Then again, I might have been right to hold my tongue, after all. I figured you'd get your britches in a twist once you knew, no matter when you found out, or how, as far as that goes."

Shaking his head, Tripp turned from the windows. "You're the only father I've got," he said, calmer now—or maybe just spent. The day had been a long one, after all. He'd been shaken by the encounter with Hadleigh and now…this. "So, yeah, I'd have freaked out in any case. Then I would have stepped up and done what needed doing on this ranch, so you could concentrate on getting well."

Jim was looking away, probably because his eyes were misty again, and he considered Tripp's words in solemn silence before offering a concession—of sorts. "I reckon we've both got a point." He blinked a couple of times, then faced his son. "You had a right to know, and I had a right to keep my own counsel. I guess we've just been coming at things from different directions." A pause. "What do you say we meet someplace in the middle?"

Tripp nodded, gulped once, got out a hoarse "Fair enough."

"Well, then," Jim decreed with obvious relief, "that's settled." He levered himself to his feet. "Now, if you can see your way clear to feeding the horses, I'll see what I can do to rustle us up some supper."

Once more, Tripp nodded. There was no point in pursuing the subject any further, not that night, anyway.

So, grimly silent, he helped himself to Jim's denim jacket, found hanging in its usual place on one of the pegs beside the back door, shrugged into it, straightened the collar.

They still had issues, father and son, but in time, they'd come to terms, hammer out some kind of mutual understanding.

But time wasn't a fixed commodity, was it? One minute, a person was there, living and breathing. The next, he or she could be gone for good.

Time. Let there be enough of it.

Resigned, Tripp left the house, crossed the back porch and descended the somewhat rickety steps to the yard. Ridley stopped exploring the flower beds and the base of the picket fence and trotted over to Tripp's side. They both headed for the barn.

The chores were familiar; Tripp could have done them in his sleep.

With Ridley tagging after him, clearly curious about the huge nickering critters standing in the stalls, Tripp filled the feeders with good grass hay, made sure the outdated aluminum water troughs were topped off and paused to greet each of the six horses with a pat and a kindly word.

Later, as he and the dog returned to the house, Tripp stared up at the night sky and watched as the first stars popped out.

Maybe, he thought, things would turn out all right.

In fact, he meant to see to it that they did.

Jim would recover, Tripp assured himself. With more rest and less worry, he'd be his old ornery self in no time at all.

As for making friends with Hadleigh... well, that would be a challenge, for sure and for certain.

And Tripp Galloway loved a challenge.

Melody was the first to arrive at Hadleigh's place that evening, looking rushed and windblown, even though she wasn't late. She'd buttoned up her black tailored coat without bothering to free her shoulder-length blond hair from under the collar, the strap of her shoulder bag was across her chest and the supermarket deli tray—cheese and cold cuts—shook slightly as she held it out to her hostess with ungloved hands.

"You've heard," she concluded after studying Hadleigh's face for a moment.

Hadleigh took the tray from her friend, set it on the nearest counter and nodded glumly, there being no earthly reason to pretend she didn't know what Melody meant. "Tripp's back," she said.

Was he still married? Did he have children?

She hadn't had the courage to ask.

Melody let out a relieved breath, put her purse aside, unbuttoned her coat and flopped it over the back of a chair before fluffing out her formerly trapped hair with a quick swipe of her splayed fingers and a shake of her head. **"And?"** she prompted, still peering at Hadleigh's face.

"And he was here," Hadleigh said. To her, this wasn't good news, but she knew Melody would be surprised, and she rather enjoyed springing it on her.

The reaction was immediate. "Here?" Melody's blue-green eyes sparkled with pleased alarm. "Tripp Galloway was **here,** in this house? When?"

"Today," Hadleigh answered. She took Melody's discarded coat from the back of the chair and carried it out of the kitchen to the foyer, where she hung it carefully from one of the hooks on her grand-mother's antique brass coat-tree.

Melody trailed her the whole way, peppering Hadleigh with questions and giving her no space to wedge in an answer. "What did he want? What did he say? What did **you** say? Were you glad to see him—or were you mad? Or sad or what? Were you shocked? You **must** have been shocked—did you cry? You didn't cry, did you? Oh, God, **tell me** you didn't cry—"

Hadleigh turned from the coat-tree,

hands resting on her hips, grinning in spite of the flash of indignation she felt. "Of **course** I didn't cry," she said. "Me, shed tears over Tripp Galloway? **That** will be the day."

As if they both didn't know she'd wept rivers for weeks after her ruined wedding, and that, as few people would have guessed, those tears had had nothing to do with Oakley and everything to do with Tripp's announcement that he was married.

How could she not have known?

Tripp would have told his dad, if no one else—wouldn't he?

Hard to tell. Jim, like many men of his generation, tended to keep his own counsel when it came to matters he regarded as personal, and he was the sort to listen a lot more than he talked.

Melody, good friend that she was, refrained from pointing out the obvious. "What are you going to do?" she asked instead, acknowledging Muggles with a casual but fond pat on the head when the retriever joined them on the return trip to the kitchen. Since the dog came and went constantly from Earl's place to Hadleigh's, her presence was nothing unusual.

Melody regarded her as part of the household.

"Do?" Hadleigh echoed. Then she giggled in a strangled sort of way and went on. "Well, let's see now. What to do, what to do." She paused, snapped her fingers. "I know. I could enter a convent. Or sign up for the Foreign Legion, provided they're accepting women nowadays. Failing that, I suppose I could take to the high seas, become a merchant marine— dangerous work, but I hear the money's good."

Melody laughed, but the expression in her eyes remained pensive. "Stop it," she said. "This is serious. We might have to scrap the whole marriage pact thing, start over from scratch."

They'd reached the kitchen by then, and before Hadleigh could come up with a response, Bex Stuart peered through the oval window in the back door, rapped on the glass and let herself in.

There was something vaguely musical about the way Bex moved; Hadleigh could almost hear the tinkling chime of distant bells.

"Have you heard?" Bex blurted, breathless with excitement the second she'd crossed the threshold.

"Tripp Galloway's back in town," Melody and Hadleigh answered in perfect unison.

This inspired a brief ripple of nervous chuckles.

Bex, disappointed that the big story had already broken, put down her purse and a box from the local bakery, then wriggled out of her puffy nylon coat, which Hadleigh took from her.

She retraced the short trek to the coat-tree, this time with Bex and Muggles as part of the caravan, Melody along for the ride, Bex spouting questions.

Déjà vu all over again.

It was comical, really.

"Will everybody please take a breath?" Hadleigh said, while two women and a dog studied her curiously there in the foyer.

"I couldn't get a thing out of her," Melody confided to Bex, as though Hadleigh were suddenly absent.

Bex's chameleon eyes, sometimes a pale shade of amber, sometimes green, widened with rising interest.

"Not only that," Melody went on, still ignoring Hadleigh, "but he was **here.**"

"Wow," Bex marveled. She glanced upward. "And the roof didn't fall in."

"You're not breathing," Hadleigh told her friends.

They **were** breathing, of course, just not in the calming way she'd meant. On either side of her, Melody and Bex each took one of Hadleigh's elbows and firmly propelled her back to the kitchen. They even sat her down in a chair, as though she'd been yanked from the jaws of certain death and might still be in shock.

Muggles, tail sweeping back and forth, tagged along, cheerfully fascinated by all this moving from room to room. **Strange creatures, these humans,** she must've been thinking**. No matter where they are, they want to be someplace else.**

Nothing was said, but Hadleigh's two best friends went into action, as if they'd choreographed the scene beforehand.

Bex slid a step stool in front of the refrigerator and climbed up to open the cupboard above, reaching past an **I Love Lucy** cookie jar and groping around for a lone and very dusty bottle of whiskey, last used to spike the eggnog at Christmas. It was still three-quarters full.

Melody, meanwhile, took a trio of squat tumblers from another cupboard, carried them to the sink, then rinsed them carefully and dried them with an embroidered dish towel.

Hadleigh watched, bemused, as did Muggles. The whole drill reminded her of the syncopated routines in the black-and-white movies her grandmother had loved to watch on TV, the ones performed in sparkling pools by bathing beauties in sleek one-piece suits and rubber swimming caps.

With a flourish, Melody poured a double shot into each of the glasses, handed one to Bex and one to Hadleigh, with an appropriate flourish, and finally raised her own high, prepared to offer a toast.

Hadleigh's whirling brain suddenly snagged on a memory. They'd been supermarket premiums, those glasses, she recalled, with a pang of nostalgia, and Gram had collected them eagerly, one by one, until she had a set of eight.

That hadn't been like her grandmother, a nondrinker and a minimalist.

Hadleigh, in junior high at the time, had finally asked Gram why she'd wanted the glasses, since they were never used. Her grandmother had smiled and said she liked the way they caught stray beams of light sometimes, giving off an unexpected shimmer, thereby brightening many an otherwise dull day.

You **were the one who brightened up the dull days, Gram,** Hadleigh thought now. **You, with your love and your laughter and with that magical smile of yours.**

Melody got Hadleigh's attention with a loud "Ahem." "To the marriage pact," she said.

"To the marriage pact," Bex repeated, with less certainty.

Hadleigh merely nodded and took a cautious sip from her glass.

The whiskey burned the back of her throat and then proceeded to sear its way down her esophagus.

Always a sport, Bex overcame her obvious hesitation, upended her glass, swallowed the contents in one gulp and immediately began to cough, choke and sputter.

Grinning, Melody crossed to where Bex stood and, with her free hand, administered half a dozen brisk whacks on the back.

Bex frowned at Melody, as though affronted, and said, "Geez, Mel, you don't have to knock me over."

"Sorry," Melody said lightly.

"And," Bex continued, "it probably isn't smart to drink on empty stomachs. If we're going to come up with a workable plan, we need to be sober, at least."

"You're right," Hadleigh said resolutely, setting her glass on the table and rising from her chair to head for the fridge, where she'd stashed the pasta salad she'd made earlier in the day. Before Earl was taken away in an ambulance, before she'd inherited a full-time dog, before Tripp had shown up, materializing on the rainy sidewalk in front of her house in the middle of the afternoon. Needless to say, she hadn't gotten around to baking the cake she'd planned to serve. "Let's eat."

The meal was simple, delicious and, from Hadleigh's viewpoint, over much too quickly. There was virtually no washing up to be done—just the salad plates and the silverware, and Melody stowed those away in the dishwasher while Bex wiped the tabletop clean and Hadleigh let Muggles out for a few minutes, filled the dog's bowl with fresh kibble and set it on the floor.

After a brief interlude, Muggles came back inside, and the three friends gathered around the table again, as in days of old.

"Since you couldn't bring yourself to ask him straight out if he was still married, did you at least check for a wedding band?" Melody asked casually.

The truth? Hadleigh had been too rattled to think of that—or much of anything else.

Melody sighed when Hadleigh didn't speak and then answered her own question. "You didn't," she said. "Well, don't worry about it. Nobody else in town seems to know either."

Just as Tripp's return to Mustang Creek had apparently caught everyone off guard, so had his marriage ten years ago. News like that usually got around Bliss County in a flash, even if it was supposed to be a secret—**especially** if it was supposed to be a secret—but he'd somehow managed to keep that particular tidbit under wraps.

Until he'd sprung it on Hadleigh in Bad Billy's Burger Palace...

"I...couldn't think," Hadleigh admitted, uneasy again, even though she'd firmly decided not to let Tripp Galloway get under her skin. All she had to do was stop remembering.

Fat chance she'd forget.

"You didn't even ask Tripp why he came back?" Bex wanted to know. Being Bex, if she didn't like an answer, she just kept asking, evidently hoping to get a better one through persistence.

"He grew up in Mustang Creek, just like the rest of us," Hadleigh retorted. "And he doesn't need to account for his whereabouts—not to me, anyway."

Melody sat back in her chair, regarding Hadleigh thoughtfully. "Spare us the act, Hadleigh," she said. "This is **us** you're talking to, your closest friends. We see all—we know all. You've been in love with the man since forever."

"I have not," Hadleigh protested, with less conviction than she'd intended.

Okay, yes—she'd had a crush on Tripp once upon a time.

And, yes, she'd stuck to Tripp's heels like a wad of gum from the first day Will brought him home from school, and she'd even shed a few tears over him.

None of which meant she was or ever had been in **love** with the guy, for pity's sake.

Tripp was one of the last links to Will, that was all, a connection to the lost brother she'd adored. Except for Gram, of course, Tripp had remembered Will better than anyone, and, at least at first, he'd been willing to share those memories.

They'd warmed Hadleigh, those recollections, like a bonfire on a cold night. She'd considered Tripp a friend, almost a surrogate big brother. And while she could have forgiven him for making a circus out of the most important day of her life, the fact that he hadn't bothered to tell her, or anyone else in Mustang Creek, that he had a **wife** tucked away somewhere—well, that had been a betrayal.

And she wasn't over it.

"The point is," Melody said, effectively bringing the informal meeting back to order, "Bex and I need to know where you stand on the pact."

Ah, yes, the marriage pact.

They'd made a personal commitment, the three of them, one summer night at Billy's, sharing an order of his fabled chicken-chili-and-cheese nachos, a year or so after Hadleigh had been carried bodily out of the church where she'd planned to marry Oakley Smyth.

After a few years, with no viable marriage prospects in sight, it had begun to seem that they were destined to be perennial bridesmaids rather than brides, and they were fed up with waiting around for their lives to start, plucking the strings of second fiddles. It was getting old, playing supporting roles in other people's splashy, romantic weddings, attending bridal showers for everybody but each other and always, always putting on a brave face.

It wasn't that they weren't modern women, not at all. They'd gotten college educations. They had career goals, and they'd accomplished most of them.

But, deep down, they all knew something was missing.

They wanted husbands, homes, families.

Was that so wrong?

And, furthermore, they'd had their fill of dating little boys posing as grown-ups.

Damn it, they wanted **men.** The real deal, testosterone and all.

So they'd made the pact.

They'd written the tenets of the

agreement on paper napkins emblazoned with Bad Billy's distinctive horned devil logo—they would support each other in the search for their individual Mr. Rights. They would meet at least once a month as long as they all lived within a fifty-mile radius. Failing that, they would do video conferences. In this way, they figured, they could keep their minds focused on the objective—a full life, no settling allowed.

It was true love or nothing. That was the agreement.

So far, there had been none of the former and plenty of the latter.

But a cowgirl never gives up.

Hadleigh, Melody and Bex had certainly stuck to their guns.

If some of the monthly meetings had turned out to be shopping trips, dancing to the jukebox in some cowboy bar or marathon movie watching in one of their living rooms, rather than actual strategy sessions, well, so what? No plan was perfect.

On other occasions, especially after

overexposure to TV, specifically the Oprah Winfrey Network, they'd renewed their efforts, gone so far as to light candles, compose affirmations, refine their intentions, really taken the New Age approach. Why, they'd even made "vision boards," gluing magazine pictures to poster-size pieces of paper. They chose photographs of spacious houses; churches decked out for glamorous weddings; honeymoon destinations the world over; handsome men in tuxes; numerous healthy, beaming children anyone could see were of above-average intelligence; and, finally, a pet or two. They'd taped these creations to the insides of their closet doors and stared at them on a regular basis.

Their friends kept getting married.

Inviting them to serve as bridesmaids.

The edges of the vision boards had begun to tatter and, eventually, out of embarrassment, they'd burned the lot of them in a barrel in Hadleigh's backyard.

Daunted but still determined, they'd signed up for an online dating service, the one boasting the most marriages.

Although their hopes had been high in the beginning, this idea, too, had quickly fizzled. When they were matched with any guys, they often discovered that they'd grown up with them, right there in Mustang Creek, and the reasons they'd never been keen to date them were all too obvious. The prospects from farther afield acted suspiciously married, or asked to borrow money, or expected sex right out of the chute.

Losers.

Still, the Three Musketeers had hung in there. While away at college, they'd attended every party, whether they felt like it at the time or not. They'd gone on blind dates with the brothers, cousins and ex-boyfriends of various friends, friends of friends and those of mere acquaintances, too, as advised by the find-a-man books they shared, devoured and discussed at excruciating length.

The results of all these efforts, though dismal, had at least left them with a few good stories to tell and a lot of things to laugh about.

While a less stubborn crop of females might have cut their losses and run, resigned themselves to the single life, Hadleigh, Melody and Bex were not quitters.

So, here they were, a mere two years from turning thirty, all of them successful in their chosen careers—Melody was a talented jewelry designer, Bex owned a thriving fitness club she was about to franchise and Hadleigh was nationally known for her artistry as a quilter. And the three of them were no closer to finding and marrying the men of their dreams than they'd been that first night at Billy's when they'd come up with the initial concept.

Hadleigh, having been distracted by these thoughts, suddenly splashed down into the flow of conversation.

"Maybe we were taking too narrow a view," Bex was saying. "Not considering men we already know as possible husband material..."

Melody nodded, brow creased with

concentration. "It could be fate." She swirled the last of her before-supper whiskey in the bottom of the supermarket glass. "Tripp coming back to Mustang Creek to stay, I mean, and stopping off to see Hadleigh before he'd even been out to the ranch."

Hadleigh blinked. "Wait a second," she said. "In the first place, who said Tripp was home for good? His dad's been pretty sick, and it's about time he came for a visit, but he's got a company to run, after all. He might still have a wife, too, and maybe a couple of kids."

Both Melody and Bex looked mildly surprised.

"You haven't been listening," Bex accused, though not unkindly.

Melody grinned. "Obviously," she added. With an index finger, she tapped the screen of her smartphone, resting nearby on the table. "The miracle of search engines," she went on. "Very recently, Tripp sold his company for megabucks. Leased his condo in Seattle out long-term and jettisoned most of its contents. And there's no mention of a current wife—only an ex. Her name is Danielle, she's been married to an L.A. architect for eight years and they have two children and a standard poodle named Axel."

Hadleigh opened her mouth, closed it again. Words escaped her.

"Axel," Bex mused, almost sadly. "Poor dog."

"Are you for real, Hadleigh?" Melody asked. Before she'd taken up jewelry design, she'd planned on becoming a trial attorney. Sometimes it showed. "You've never checked up on Tripp, not even once, in all these years?"

Hadleigh felt color bloom in her cheeks. Muggles, asleep under the table last she knew, got to her four feet and rested a sympathetic muzzle on Hadleigh's right thigh. "No," she said, trying not to sound defensive. "I was in denial, okay? I'm only human, you know."

Melody and Bex exchanged a glance, but neither of them responded.

"Apparently," Hadleigh pressed, "neither of you did any checking, either."

"We weren't crazy in love with the man our whole lives," Melody said.

"He hurt you," Bex added, watching Hadleigh. "I didn't **want** to know anything about him. For all I cared, the man could have signed up for a one-way mission to Mars or any other planet—the farther from earth, the better."

"I was never and am not now," Hadleigh reiterated, "in love with Tripp Galloway. He was my big brother's best friend. I looked up to him. There might even have been some hero worship in play—before I got my braces off, that is. But I was never, I repeat, **never,** in love."

Melody and Bex exchanged another glance, smirking a little in the process. "Right," Melody said sweetly.

"Whatever you say, Hadleigh," Bex agreed.

CHAPTER FOUR

Tripp spent the better part of the next week riding the fence lines, counting cattle bearing the Galloway brand and rounding up strays to be returned to neighboring ranches. He checked out the roofs of the house and barn, both of which needed serious repairs, took care of the horses and assessed the state of the hay shed on the range.

Basically a roof supported by poles set in crumbling concrete, the shed was empty except for various nests and a lot of bird droppings. The whole shebang listed to one side and was sure to come crashing down with the first snowfall.

Looking up at a slate-gray sky already hinting at the approach of a Wyoming winter, the collar of the sheepskin coat he'd forgotten he owned drawn up to shield his ears from the wind, he'd made a mental note to rebuild the open-sided barn and order several tons of hay, pronto. Once the blizzards began, it would be next to impossible to haul feed to the cattle by truck, so there had to be a supply out on the range, ready and waiting. Since horses wouldn't be able to get through if the snow was too deep, most ranchers owned at least one snowmobile.

In any event, water wasn't a problem; a creek bisected the spread, too fast moving to freeze over, although that had been known to happen once in a great while. When the ice was too thick, the cattle couldn't drink, so the surface had to be broken by hand, with posthole diggers or sledgehammers or, in extreme cases, melted beneath a few strategically placed bonfires. Snow would have slaked a cow's thirst, but the beasts didn't have the brains to know that, so they'd go right ahead and dehydrate, even if they were up to their chins in the stuff.

All of which added up to a lot of cold, hard work for a cattleman and any ranch hands he might be lucky enough to have on the payroll.

Now, after spending years dressed in three-piece suits instead of jeans and a shirt and boots, after flying a desk instead of an airplane and riding a swivel chair instead of a good horse, Tripp relished the prospect of using every muscle in his body, despite the inevitable aches and pains, and not, as Jim would have phrased it, just the ones between his ears.

"It's a damn wonder this place didn't fold up and disappear into a sinkhole," he announced to Jim as he walked into the ranch house kitchen one evening, the barn chores done.

Jim was seated at the table, a cup of fresh coffee steaming beside him while he pored over a sheaf of colorful travel folders. A single week of taking it easy had done wonders for his disposition; he was starting to flesh out, and that sickly pallor was gradually fading.

So far, so good, by Tripp's reasoning.

Jim acknowledged the remark, or maybe just Tripp's existence, with a distracted nod. Ridley, that traitor, had thrown in with Jim after spending a single day on the range with Tripp—some sidekick **he** was —obviously preferring to lounge around in the house, where it was warm and there was always a bowl of kibble close by.

Both resigned and amused, Tripp had saddled up and ridden off by himself after Ridley flaked out on him.

"I'm thinking I might like to go on one of these singles cruises," Jim said, while Tripp ran hot water at the sink and reached for the requisite grubby bar of soap to scrub his hands and forearms. "They've got some fine ones, it looks like."

So that was the reason for all those glossy brochures. Jim must have called an eight-hundred number—he was computer phobic—had them sent and gotten them in that day's mail, since this was the first Tripp had seen of them.

A singles cruise?

Tripp couldn't help smiling at the image of his dad, decked out in polyester pants, a loud Hawaiian shirt and a couple of gold chains. As far as he could remember, Jim had never worn anything but jeans, work shirts and boots, though he did own one outdated suit, taken out of mothballs only for weddings and funerals.

"I'll say this for you, old man," he responded, grinning. "You're full of surprises."

Jim waggled his bushy eyebrows. "Lots of man-hungry females on those boats," he said. "I might have lost some of my charm along the way, but maybe I can work the sympathy angle."

This time, Tripp laughed outright. "You're serious, aren't you?" he said.

"Hell, yes, I'm serious," Jim answered. "Ellie's been gone a long time. A man gets lonesome, knocking around all by himself, like the last dried bean in the bin."

Tripp dried his hands, still trying to imagine his rancher father whooping it up with the ladies on some ship. It was a hard concept to grasp.

"I've been hounding you to ramp up your social life for years now," he pointed out with pretended annoyance. He and Jim hadn't really talked in any depth or at any length since the day Tripp got home, but the gentleman's truce was holding so far. "You wouldn't join the singles group at church or do anything else that might have led to female companionship. What's different now?"

He knew the answer, of course, but getting more than two consecutive sentences out of his dad was like trying to herd feral cats through a nail hole in the wall. Being on a roll, he meant to keep the conversation going if he could.

"It's a funny thing, when a man gets to thinking about dying," Jim replied, leaving his chair and his brochures to stroll over to the counter and lift the lid off the Crock-Pot, where a batch of elk stew was bubbling away. The scent was tantalizing; turned out the old man had become a pretty fair cook, living by himself. "It gives a fella some perspective. Life is short—that's the message. And damn unpredictable, too."

Tripp, leaning against the counter and folding his arms while Ridley roused himself enough to sniff at the knees of his jeans, indicated the colorful pile of glossy paper heaped on the table. "All right, then," he said. "So what's your first port of call?"

Jim frowned, turning from the Crock-Pot. "My what?"

"Where do you want to go?" Tripp translated patiently, heartened by what was, for Jim, a pretty wild plan.

Jim grinned and eased himself down into his chair again, causing Tripp to wonder if he was in pain, though he knew better than to ask. "I reckon Alaska would be my pick," he replied. "Always wanted to see some glaciers and maybe a polar bear or two."

"You might have to go a little farther north to find polar bears," Tripp said. He was no wet blanket, but he didn't want his dad to travel all that way and then be disappointed.

Jim rolled his shoulders in a shruglike motion. "It's really the ladies I'm interested in anyhow," he admitted. "Totem poles, too. I'd like to see a few of those."

Tripp's stomach rumbled as he passed the simmering pot of stew to join his dad at the table. "When are you taking off?" he asked mildly.

"Don't be in such a hurry to get rid of me," Jim said, his eyes dancing with good humor. A moment later, though, the sparkle faded. "I've got to check with my doctor first, and then there's the matter of paying the fare." He tapped one of the brochures with a calloused index finger. "It's half again as much for a cabin of my own, and I'm not of a mind to bunk in with a total stranger just to get the lower rate."

Tripp was having a hard time keeping a straight face. "I had no idea you were such a high-grader," he joked. "You planning on flying first class when you head for the departure city? Putting up in a five-star hotel for a few days?"

Jim laughed. "Not me," he said. "I figure a person gets where he's going just as fast in the back of the plane as up front."

"So I guess a private jet is out as a mode of transportation?"

"What?" Jim shot back jovially. "No spaceship?"

Tripp smiled. "A vacation would be good

for you—and things are going to be pretty crazy around here for the next month or so. You probably wouldn't get much rest if you stayed put."

Jim's expression was serious again. "I repeat—are you trying to get rid of me, son?"

Tripp shook his head, briefly exasperated. "I'm having new roofs put on the barn and the house, and the hay shed needs to be replaced. The fences are down in more places than they're up, and the whole outfit will be crawling with construction crews. There won't be much peace and quiet around here."

The projects he'd named were a sketchy outline of what he had planned. He'd be buying cattle, hiring a few ranch hands— an expense Jim had always avoided if he could—and bringing in trailers to house them, arranging for electrical hookups and digging at least one well, acquiring a truck or two and several horses, since the current barn population wasn't good for much except pleasure riding. Figuring Jim would feel he ought to stay home and lend a hand if he knew exactly what bringing the ranch back up to speed would mean, to say nothing of fretting over the costs, Tripp wasn't inclined to elaborate further.

"I always meant this ranch to be yours," Jim said, very quietly. A faint flush appeared under his cheekbones. "I was never sure you'd want it, though, what with that high-falutin' life you were living, flying jets and running with the big dogs." He sighed. "I admit I had hopes you'd come to your senses one day. Hightail it back here, settle down with a good woman—like Hadleigh Stevens, for instance—and have a bunch of kids." Another sigh, this one deeper than the one before. "I did expect things around here to be in better shape when I handed the place over to you, however."

The backs of Tripp's eyeballs burned something awful for a few moments, and his voice came out sounding croaky. As for the part about marrying Hadleigh and raising a family, well, he couldn't even think about that just yet. "No matter where I went," he said, "this ranch was always home, and I'm glad you trust me to keep it going. I just wish I'd come back sooner, that's all." The words chafed his throat raw, as if they were made of coarse-grit sandpaper. "Dad, you knew I had money. Why didn't you **tell** me you needed help?"

"Because I have my pride, that's why," Jim almost growled. His brows were lowered and his eyes flashed. "But I'm tired, son—plumb wore out. I can't run this ranch any longer. I don't even want to **think** about keeping a few scruffy cattle alive through another hard-ass Wyoming winter, or the pump freezing up, or the furnace breaking down. Be that as it may, if you don't want to be saddled with this sorry excuse for a spread, I'll understand, and I won't blame you one bit. You're used to big cities and everything that goes with them." He paused, and his voice softened to the point where Tripp could barely hear him. "If you'd rather be somewhere else, well, that's fine—all I ask is that you haul off and say so straight-out. No beating around the bush. We'll put the place on the market as it is, get the best price we can and go on from there."

Tripp was quiet for a long time. The ranch was Jim's; it had been in the Galloway family for over a hundred years, in fact. The old graveyard on the other side of the cottonwood grove a mile west of the house served as the final resting place for a lot of sturdy folks, most of them related to Jim by blood.

Ellie, Tripp's mom, was buried there, too.

"I'll maintain the place for you, Dad," he said quietly. "You know I have the resources to do that. You don't have to sign it over, though. It's rightfully yours."

"This ranch," Jim said crisply, "has always been passed down from father to son. And you're **my** son, in every way that counts. I'd like to think that someday these acres will belong to **your** son, and his son after him, but things have changed. I realize that. The old ways are gone for good, more's the pity, but you can't fault a man for hoping."

"No," Tripp managed to reply. "You can't

fault a man for hoping."

"I loved your mother more than I ever thought it was possible for a man to love a woman," Jim went on, pushing out the words as though he was determined to say them before his fierce pride stopped them altogether. "And when she came into my life, she brought a fine boy along with her. I was proud to claim you then, and I'm proud to claim you now."

They were both quiet for a while, Tripp bruised by the depths of his feelings for this man who had taken him in, raised him well, loved him without reservation, and Jim thinking thoughts of his own.

Eventually, Tripp broke the silence. "Suppose you go on this cruise and you meet the perfect woman and you bring her home to Mustang Creek. Then what? You'll need a place to live—a threshold to carry her over."

Jim raised one eyebrow and replied with a twinkle, "I reckon I could figure something out. And any woman I met on a cruise would probably have a few ideas of her own when it came to living arrangements."

Tripp shook his head. For most of his adult life, he'd have bet money that ten tons of dynamite couldn't blast Jim Galloway off this place, and now here he was, talking about singles cruises and opting out of ranching and taking up with women who had minds of their own. Not that Tripp's mother hadn't had one of those herself, because she definitely had, but she'd been a little on the old-fashioned side, too, expecting Jim to head up the family, deferring to him most of the time. "I know," he said now, as though struck by a revelation. "Aliens kidnapped the real Jim, and you're an imposter. Some kind of clone."

Jim chuckled. "And here I thought I had you buffaloed," he said.

Ridley whined just then, reminding Tripp of his presence, and headed for the back door, where he proceeded to scratch at the wood.

Tripp let the dog out, went to a cupboard and took two bowls down from the middle shelf. "Go on your cruise," he told his dad.

"I'll get the repairs rolling, and we'll talk about living arrangements when you get home. As for the expenses involved, let me worry about that."

Jim acted as if Tripp hadn't said anything at all. More surprising yet, he didn't kick up a fuss about who was going to pay for what. "Speaking of brides," he said craftily, "the way I see it, you owe Hadleigh Stevens a wedding."

"**Were** we speaking of brides?" Tripp retorted lightly, while everything inside him turned molten at the thought of marrying Hadleigh, then settled painfully in his groin.

Jim merely chuckled again.

So it was up to Tripp to keep things going. "Maybe you've got marriage on your mind," he said. "But that doesn't mean **I** do." He took the lid off the Crock-Pot, ladled a healthy portion into one of the bowls and brought it to Jim.

"Hmm," Jim said.

Outside the back door, Ridley yelped companionably and Tripp let him in, then gave him his kibble ration and a fresh bowl of water.

"Hmm yourself," Tripp told his dad, dishing up some stew for himself. One thing about ranch work and fresh September air—the combination made a man hungry as all get-out.

"You'd sure make some dandy babies, the two of you," Jim ruminated between bites of stew.

Tripp pictured Hadleigh in his bed. He wasn't proud of it, but this was nothing new, since, on some level, he'd been fantasizing about her for ten years—or more. In the vision, she was warm and flushed and impishly willing. He imagined conceiving a child with her, the two of them bringing up a son or a daughter or better yet, several of each, raising them to be good people, right here in this venerable old house, where he'd grown up.

And his need for her slammed into him, all but doubled him over.

"She's not exactly my biggest fan," he said in a reasonable voice, and this was a reminder directed to himself as much as it was to Jim.

Jim smiled, his spoon poised halfway between his mouth and the bowl. "Oh, I bet you could win her over if you tried," he said. "Why do you think a beauty like Hadleigh is still single after all this time? You think she let you haul her out of that church like a sack of potatoes way back when, and right in the middle of the wedding of the year, no less, because she didn't like you? If you do, you're not as bright as I've always bragged you up to be."

Tripp realized, with incredulity, that he'd never once thought of the event from that particular angle. Then he decided it was too good to be true.

"Because she was unarmed, so she couldn't shoot off my kneecaps on the spot?" he ventured.

This time, Jim laughed out loud. "Because she didn't want to marry Oakley Smyth in the first place, you damn fool. She must have thought you'd come to claim her for your own." The old man spooned up some more stew, chewed thoughtfully, swallowed. "Women are romantic, son, in case you didn't get the memo. It must have come as a nasty shock to Hadleigh when you told her you'd already been roped in by that Danielle woman."

That **couldn't** have been the reason she hadn't put up the fight of her life to stay at the church—could it? Sure, she'd kicked and fussed the whole way down the aisle and out to the truck, but if she'd really **wanted** to escape, she would have.

Wouldn't she?

And why in hell would she have let things go so far—the dress, the flowers, the invited guests and the ceremony itself—if she **didn't** want to become Mrs. Smyth?

All those questions ran through Tripp's mind as he remembered the hurt in those golden-brown eyes when he'd told Hadleigh the stone-cold truth about Oakley and his ongoing relationship with the mother of the two children she hadn't known about. He remembered how she'd asked him to take her with him when he left Mustang Creek, and her wounded surprise when he'd told her he was married.

Even now, years later, he felt guilty—not because he'd tied the knot with Danielle, but because he hadn't told Hadleigh sooner.

Hell, he hadn't told anybody in Mustang Creek, including Jim, until weeks after the fact.

Why was that?

Given a second chance, he wouldn't have dropped the news on her like that, but what exactly could he have told her instead? That he'd thought he loved Danielle, the sophisticated jet-setter he'd met at a friend's party? That he'd married her in haste and repented at leisure, as the old saying went? That the marriage had been over before it began, for all practical intents and purposes, if only because, once the initial heat had subsided, he and Danielle had promptly discovered that they had nothing whatsoever in common?

Oh, yeah. He would've sounded like the original asshole, a cheating husband looking for a little side action.

And explaining that Danielle had already had one foot out the door wouldn't have improved matters, either. Didn't men always say stuff like that, to justify selling out a person who had every right under heaven to trust them?

Tripp ran the splayed fingers of one hand through his hair.

Hadleigh had been a very smart girl, and she was a smart woman. What little respect she might have had for him after the thwarted wedding would have evaporated on the spot. And, while a man and a woman might well make a relationship work without money, without a place to call home, even without love, no union stood a chance in hell without respect.

"We'll see," Tripp said evasively, since he knew Jim wouldn't drop the subject if he flat-out rejected the idea of pursuing Hadleigh.

Jim's eyes sparkled again. "Yes," he agreed. "I believe we will."

Hadleigh called the local hospital every

day for almost a week to ask about Earl, and each time she was told he was holding his own but still in intensive care and still not up to having visitors.

The rest of the time, she kept busy, running the shop, working on one quilt or another, brainstorming ideas for a new online class. With the growth of the internet, cyber-instruction had become a major source of income, and sell her one-of-a-kind quilts to customers all over the world. The profits far exceeded what she brought in selling fabric and thread and patterns over the counter.

Muggles, thankfully, was her constant companion.

She might have been lonely without the dog to keep her company, since Bex and Melody were both busy with their own projects, Bex meeting with lawyers in Cheyenne as she finalized her plans to franchise the workout studio, Melody working long hours to fill a special jewelry order for a major retailer.

Despite all that, the three women kept in touch via text and email, and the marriage pact remained the hot topic, though Hadleigh would have preferred to discuss something else—the weather, maybe. Even politics or religion.

Anything but marriage, because if she thought along those lines, she had to think about Tripp Galloway and, damn it, she didn't **want** to think about him.

He was a sore spot, to say the least.

So she stayed as crazy-busy as possible.

When Earl was finally moved out of intensive care and into a regular hospital room, she went to visit him, bringing flowers and showing him phone pictures of Muggles, who was waiting patiently in the station wagon.

Earl smiled at the photos, but he seemed smaller, thinner, somehow less substantial than before his heart attack. He wouldn't be coming home after his release, he confided sadly—it was Shady Pines Nursing Home for him. The sooner he turned up his toes, as he put it, the better.

Although she kept a smile plastered on her face, Hadleigh was thoroughly depressed by the time she kissed Earl's wrinkled forehead and said goodbye, after promising she'd be back again soon.

She was at the store, reopening after the lunch break, the faithful Muggles at her side as always, when a familiar truck pulled up at the curb.

Tripp, being the last person Hadleigh wanted to run into just then, was at the wheel. **Murphy's Law strikes again.**

"Oh, hell," she told Muggles in an undertone. Her breath quickened, and she fumbled with the shop key as she struggled to work the lock, her heart kicking hard at the back of her breastbone.

Muggles gave a happy bark, maybe because Tripp's dog—she'd forgotten his name—was along for the ride and therefore visible through the respectably dusty windshield.

Tripp was grinning as he got out of the truck, stepped up onto the sidewalk and came toward Hadleigh. "At least one of you is glad to see me," he said, bending to pat Muggles on the head.

Hadleigh felt her cheeks start to burn, and that was **really** irritating, because

Tripp was bound to notice and to misunderstand, think he'd rattled her, gotten under her skin, by showing up unexpectedly.

Again.

"I think," she replied coolly, "that you're flattering yourself. Muggles is glad to see another dog, not you." **You vain, ridiculously, unfairly hot jerk.**

Tripp looked cowboy-perfect, wearing jeans, a white shirt, a denim jacket and all that effortless sex appeal. "My mistake," he said with a little bow.

Hadleigh practically fell through the shop door when it opened, and that made her blush even more, because she'd forgotten, for a moment, where she was and what she was doing. Busy recovering her dignity, she said nothing.

He followed her into the shop, obviously enjoying her discomfort.

The bastard.

"Taking up quilting?" she asked, moving behind the counter, putting her purse away beneath it and shouldering out of her coat.

Still grinning, Tripp shook his head. "Not in this lifetime," he answered drily.

Standing on the other side of the counter—which was entirely too close, even with a barrier between them—he didn't speak again. No, he just watched Hadleigh, making nerves jump under her skin wherever his gaze happened to land—which was on her mouth, then the hollow of her throat, followed by a quick dip to her breasts, and finally back to her face and directly into her eyes.

"What?" she demanded, angry because she couldn't seem to look away no matter how she tried. What was the guy, some kind of hypnotist?

"Will you go out to dinner with me?" Tripp asked, as though that was a perfectly ordinary request to make, and never mind all that water under the bridge. Oceans of it.

"Why would I do that?" she countered, furious to discover that she wanted to accept his invitation, audacious and presumptuous as it was.

She needed her head examined.

Tripp's comeback was immediate and typically smooth. "Because you have to eat, like everybody else?" he suggested.

What was she supposed to say now? Nothing came to her, except "Yes, of course I'll have dinner with you" and she was damned if she'd say **that.**

Tripp's expression turned solemn, probably a ruse. "Or maybe because your brother was the best friend I ever had, and it seems wrong that you and I can't at least be civil to each other?"

Hadleigh managed to drag her gaze free of his, only to look back. She swallowed, and her eyes scalded at the mere mention of Will because, for her, grief was like that. It lay in wait, despite all the years that had passed, and pounced when she least expected.

"Hadleigh," Tripp prodded gently. "It's okay. We're talking about a burger and fries at Billy's, that's all. Just a friendly meal—no obligations on either side."

She stifled a sigh, folded her arms across her chest, classic body language for "back off, buddy," but her next words were out of her mouth before she could stop them. Before she even saw them coming.

"Why are you pushing this, Tripp?"

He braced his hands against the counter and leaned forward slightly. "Partly because I think Will would want it," he said, his delivery calm and earnest and damnably convincing. "And partly because I've finally noticed that you're not a gawky kid anymore. You're a woman, and a beautiful one at that."

Was there the slightest hint of a caress in the way he'd said the words **a woman?** The "beautiful" part was probably flattery—so why had it touched her so deeply?

"I was a woman when you ruined my wedding." She bristled, hoping Tripp wouldn't guess how shaken she was.

The flattery theory lost some of its zip when he shook his head. "No," he said. "You were an eighteen-year-old girl with stars in her eyes and a lot of naive fantasies about what it would mean to be married." A pause, during which Hadleigh struggled to catch her breath. She wasn't sure just then **what** she was feeling. Then he went on, so gently, so seriously. "But the promise was there all along. There were glimpses of the woman you'd be one day—the woman you are now."

Hadleigh opened her mouth, found herself wordless and closed it again as more heat surged into her face.

Tripp chuckled gravely. Then he lifted his right hand, cupped it under her chin, ran a surprisingly calloused thumb across her mouth. "One dinner," he said. "That's all I'm asking for, Hadleigh."

Her lips tingled from his touch, and she couldn't help imagining what would happen inside her if he ever actually kissed her.

She was reluctant.

She was eager.

She was wary, and she was intrigued.

"One dinner," she agreed in a near whisper.

CHAPTER FIVE

Because Hadleigh never got away with much of anything, Melody blew in like a spring breeze just as Tripp was turning to leave the store.

"Hey," Melody greeted him, after catching Hadleigh's eye briefly and then shifting her gaze to Tripp's face. "Nice to see you again."

"Melody," he acknowledged with a cordial nod.

With that, Tripp Galloway went around Melody, stepped out onto the sidewalk and closed the door behind him. The bell above gave a merry little jingle. Muggles drooped with evident dog-despondency at his departure, plopping down beneath a table display of quilting-related gift items with a soulful sigh.

Hadleigh might have found the retriever's

response depressing if she hadn't been busy pretending not to watch out of the corner of one eye as Tripp opened the door of his truck, the bright September sun catching in his wheat-gold hair, swung up behind the wheel and reached over to ruffle his dog's ears before starting the engine.

"What was **that** about?" Melody asked.

As if she—knowing Hadleigh as well as she knew herself—hadn't already guessed what "that was about."

"I might as well tell you," Hadleigh said without enthusiasm.

"Yep," Melody agreed, grinning. "You might as well. If nothing else, it'll save me some arm-twisting."

"He asked me out," Hadleigh admitted.

Tripp, meanwhile, backed the truck onto the street and drove away.

Hadleigh wondered fretfully if he was gloating right now. Congratulating himself on getting his way. Didn't he **always** get his way?

Melody gave a shrill whistle through her front teeth. She'd been the envy of every other girl on the playground, back in grade school, when it was commonly believed that only boys could make that ear-piercing sound. At the moment, she was just irritating. "And you said yes," she guessed, although it was obvious that she already knew.

Hadleigh felt her shoulders sag as she nodded. "Like a fool," she confirmed.

Melody beamed. "Hardly," she told her brightly. "A **fool** would have said no. Surely you've noticed, my friend, that the man is one finely manufactured cowboy?"

Hadleigh's color flared again, mainly because she privately agreed and she was furious with herself for it. "If you think Tripp's so great," she snapped, "why don't **you** go out with him?"

"I would," Melody replied, still grinning, "except for two tiny facts. One, he didn't ask me, and, two, even if he had, I'd be honor-bound to turn him down, since I happen to be a very loyal friend."

Sudden and totally embarrassing tears flooded Hadleigh's eyes. She came out from behind the counter and stood facing

Melody. "What's the matter with me?" she asked. "Am I self-destructive or stupid or what?"

Melody immediately put her arms around Hadleigh and hugged her hard before taking her by the shoulders and holding her at a distance so she could look straight into her eyes. "Oh, honey," she said, tearing up herself, "**nothing** is the matter with you. Tripp's hot, you've always had a thing for him, whether you're willing to admit it or not, and you haven't had a real date in—what? Two years?"

"Longer," Hadleigh confessed. Melody and Bex hadn't had a "'real date"—which meant something more than meeting some guy for coffee—in a month of Sundays, either. Pointing that out would not only have been unnecessary but unkind, too.

"Where's he taking you?" Melody asked, smiling again, looking as twinkly as Disneyland on a December evening.

Hadleigh knuckled away her tears and straightened her spine. "We're going to Billy's," she said. "It's just a friendly dinner

—Tripp said so himself—nothing fancy. No strings, no obligations."

Melody looked both skeptical and delighted. She tilted her head to one side as she studied Hadleigh's face. "It's a start," she insisted.

"It's an **ending,**" Hadleigh said, for the sake of clarity. "Tripp and I have an agreement. **One dinner.** Nothing more."

"Why all the resistance?" Melody asked, her voice soft now and a little sad. "Tell me the truth. Are you afraid of him—or of yourself? Because you're sure as heck scared of something, any idiot could see that, so kindly don't insult me by saying you're not."

Sure, she was scared, Hadleigh reasoned silently, privately.

She was **terrified,** actually. Why? Because Tripp had single-handedly broken her heart, a heart she'd spent a decade mending, without even knowing what he'd done. And he had the power to do it all over again.

She'd felt close to him as a child, regarded him as **her** friend, too, and not just Will's, because he'd treated her that way. She'd grieved with Tripp after Will's death, cried on his shoulder, held on to the happy memories he'd shared and the wise, even tender, counsel he'd given her, drying her tears, urging her not to let her brother's life be all about the tragic, senseless way he'd died. Moreover, Will's time on earth, however brief, was worth celebrating.

And after all that, Tripp had **gotten married,** without so much as telling her— **her,** Will's sister, the orphaned child he'd charmed and teased and protected. If Tripp had felt pity for her, he'd never let it show. No, he'd nourished her as she grew, simply by accepting her as she was, joking with her, including her even when Will would have preferred that she make herself scarce.

Had Will lived, he would've known his closest friend had fallen in love, way off in some faraway city, known that Tripp had asked some strange woman to marry him. Will would have served as best man at the wedding, in fact, and Hadleigh, while there was no denying that she'd have been hurtin'-for-certain, wouldn't have been blindsided, sideswiped, **crushed** by the discovery.

Melody, still grasping Hadleigh's shoulders, gave her a gentle shake. "You're not thinking of begging off, are you?" she asked. "Give Tripp a chance, Hadleigh. He deserves that much."

Hadleigh nodded, her patched-together heart aching, afraid of being shattered again. If that happened, there would be no putting the pieces back together. No matter how many good and decent men she met after that, men she might have loved, married and had children with, her ability to trust, let alone love, would be gone. She'd have nothing to offer as a wife and mother.

"I'd be risking so much if I let myself care," she finally choked out. It was something she hadn't meant to say, even to one of her two closest friends, but it was out there now and she couldn't take it back.

Melody pulled a ruefully affectionate

face, squeezed Hadleigh's shoulders lightly and let go, her hands falling to her sides. "It's **always** a risk, caring deeply for another person, it's a risk for **everybody**—that's how the game is played, kiddo. Sorry, but you don't get to be the exception, the one with a written contract from on high, happily-ever-after guaranteed. No one gets that."

"I know," Hadleigh whispered, after biting her lower lip. "But I'd like to go on record: I wish there **were** guarantees."

Melody laughed, even as her own eyes glistened with sympathetic tears. "If you want a guarantee, sweetie, buy a major appliance."

Hadleigh choked out a moist chuckle. "Gee," she said. "Thanks for that."

Melody's face softened again. "Know what's worse than getting your heart broken? Playing small, staying safe, hiding from life. Get a clue, Hadleigh—you're beautiful, you're smart and you're one damn fine human being." She sucked in a breath, then huffed it out, causing her bangs to flutter slightly. "If Tripp's putting the moves on you, it shows that he's nobody's fool."

Hadleigh was moved by what Melody had said, and a little saddened, too, because for all that positive reinforcement, there'd been a hint of wistfulness running beneath her words. Had Melody, who never failed to champion the marriage pact, even when Hadleigh and Bex expressed doubts, secretly stopped believing that true love would ever come her way?

"We're making a very big deal out of this," Hadleigh said in an effort to lighten the moment. "Tripp's taking me out for burgers and fries, not sweeping me away to Paris so we can kiss on bridges and hold hands in sidewalk cafés. Billy's, as you very well know, is not exactly a romantic setting."

Melody's response made Hadleigh wonder if her friend had heard a single word she'd said.

"When?" she asked, straight out of left field.

"When what?"

"When is this not-a-date date supposed to happen?"

As easily as that, Hadleigh was a nervous wreck again. "Tonight," she said, with a small quaver in her voice.

"Close up the shop," Melody commanded, linking her arm with Hadleigh's and steering her toward the counter. "Right now. We need time to decide what you're going to wear, girlfriend, because you can't go like that."

Hadleigh looked down at her jeans and rust-colored pullover sweater. "What's wrong with—"

"I swear," Melody said, shaking her head.

"I thought I'd change into jeans and a long-sleeved T-shirt when I got home," Hadleigh offered weakly. After all, Billy's wasn't a black-tie kind of joint.

Though she **had** gone there in a wedding dress once.

Better not to remember that, especially when she'd be sitting across the table from the same man she'd been with back then.

Besides, she had things to do here at Patches, and closing time was hours away. All the same, she knew when she was beaten. She collected her bag from its place under the counter, rummaged through it for her key ring, then snatched up her coat from the top of the nearby glass display cabinet, where she'd tossed it after Tripp had followed her into the store.

"Well, **of course** jeans," Melody chirped, all business. "I'm not **completely** fashion-deficient. The question is, **which** jeans? What color? How tight? With or without fancy stitching or rhinestones?"

All the while, Melody was shuffling Hadleigh toward the door.

Muggles, of course, followed.

"Rhinestones?" Hadleigh echoed, a beat or two behind.

"Do you want to impress Tripp or not?" Melody opened the door, extended a hand for the keys once both of them, plus the dog, were on the sidewalk, standing under the faded, green-striped awning with the name **Patches** scripted across the ruffled part.

"Actually," Hadleigh replied, "no. I **don't** want to impress him."

He'd said she was beautiful. Did he really think so, or was he playing some kind of game?

Back in her junior high days, when she was all teeth and knees and elbows, Tripp had often tugged lightly at one of her braids and told her she'd be a looker someday, but there was no rush to grow up, so she ought to just "be a kid" while she still could.

"Well," Melody retorted, "that's why you need a little friendly guidance."

And that was that.

The next thing Hadleigh knew, the shop was locked, and she and Muggles were on their way home in the station wagon. Normally, she walked to work, since she lived only six blocks from the store, but that day, because she'd finally gotten permission to visit Earl in the hospital, she'd brought the car.

Melody's spiffy little BMW was on her rear bumper, sort of shooing her along. If

Hadleigh so much as let up on the gas pedal, Melody honked her horn.

Two or three minutes after they'd left Mustang Creek's main street, which was seriously touristy except for Patches and one or two other small businesses, Hadleigh turned into her driveway, looked over at Muggles and sighed.

"I guess I'm not getting out of this one," she told the attentive dog. "But one thing's for sure. I am **not** wearing rhinestones."

Muggles whined softly in response.

Melody whipped in behind Hadleigh's car, blocking the driveway, just in case there was an escape attempt in the offing, apparently.

Five minutes later, the three of them, two women and a golden retriever, were in Hadleigh's bedroom, closet doors wide-open, dresser drawers pulled out. Melody was flipping through Hadleigh's limited sweater collection, looking for something with, as she phrased it, "a bit of pizzazz."

"Don't you own anything but turtle-necks, men's sweatshirts and sweet little twinsets?" Melody demanded at one point, growing more frustrated with every passing moment.

"I **like** turtlenecks," Hadleigh protested. She felt swept along by strong currents, just as she had on Snake River once, when she'd fallen out of a rubber raft and Will and Tripp had had to jump in after her, nearly drowning themselves before they got her to shore.

The raft was a total loss.

"So I see," Melody fretted, continuing to ransack Hadleigh's dresser drawers. "Honestly, Hadleigh—**turtlenecks?** If that isn't symbolic, I don't know what is. And, I might add, I had no idea you were so wardrobe-challenged. Why, I remember some of this stuff from college. Don't you ever **shop?**"

Hadleigh gaped at her frenzied friend, feeling helpless and more than a little indignant. "Yes," she said testily. Her closet, after all, was packed with clothes. "I do."

Melody shook her head in tolerant dismay. "Anywhere besides the Western-wear place and the discount heaven out on the highway?" she asked. Then she answered her own question. "I think not."

"Melody," Hadleigh said. "I love you dearly, but isn't it time you went home or back to your studio or perhaps jumped into the nearest lake?"

"You'll thank me for this someday," Melody replied, finally settling on a clingy pink T-shirt with long sleeves and a V-neck.

"That 'someday,'" Hadleigh answered, "is a long way off."

Melody flung the pink T-shirt in Hadleigh's direction and began rooting through stacks of jeans neatly arranged on shelves inside the closet. Hadleigh had meant to toss the T-shirt ages ago—it was a remnant of a long-ago girlie-girl phase, around the time she'd finished college. Fortunately, she'd gotten over the pink penchant as quickly as she'd gotten over the guy she'd been trying to please at the time.

Joe? Jeff? Joshua?

Something that started with a **J.** She

couldn't quite remember.

"Yes!" Melody crowed triumphantly, holding up a pair of skinny black jeans with—sure enough—sprays of rhinestones trailing down both legs and shimmering across the back.

"I've had those forever," Hadleigh said, almost desperately. "You remember, we bought matching pairs, you and Bex and me, to wear to a rock concert. I might not even be able to zip them up."

"Nonsense," Melody answered. "You probably weigh what you did in high school. Which, may I say, is downright annoying?"

"Go **home,** Melody."

"Not until you try on the outfit," Melody said, digging in her figurative heels. "If it doesn't fit, fine. You can go out with one of the hottest guys this town has ever produced looking like a homeless person. It's up to you."

Knowing she'd need all her strength to get through the burger date at Billy's, and already half worn-out from arguing with her friend, Hadleigh took the coward's way out, carrying the jeans and shirt to her bathroom.

She'd be vindicated in a few minutes, she told herself, because whatever Melody thought, she **had** gained weight over the years. Enough, she hoped, to take those jeans and that gaudy pink T-shirt out of the equation—permanently.

She might have slammed the bathroom door if she hadn't been afraid the noise would startle poor Muggles, who was an innocent bystander.

The jeans still fit, it turned out. This development was irritating, but it was also somewhat gratifying.

The T-shirt was a little tight, especially around her breasts, but it was a lot more modest than Melody probably hoped it would be, not so low-cut that her belly button showed and all.

She swept out of the bathroom, modeling the outfit.

"**That's** what I'm talking about," Melody cried gleefully.

Hadleigh wouldn't be jollied out of her mood. "**Now** will you go home?"

"Go home?" Melody echoed. "So you can change into baggy sweatpants and one of your brother's flannel shirts the minute I'm gone? No possible way."

True to her word, Melody stayed, giving Hadleigh unwanted pointers on makeup and debating whether she ought to wear her hair up or down.

Reminding her friend, ad infinitum, that she and Tripp were going to a fast-food place, not some swanky restaurant, did absolutely no good at all.

When Tripp showed up at six o'clock, according to plan, Melody was still hanging around, sitting cross-legged on the couch, shoes off, feet up, spooning yogurt into her mouth from a plastic container. She wasn't going anywhere, she'd long since declared. She was going to stick around and keep the dog company until Hadleigh came back and told her **everything.**

"**If** you come back," Melody added slyly, hurrying over to the front window to peer out at the street. For her part, Hadleigh wouldn't have been caught dead watching for her so-called date to arrive. "Wow," her pushy friend murmured. "The man **washed his truck** for the occasion. And he looks like seven kinds of heaven, too—right down to the shine on his boots."

"Will you stop?" Hadleigh whispered fiercely.

"He's opening the gate," Melody reported between spoonfuls of yogurt. "Coming up the walk. Now he's on the porch steps—"

He knocked.

Hadleigh rolled her eyes.

Melody gestured wildly, mouthing the words, "Open the door."

Hadleigh glared.

"If you don't let him in right now," Melody told her, too loudly, "I **will.**"

Tripp knocked again, a sort of offhand rap.

Hadleigh shoved past Melody and practically pulled the heavy door off its hinges, she yanked so hard on the knob.

Melody had been right—Tripp **did** look better than good, clad in jeans that fit him with casual perfection, a crisp long-sleeved shirt the same arresting shade of blue as his eyes and a pair of boots that had probably cost more than the entire contents of her quilt store. He took in her appearance with a subtle but thorough sweep of his eyes, and a corner of his mouth tilted upward.

Hadleigh lifted the hook on the screen door, trying to appear suitably disinterested. "You're here," she said, and then could have bitten off her tongue. **Well, duh,** gibed her inner teenager.

Tripp's grin twitched again but, mercifully, he didn't make a smart remark. Instead, he just said, "Ready?"

Hadleigh nodded, making a production out of getting her purse, hoping he hadn't noticed that he'd made her blush again.

Am I ready? Oh, Cowboy, you have no idea how ready I am.

Melody hung back, like a vigilant parent trying to be subtle, her face wreathed in smiles and her eyes dancing. Muggles ambled into the foyer from the living room, tail waving tentatively as she gazed adoringly up at Tripp.

"Hey, dog," Tripp said warmly, bending to tug gently at Muggles's floppy golden ears, first one and then the other.

Muggles, apparently satisfied with the attention, licked Tripp's hand and sway-tailed it back to the living room.

Hadleigh headed for the open door, putting one arm through the shoulder strap of her purse. She was about to offer a slightly acid goodbye to her friend when Melody raised a finger to her lips, shushing her.

Tripp poked his head around the door, grinned and said companionably, "Don't wait up for us, Melody."

"Do feel free to move your car, though," Hadleigh told her sweetly, since the BMW was still blocking the driveway.

Melody merely grinned, executed a little salute and trailed after Muggles to the living room, no doubt planning to make herself comfortable on the couch again.

There was a certain sense of déjà vu, Tripp thought, as he drove into the parking lot at Billy's, with Hadleigh riding in the passenger seat of his truck.

Not that a lot of things weren't different now. She wasn't wearing a bride's getup this time, for one, and he hadn't had to abduct her from a church to get her here, either. Hadleigh had been a girl back then, but now she'd ripened into a woman—and **what** a woman.

She made his mouth water and his heartbeat quicken.

Little girl, all grown up.

Tripp sighed.

Hadleigh had come along willingly, for all her protests—he wouldn't have forced her in any case and she knew it—but that didn't mean she **wanted** to be there, not with him at least. She was sitting up very straight, with her chin jutting out slightly, her gaze fixed straight ahead.

Tripp parked the truck, got out, walked around to Hadleigh's side and opened the passenger door. She wouldn't look at him, ignored the hand he offered, stepped onto the running board and then the gravel-covered ground.

There'd be no fence-mending tonight, he thought with grim amusement. Not if

Hadleigh Stevens could help it.

As they walked toward the entrance to Billy's, Tripp wondered what, if anything, he could say or do to get on her good side.

Short of leaving town and staying gone, he couldn't come up with a single idea. Not one that was workable, anyway.

He opened the door for her, and she stopped, right there on the worn rubber mat where folks had been wiping their boots free of dust and manure for some forty years, and looked him directly in the eyes.

It wasn't a victory.

"Guess I could throw you over my shoulder and carry you inside," he said mildly, with a smattering of bravado and very little conviction that she'd let him get away with any such thing. "Of course, that would make a scene."

Hadleigh glared at him for a moment longer, then released a disgusted breath and stalked into the restaurant.

Tripp's delight, not to mention his relief, was out of all proportion to winning one small battle, but something good came out of everything. He had a few minutes to admire her very shapely backside, high and tight and deliciously round beneath black denim and a splash of rhinestones.

And that stretchy pink shirt she was wearing? **Damn.** There was only one way Hadleigh could look better than she did with it on, and that was with it **off.**

"Come in or go out," the legendary Billy barked from behind the cash register, effectively breaking whatever spell had turned Tripp to stone, still holding the heavy glass door open long after Hadleigh had crossed the threshold. "I ain't paying to heat the whole state of Wyoming, you know!"

Tripp laughed.

Remarkably, Hadleigh did, too.

Tripp entered and then shut the door behind him.

Maybe, just maybe, there **was** a chance for him and Hadleigh, after all.

But a chance for what?

A new start? Friendship? Some kind of truce, be it easy—or armed and dangerous?

Once, Tripp had believed he knew all the answers, at least where the breach between him and Hadleigh was concerned.

Now, with his heart shinnying up his throat and pounding there like a drumbeat, with his brain reeling, his blood running hot and his groin aching, he wasn't so sure he knew a damned thing.

CHAPTER SIX

Here she was, Hadleigh thought, out on what amounted to a date—a casual one, thank heaven—with none other than Tripp "The Heartbreaker" Galloway. The very thing she'd sworn she'd never do, no way, no how.

Not that she'd actually expected to get the chance....

Now, after all the fretting and fussing she'd done earlier, standing by helplessly while Melody ransacked her closet and bureau drawers for just the right outfit, she felt strangely calm as she breathed in the familiar scents of Billy's place. She would have known where she was by the aromas alone, even if she'd been blindfolded: French fries and onion rings bubbling in hot grease, burgers sizzling on the grill, freshly baked pies, scorched coffee and a hint of the disinfectant the janitor used.

However self-possessed she might feel—please, God, let it last—Hadleigh was conscious of Tripp in the charged nucleus of every cell and every space in between, even though he was still somewhere behind her. Masculine to the core, the man virtually exuded heat and vitality; it struck her with a visceral impact.

Oh, yeah. She was definitely picking up some interesting—okay, **sexy**—vibes from him, and she couldn't help responding, not just physically, but emotionally as well, and maybe beyond that into sacred and uncharted personal territory.

Moreover, the near panic she'd experienced until just moments before had subsided so subtly that she hadn't consciously registered the shift. She'd undergone a lasting change both swift and gradual, like the nearly imperceptible brightening of the sky as dawn stretched tentative fingers over the eastern horizon and, after moments measured in miniature eternities, spilled floods of dazzling light everywhere.

Yep, something was different, all right. **She** was different.

And more truly **herself** than she'd ever been.

The epiphany was a delicious one, bordering on the mystical, but it was startling, too, because now, Hadleigh knew, she was going to have to push up her figurative sleeves, wade in and get to know this confident stranger, this **someone** she'd probably always been without even being aware of it.

But didn't transcendent experiences like this usually happen in meditation or in church, on mountaintops or beside quiet streams—provided they took place at all? Surely, not many personal miracles took place in joints like Bad Billy's Burger Palace on a busy evening?

Okay, the tectonic shift, while obviously exciting, was a little on the bizarre side, but what choice did she have besides going with the flow? She was bound to wash ashore downstream somewhere, regretful and bedraggled, but why not enjoy this gentle, crazy joy while she could?

With all this going on in her heart and mind, Hadleigh's motor skills were on autopilot. She found herself standing dutifully beside the please-wait-to-be-seated sign next to the counter holding the cash register, and looked around, taking in the busy scene while Billy blustered away at Tripp about shutting the door, damn it, because he had no desire to heat the surrounding countryside.

She smiled, savoring the ordinary in a very special way, and allowed herself to think idle thoughts, noting, for instance, that every stool at the counter was occupied by a customer, and most of the booths and tables were, too. Waitresses bustled to and from the kitchen in back, where twin fry cooks named Peter and Paul labored amid steam vapors and wisps of smoke from the fryers. Conversations buzzed on every side, creating a companionable cacophony.

She went on to consider "Bad" Billy himself, a sixtyish man she'd known virtually all her life. Billy tried to disguise his true nature—to all appearances, the man had all the warmth and charm of a badger swatting away a swarm of bees. No one who'd known him long took his curmudgeonly rants seriously, though. A longtime widower with no children, Billy played Santa every Christmas, and not just at the town's tree-lighting ceremony, either. No, he delivered whole holiday dinners to folks who were sick or out of work or grieving the loss of a loved one. He bought new toys all year long and stashed them in a unit over at the storage place, and sometime on Christmas Eve, those same toys turned up on certain front porches all over town and out in the country, too.

Although Billy always tried to keep this philanthropy a secret, most likely because he wanted to preserve his reputation as a Grinch, everybody knew what really went on. In fact, lots of locals dropped off shopping bags full of nonperishable food and gifts right there at the Burger Palace, starting the Friday after Thanksgiving.

And that wasn't all there was to Billy, either, of course. He and several of his equally crusty cronies had formed a band somewhere along the line, and they entertained the residents over at the senior center at least once a month, Billy's accordion wheezing out lively polkas while the other band members backed him on banjos, guitars and a set of snare drums.

It was Tripp's wry response to Billy's gruff chiding that brought Hadleigh back from her pleasant mental meanderings.

"I see your personality hasn't changed since my last visit, you miserable old reprobate," Tripp said in a good-natured way. "Good to know there are still a few things a man can count on."

Billy made a huffing sound, a combination of laughter and disdain, and Hadleigh finally glanced back at the two men, amused by the exchange. It was typical Mustang Creek banter between old friends who hadn't seen each other in a while, man-speak for **it's about damn time you came back home, you sorry so-and-so.**

In this context, those were words of affection.

"I'll tell you what **else** a fella can reckon on for sure," Billy grumbled. "No matter how often you leave town, or how long you've been gone, Galloway, you're still a smart-ass when you show up again."

Tripp laughed. "Now, that isn't very original," he drawled. "I hear it all the time."

"Don't need to be original," Billy blustered. "Just needs to be true."

That time, Tripp didn't answer. Maybe he was remembering that when it came to arguing with Billy, getting in the last word would take way too long, if it could be done at all.

Ginny, an aging waitress who'd worked at Billy's since opening day, bustled over to greet Hadleigh with a nudge of one elbow and a stage-whispered, "I **heard** you and Tripp were seeing each other—and it's a fine idea, if you ask me!"

Hadleigh blushed slightly and refrained, out of respect for an elder, from pointing out that she **hadn't** asked, and she didn't bother to say that she and Tripp weren't "seeing each other," either, because that would have been a waste of time. Once the wheels of the local gossip mill started grinding, there was no stopping them.

Anyhow, Ginny Clooney was a good woman, and she'd been one of Gram's closest friends.

So Hadleigh suppressed a sigh, smiled warmly and asked, "Is there a place open near one of the windows?"

She'd barely completed the question when she felt Tripp's hand come to rest, lightly but firmly, on the small of her back. As attuned to him as Hadleigh was at the moment, he'd still managed to catch her off guard. His touch made her jump, sent a fiery ache blazing through her system, zapping her nerve endings with enough heat to short-circuit them. Why, she might as well have tried to climb over an electrified fence in a lightning storm and gotten herself high-centered on the top rail—or been goosed from behind with a cattle prod.

Except that either of those things would have been painful, and this **wasn't.**

Instead, it felt dangerously, treacherously, deliciously good.

Hadleigh reined in her runaway imagination, and fast, but not before she'd thought about how it would feel to be skin to skin with Tripp in some private place.

"Sure, you can sit by the window, honey," Ginny prattled as she moved through the jam-packed restaurant, wending her way past people-filled booths and chairs encircling tables, finally coming to a stop next to the one where Hadleigh would have preferred not to sit. "How about this?"

Whether by design or coincidence, Ginny had chosen the very same booth Hadleigh and Tripp had shared the day of her wedding-that-wasn't.

In her mind's eye, Hadleigh saw the two of them as they must have looked then, Tripp determined, stubborn, unapologetic, herself, eighteen years old, hopelessly romantic, with the lace of her voluminous bridal gown billowing up around her, sparkly veil straggling down her back, holding on by a single hairpin. Her makeup had been smudged, her glue-on lashes long gone and her intricately braided, salon-styled chignon had drooped sadly, nearly resting on her right shoulder.

Hadleigh, stricken by the memory, blinked the scene away.

"It'll do just fine, Ginny," she heard Tripp say very quietly.

Ginny made some lighthearted reply, and the next thing Hadleigh knew, she was seated, with Tripp across from her, a slight grin tugging at his mouth but not quite rising into his eyes.

The waitress handed them each a menu, promised to return in a few minutes and rushed away. By then, more hungry people were arriving at Billy's, while others, having finished their meals, prepared to leave, gathering coats and handbags and backpacks, tossing crumpled bills onto debris-strewn tables for the tip, bundling babies into carriers, lifting sticky-fingered toddlers from high-chairs, herding older children away from the gumball machine and the arcade games and toward the exit.

Hadleigh's throat tightened at the ordinary poignancy of it all. She loved living in Mustang Creek, always had, despite bittersweet memories of her lost parents and Gram and, of course, Will. Then, aware that Tripp was watching her, and possibly seeing a few of the soul bruises she usually kept hidden, she turned her gaze to meet his.

"Did you arrange this ahead of time?" she asked, with a touch of irony. "Our being seated in this particular booth, I mean?"

Tripp's own gaze was steady as he looked back at her, and his expression was still serious. "No," he answered, with a raspy half chuckle. "Must have been plain ol' dumb luck."

Hadleigh picked up her menu with a flourish. "If you say so," she replied in a breezy "whatever" tone, studying the list of offerings she could have recited from memory.

He chuckled again, shook his head. "Now, why would I do that, Hadleigh? I'm trying to get on your good side, if I haven't made that clear."

She closed her menu, having decided, during the tense drive from her place to Billy's with Tripp, on her default dish— a Cobb salad with Thousand Island dressing. Since Hadleigh 3.0 was in charge, having ousted Chicken Little, hopefully for good, she asked the same question she'd asked a week ago, when Tripp suddenly turned up in her life again, the question he'd sidestepped before.

She thought she knew the answer, but it was just a guess. She needed to hear Tripp's take on the situation. "What brings you back to Mustang Creek after all this time?"

Tripp hadn't opened his own menu; maybe he'd already planned his order, too. He sat with his hands resting on the vinyl-covered folder, fingers loosely interlaced, at ease now, but he was still watchful. "I'm here because of my dad, mainly," he said, as expected. Everyone knew Jim Galloway had been battling prostate cancer for a while now, even though the man personified the strong, silent type. "He says he's past the worst of it and that's probably true, since he's no damn good at lying and never has been." Tripp paused, gave a sigh. "The ranch, on the other hand, looks as if it's been going downhill for a while."

Just then, Ginny was back, with her lipstick-bright smile, her perky wash-and-wear uniform and her crepe-soled shoes, armed with an order pad and a stubby pencil. The interruption was fine with Hadleigh, because the Galloway ranch **did** look pretty forlorn, reminding her of those old photos of once-prosperous family farms, foreclosed on or simply forsaken when the Great Depression hit back in the 1930s.

She bit her lower lip rather than give an opinion, not just because Ginny was standing right there, all ears, waiting to take their orders, but because she knew that the present state of the once-thriving ranch was none of her business.

Hadleigh asked for the salad, the lunch-size one instead of the dinner portion, along with a glass of unsweetened iced tea.

Tripp chose the chicken-fried steak and said he'd have plain water with extra ice, if Ginny would be so kind.

Ginny, flattered and humming under her breath, quickly went on her way again, leaving them alone. Since Billy's was one of the busiest eating establishments in the county, however, they weren't by themselves for long.

Folks stopped by to say hello to Tripp— they greeted Hadleigh, too, of course, but most of them saw her around town all the time. They wanted to ask how Jim was holding up and whether or not Tripp meant to stick around and run the ranch, things like that.

Tripp was cordial to all of them, patiently answering the same questions over and over again: yes, Jim seemed to be getting better, and he was even thinking about taking himself a vacation on a cruise ship. And, yes, Tripp would be staying on to help out as much as he could.

Did that mean he was home for good?

Hadleigh was still trying to work out

whether she hoped the answer would be yes or no when Spence Hogan, the local police chief, came through the door, crossed the restaurant and came to a stop beside their table.

He smiled at Hadleigh, then turned almost immediately to Tripp.

Spence had gone to high school with Will and Tripp, and the three of them had been buddies. Dark haired and handsome, with indigo-blue eyes and a quick smile, Spence, at thirty-five, was perennially single and, thus, by the rules of the marriage pact, he qualified as potential husband material—technically, anyway.

Because nothing and no one is perfect, there were drawbacks, even without the hometown-guy, familiarity-breeds-boredom factor.

Spence loved being a cop, and he was a good one, committed to his job and his community. He was honest, upright and solvent, and definitely a pleasure to look at, no question about that. All points in his favor.

But when it came to settling down, well,

he wasn't about to limit his options that way. Spence was about keeping options open, **all** of them. Not surprisingly, he had all the women he had time for, and then some.

Melody had gone out with him on a few dates, in both high school and college, and that second time around they'd seemed serious about each other—until something had gone wrong and they'd broken up. After that, all Melody would say was that they'd both come to their senses and agreed to call it quits.

"I was wondering when I'd run into you," Spence was saying to Tripp when Hadleigh tuned back in on the conversation. "My office is still in the same place it always was, you know. After better than a week back home, I'd have thought you could find your way over there and say howdy."

With that, Spence commandeered a chair from a nearby table, dragged it over and sat down.

"Make yourself at home," Tripp told his friend drily. "And, by the way, the ranch hasn't been relocated, either."

Out of the corner of her eye, Hadleigh spotted Ginny heading toward them with the drinks they'd ordered a few minutes before.

She set the glasses down with a simultaneous **thump** and nudged the police chief lightly in one shoulder. "I suppose you want something to eat?" she asked, cheerfully affronted.

Spence gave the older woman one of his famous grins bordering on impertinence—a brief flash of white teeth, a twinkle in his too-blue eyes, a dimple denting his right cheek for an instant.

And sure enough, he made even Ginny blush. Ginny, who could stand toe-to-toe with any other charmer in all of creation and hold her ground.

"Just coffee, please," Spence said. "Black, as usual."

Ginny, who prided herself on being, as she put it, "a tough old broad," grunted, then turned and beelined it for the big java machine behind the counter.

Spence sighed, as if to say it was all in a day's work, and it wasn't **his** fault he appealed to women of all ages, types and descriptions.

"Was there something you wanted, old buddy?" Tripp asked, not unkindly. "Because if you're just here to while away your coffee break shooting the breeze, well, I happen to be a little busy right now."

Spence's gaze moved smoothly to Hadleigh's face, stayed there a moment and then, after a slight twitch of a grin and an almost imperceptible lift of his eyebrows, turned his attention back to Tripp. "So I see," he replied, pretending to be miffed. "I won't keep you long."

"Good," Tripp said.

Ginny bustled over with Spence's coffee and set it down in front of him. The heavy stoneware cup rattled against its matching saucer.

Too smart to make eye contact with Spence again, she gave Hadleigh a meaningful look instead.

Hadleigh smiled reassuringly.

A second later, Ginny was gone.

Spence took a sip of his coffee, deliberately lingering. "How's Jim doing?"

he asked presently, in an offhand tone.

It was a gibe, though a mild one, and subtle. Hadleigh might not have picked up on it at all if Tripp's eyes hadn't looked hot enough to come to a blue boil—and if she hadn't seen this kind of masculine interaction a million times growing up around Will and his friends. They would've done just about anything for each other, the three of them, and yet those line-in-the-sand challenges arose occasionally, as though they were young bulls, marking out their separate territories.

Close as they were, Will and Tripp had tangled more than once, bloodying their knuckles, blackening each other's eyes, rolling in the yard like a pair of fools until one of two things happened. Either Gram came outside and sprayed them both down with the garden hose or, because they'd been so equally matched, they'd finally worn themselves out and lain side by side on their backs, gasping for breath and laughing up at the sky. And, of course, if Spence was around, he'd jump right in at the first sign of a brawl.

At first, these tussles had scared Hadleigh—her brother and his friends went at it full throttle and in high gear—but she'd eventually figured out, with a little help from Gram, that fighting was like a sport to them, a way to vent excess energy and prove something to themselves as well as each other.

Tripp took his sweet time replying to Spence's question about Jim Galloway's well-being. When he did, he rested his forearms on the table, leaned a fraction of an inch in his friend's direction and replied, "My dad's doing all right, Spence. Thanks for asking."

Spence rolled his eyes. "No **problem,**" he said.

Then he scraped back his chair, stood up and favored Hadleigh with a courtly nod of farewell. His coffee, half-finished, remained on the table, apparently forgotten.

"**That** was neighborly of you," Hadleigh observed once Spence had walked away.

Since Ginny was headed their way with the food, Tripp waited until she'd served

Hadleigh her salad, plunked his plate down, picked up Spence's abandoned cup and saucer and left them again.

"I thought Spence was your friend," Hadleigh persisted when Tripp didn't speak right away.

"He is," Tripp said, picking up the pepper shaker and seasoning his meal generously.

Hadleigh lowered her voice. "Well," she retorted, "nobody would have guessed that from the way you acted just now."

Tripp chuckled. "Everything's fine, Hadleigh," he assured her. "In fact, a bunch of us are getting together for a poker game real soon."

She picked up her fork and stabbed halfheartedly at a chunk of the blue cheese that garnished her salad. "I still don't understand," she admitted, practically whispering. "You and Spence go way back, and you were **rude.**"

Tripp grinned, taking his own fork in hand and watching Hadleigh from the other side of the table. "Because men aren't conciliatory, like women," he said, with a maddening air of mirthful reason. "Spence wanted to get under my skin for not getting in touch right away, it's true, but what just happened wasn't about him and me. It was about **you** and me."

Hadleigh opened her mouth, closed it again. She still hadn't gotten the morsel of blue cheese more than halfway to her face.

"What?" she finally managed, confounded.

Tripp's grin broadened. He took the time to savor a forkful of gravy-laden mashed potatoes and swallow before he troubled himself to answer. "This is a small town," he said at long last—and quite unnecessarily. "Everybody knows we've mixed about as well as oil and water these past ten years." He paused, picked up his knife and began to cut up the gigantic slab of breaded chicken, also awash in gravy, and taking up most of the space on his plate. Just when Hadleigh began to fantasize about stabbing him with her fork out of sheer frustration, he went on, "We have a legend to live down, you and I. I'm the man who carried you out of your wedding before you could get yourself saddled with the wrong husband, and you're the spitfire bride who fought me every inch of the way. So, naturally, our having a peaceable meal together in a public place is bound to raise some speculation."

Hadleigh's mind snagged momentarily on the phrase "the spitfire bride who fought me every inch of the way." **Had** she put up a real fight? Or had she been, for all her kicking and squirming and loud protests, well, just a **little** bit thrilled?

It was a possibility she'd never seriously considered, though of course it **had** crossed her mind. Gram had hinted once or twice that Hadleigh might actually have been hoping, in some hidden corner of her heart, that Tripp would come to her rescue like a hero in a romantic movie, stop the wedding and carry her off like pirates' plunder. Next stop: happily ever after.

At the time, she hadn't been conscious of any such plan.

But what about her **un**conscious aims?

She frowned. No, she decided. Even at eighteen, she hadn't been **that** much of an airhead. For one thing, she'd had no way of knowing how Tripp would react to the news that she was getting married to Oakley—hearing about the wedding, he might well have dismissed Will's little sister as a dingbat and never given her another thought.

Except, she **had** known he'd come back to Mustang Creek, she realized with a start, known he'd storm straight into the church and call a halt to the ceremony if it came to that, and have no qualms at all about raising hell.

How had she known? That was no great intellectual leap. Her brother, never a fan of Oakley's, would probably have done the very same thing. Will and Tripp had always thought along very similar lines, allowing for the occasional loud disagreement, usually over a girl.

Slowly, Hadleigh set her fork down, leaned back in her seat and marveled at how she'd kept herself in the dark about her real motives, both at the time and right on through the next ten years.

Tripp, watching her, stopped eating. "Something wrong with your food?" he asked.

Hadleigh swallowed, shook her head. "I was having a flashback," she said.

He didn't seem annoyed, just puzzled. "Look, Hadleigh, I'm sorry if sitting here bothers you—"

She interrupted quickly. "No," she told him, "it's not the booth. Or the food."

"Then what?" It was a patient question, although that didn't mean he'd let her skate over the issue.

Hadleigh turned her head to see if any of the other customers were watching— they were—and lowered her voice to a whisper. "I can't talk about it here," she said. "Maybe I can't talk about it **anywhere,** ever."

Tripp frowned. Now, she could see, bewilderment **was** giving way to exasperation. "If it concerns me," he said evenly, "then we're going to talk about it— whatever 'it' is."

"What makes you think everything in the universe somehow affects you?" It was a lame attempt to make Tripp back off, and she saw right away that it had failed.

"Hadleigh." That was all he said, just her name.

She tried again. "Really, it's nothing—"

There was a short, uncomfortable silence.

"Look me in the eye and tell me I don't figure into whatever's going on in that beautiful head of yours," Tripp challenged quietly, **too** quietly, "and I'll take you at your word."

"You...you'd believe me?"

"I didn't say that," he replied tersely.

She couldn't do it, couldn't lie to Tripp's face or anyone else's, and he knew that as well as she did.

Hadleigh sighed, and it seemed to her that she was deflating like a punctured tire.

Tripp waited. And though he held up one hand to signal a passing Ginny for the check, his eyes never left Hadleigh's face.

Ginny hurried over with the bill. Her earlier glee was gone—she looked worriedly from Tripp's plate to Hadleigh's. While Tripp had at least made a dent in his supper, Hadleigh's salad was practically untouched, and the fact was all too obvious.

"Is something wr—"

Tripp broke in before Ginny could finish her sentence. "Everything's fine," he said, flashing a grin at the woman that probably would have made Hadleigh's clothes fall off, then and there, if it had been directed her way. "We just remembered we're supposed to be somewhere in a couple of minutes, that's all."

Ginny fairly melted at the explanation, beaming and handing over the tab.

After a glance at the total, Tripp took a bill from his wallet and held it out to Ginny with the cash register slip.

"I'll get your change real quick, since you're in a hurry and all," Ginny promised, flushed and eager to please.

Tripp was already out of the booth, on his feet. "No need," he said, extending a hand to Hadleigh as she slid over the seat, fumbling with her coat and handbag.

Hadleigh ignored his offer, partly because she was watching Ginny and partly because she could still stand up on her own last time she checked.

Tripp leaned in to whisper, his breath warm as it met Hadleigh's ear. He was fully aware, damn him, that just about everyone in the place was watching them, speculating. "Your place or mine?" he asked.

Hadleigh felt color surge into her face, even as her ear and neck tingled, but her smile was radiant, if a little forced. "Neither," she said very sweetly. If Tripp could put on a show, so could she. "Our deal was dinner and nothing more. Now dinner's over—and so is the evening."

Tripp's responding smile was like a flood of sunlight parting the clouds after a rainstorm. "Not until we have that talk I mentioned, it isn't," he told her firmly. Anyone looking on would have thought the two of them were bound to fall into bed together the instant they were behind closed doors.

As if she'd just tumble onto the nearest mattress for Tripp Galloway! **That** wasn't going to happen, and a damn good thing, too.

Mostly.

"We had an agreement!" Hadleigh argued under her breath.

Tripp held Hadleigh's coat for her. Now it wasn't just his smile that heated her through and through; the blue heat in his eyes made her so warm she was afraid she'd start sweating or even faint. "Our **agreement,**" he reminded her, taking her hand, lifting it and brushing his lips ever so lightly across her knuckles, "didn't cover ducking out early because you don't want to talk about whatever's on your mind with so many people around."

Hadleigh smiled her widest smile. Two could play his game.

Only Tripp was one move ahead, as it turned out. Before she could tell him what he could do with his agreement, he **kissed** her, the bastard.

Right there in Bad Billy's Burger Palace

and Drive-Thru, with fully half the county looking on.

Hadleigh didn't exactly kiss Tripp back, but she didn't push him away, either.

She was lost.

The other diners didn't even pretend they hadn't seen what happened. There were fond murmurs, chuckles and a smattering of applause.

Every bit as self-assured as he'd been on her almost-wedding day, Tripp took Hadleigh by one elbow and squired her past the tables and booths and the crowded counter to the main door.

He held it for her, gentlemanly as could be.

Twilight had fallen by then, and the half-moon seemed huge and regal and impossibly bright—so bright the stars couldn't compete.

"You can let go of my arm now," Hadleigh told Tripp. "The performance is over."

Suddenly, Tripp stopped, turned Hadleigh to face him and cupped a gentle hand under her chin. "I'll ask you again," he said. "Your place or mine?"

CHAPTER SEVEN

Your place or mine?

That was **so** not a choice, Hadleigh thought, delighting in her own outrage.

Refusing Tripp's help, beyond allowing him to open the passenger-side door of his truck for her, mainly because he got there first, she climbed onto the running board and planted herself in the seat. He merely smiled, closed the door, then walked around the rig to the driver's side.

Hadleigh, having already fastened her seat belt, glared stubbornly through the windshield as Tripp got behind the wheel, started the engine. She felt like one big contradiction—going along with this ridiculous game they were playing even though she certainly didn't have to, dreading telling the truth, and yet gripped by a driving, powerful need to do just that—whatever the consequences. Heaven help her, she wasn't even capable of lying by **omission.**

Where, exactly, was Hadleigh 3.0 at this moment, and why didn't she get her perky little emotionally balanced self the hell back here?

"I figure we ought to head for my place," Tripp said, sounding maddeningly reasonable, which was hard to take because Hadleigh felt anything **but** reasonable as the truck rolled out of the parking lot and onto the highway. "Since Melody is hanging out at yours."

Hadleigh felt a frisson of alarm—and something else. Something she didn't even try to identify.

"What about your dad?" she asked, suppressing an urge to leap to Melody's defense, a silly idea, since Tripp hadn't said anything negative in the first place.

At least one thing was for sure: he didn't intend to take her home just yet.

While a part of Hadleigh wanted Tripp to drop her off on the sidewalk in front of her house and leave her alone forever after, **another** part of her was determined to see this through, no matter what, go for broke and see what came of it.

"He's probably turned in by now," Tripp answered easily. "And even if he hasn't, he'll have enough sense to give us some space—which is more than I can say for Melody."

Hadleigh folded her arms. Okay, now he was asking for it.

"Melody," she said tartly, "is only trying to look out for my best interests." That was an understatement; Melody had **insisted** Hadleigh go on this date, had even chosen her clothes.

Tripp threw a grin Hadleigh's way, but mostly he was keeping his attention on the road, an admittedly sensible thing to do, considering the alternative. "You're probably right about that," he conceded with gruff amusement. "But, bottom line, Melody's good intentions are beside the point. I'm not planning to take liberties, Hadleigh, so you don't need a bodyguard."

For some reason, Hadleigh thought of

the long-ago day when she and Bex had gotten the bright idea to paint the concrete floor of Bex's mom and dad's garage. They'd been an industrious pair, clearing the space, sweeping and then mopping. They'd mixed sand with some canary-yellow paint they'd found in the storage shed, congratulating each other on their ingenuity. Bex's mom would be **so** happy when she saw what they'd done. Wasn't she constantly fretting that the garage floor was so slick in bad weather, and somebody was bound to break their neck one of these days?

Laboring side by side, on their knees, the girls wielded their brushes, happily slopping on the gritty yellow goop, working their way from the front of the garage to the back—only to realize, when it was too late, that they'd literally painted themselves into a corner.

Not wanting to spoil their handiwork—or the soles of their sneakers—by crossing the wet expanse, they'd waited hours for the floor to dry.

Hadleigh smiled ruefully at the

recollection and the correlation between that incident and the choices she'd made this very night. Here she was, trapped in another corner, albeit not entirely against her will.

What was she supposed to do now?

She didn't owe Tripp any explanations; she knew that and so did he. He was basically teasing her, trying to get some kind of reaction.

It would be way too humiliating to tell Tripp about the realization, back there in the booth at Billy's, that had left her so thunderstruck she'd had no time to compose herself.

The **same** booth, damn it, where her own immaturity and magical thinking had bitten her in the butt ten years before.

Lying wasn't an option, either; Hadleigh was not only notoriously bad at it, she was constitutionally incapable. And even if she **did** manage to invent some trumped-up explanation and deliver it without stepping on her own tongue, Tripp would see right through her.

But he **had** said he'd let the subject drop

if she could look him in the eye, as he'd put it, and tell him why, between one moment and the next, she'd lost her appetite and, very nearly, her composure, too. Only bravado, and, okay, a bit of an ornery streak, had carried her through the act the two of them had put on before they left the restaurant.

They'd been gone for just a few minutes, but by now, some of the spectators were surely comparing notes, texting their friends, maybe posting a blow-by-blow description of tonight's events on social media sites. There might even be pictures, for heaven's sake, since so many people carried smartphones these days.

She could imagine it all too well. **They kissed. Hadleigh Stevens and Tripp Galloway,** the gossips would tell each other, **right there in Bad Billy's Burger Palace, in front of God and everybody. We're not talking about a friendly peck on the cheek, either. There was probably tongue involved. And then, all of a sudden, they took off. It's not too hard to figure out what happened**

next, is it?

Hadleigh bristled at the thought and at the lingering effects of that stupid kiss. The grapevine would probably catch fire if any of those well-meaning busybodies knew how much she wanted what wasn't about to happen next.

Yes, sir, she reflected, she might have been able to preserve some shred of her dignity if Tripp hadn't hauled off and kissed her.

Dwelling on the kiss, however, would not do, Hadleigh decided. She was already finding it difficult to sit still.

Torn between her best intentions and her internal evil twin, she sighed with gusto, pressed the fingertips of both hands to her temples and wondered if she was going crazy.

She, or rather, the person she'd always been, wanted to do the right and sensible thing, and that certainly wasn't what she had in mind. Her inner twin, however, was filibustering for hot, sweaty, sheet-twisting **sex,** and the sooner, the better.

Hadleigh groaned aloud.

Tripp, who never seemed to miss a darned thing, chuckled again. "Suppose you just get whatever it is off your chest right now. It can't be all **that** big a deal."

"Easy for you to say," Hadleigh retorted. "You're not the one who's going to feel like a total idiot." This truth compulsion of hers might just turn out to be her ruin.

"You might be a lot of things, Hadleigh," Tripp said seriously, "but you're not **any** kind of idiot, total or otherwise."

He'd gotten to her—again. Paid her what sounded like a sincere compliment, however backhanded, just when she least expected it to happen and was least prepared to think up a countermove.

"You've changed your tune," she said in a singsong voice after they'd covered several country miles, "since the **last** time you kidnapped me."

Tripp was in profile, of course, and the cab of the truck was dark except for a few lights on the dashboard, but Hadleigh saw his brief grin. "To my way of thinking, what I did 'last time' was get you out of a fix that would have led to disaster—the kind that takes years to untangle." A studied pause, followed by a studiously casual, "How is ol' Oakley these days, anyhow?"

"Are you going to pretend you don't know all about him?" Hadleigh asked coolly. "This isn't Los Angeles or Seattle, Tripp. It's Bliss County, Wyoming, where everybody knows what everybody else is up to at any given moment. Oakley's been in and out of rehab—sometimes for alcohol, sometimes for prescription meds, sometimes both. The executor of his father's estate has cut off direct access to his trust fund, his mother remarried and moved to Quebec and his siblings wrote him off long ago. Oh, and he just got either his second or third divorce. I forget which."

Tripp slowed, signaling a right turn off the dark county road onto an even darker dirt driveway. "Third," he said without inflection.

She'd been right. Tripp had kept track of local goings-on while he was away getting rich and getting married—too bad she'd been too much of a coward to do some checking. If she had, she might have spared herself some angst.

"But who's counting?" They were passing the ancient mailbox with **Galloway** stenciled on its side, so she knew they'd be at their destination any minute now.

Hadleigh had only been to the Galloway ranch a few times—once or twice when she wouldn't let Will ditch her—and the day of Tripp's mother's funeral. There had been a wake at the house, following a graveside service in the small and very historic cemetery behind the orchard. Still numb from the loss of her own parents just eighteen months before, she'd watched the proceedings in somber silence, sticking close to Gram's side. Will, sixteen by then, must have been drawing a few grim parallels of his own, but he'd kept his head up and his shoulders straight, if only because his best friend was counting on him to be strong.

Tripp, also sixteen that year, was stoic throughout the whole ordeal, saying little or nothing, probably taking his cues from his stepfather. Jim Galloway had been about broken in two by the loss of his wife, everyone said so, but if he did any weeping, he did it in private. By the same token, the older man wore his grief in his eyes from then on, in the set of his shoulders and the way his strong hands hung limply at his sides. Once, Jim had been outgoing, gesturing when he talked, laughing a lot.

That part of him had been buried with his wife. For all intents and purposes, Tripp had been on his own after that, emotionally, anyway. He'd spent even more time at Gram's from then on, and Gram had made room for him without fuss or fanfare.

This cascade of memories made Hadleigh regret her flippant remark, but it also took her mind off the conversation she and Tripp were about to have—not that he was forcing her into anything. Oh, no, she'd **chosen** to play along with his caveman act.

Again.

Hadleigh sat up straighter, bracing herself for at least one bumpy cattle guard and about a mile of ruts beyond that.

"Your dad must have been pretty lonely, living out here all by himself for so long."

Tripp glanced her way, but she couldn't read his expression, since his face was in shadow. "Yeah," he agreed, his voice low and a little wary. "Dad put a good face on things whenever I came home for a visit or we talked on the phone, but it couldn't have been easy for him."

On impulse—one she might come to regret—Hadleigh reached past the console and the gearshift to rest her hand on Tripp's forearm. Even through the sleeve of his denim jacket and the shirt beneath it, she felt his muscles tense, and the warmth of his skin came right through all that cloth.

She withdrew her hand. "Tripp, I wasn't saying— I didn't mean to imply—"

"That I should have been here?" He didn't sound angry, just resigned and a bit sad. Did he get this a lot? Did he feel guilty for making a life somewhere else after his discharge from the service?

She hoped not, because whatever her own issues with Tripp might be, she knew he was a good man and always tried to do what was right.

"You had college ahead of you, and then a hitch in the military—"

Hadleigh's voice fell away, like a power line weighed down by snow and ice. The military equaled Afghanistan equaled Will dying long before his time. She turned her head away from Tripp, looked out, eyes burning, at a landscape she couldn't see, except by remembering.

A moment later it was Tripp who reached out. He took hold of Hadleigh's hand and squeezed firmly. "Hey," he said hoarsely. "I know you miss Will a lot, and that's okay. To this day, I think of things I mean to tell him. I remember that he's gone a split second later, but that's time enough to feel the loss all over again."

Tripp was still holding her hand, and she made no move to pull it away. "I think I liked it better," she told him, with a broken laugh and a slight sniffle, "when we were arguing."

Tripp laughed, and the tension eased up considerably. "All right," he said, Mr.

Agreeable. "We'll argue." An expectant pause followed. "You start," he finally added.

The invitation made Hadleigh laugh, too. "Give me a minute, okay?" she joked. "I'll come up with something that's sure to spark a raging disagreement."

"It's what you do best," Tripp replied.

She was about to protest that it took two to argue when they rounded the last bend and there was the log ranch house, a long, low-slung shadow of a place in the light of the moon. Some of the windows glowed, spilling a golden shimmer of welcome into the yard.

Maybe Jim was waiting up for Tripp; Hadleigh let herself hope he was, because her practical side had finally gotten the upper hand over the evil twin, and suddenly she wasn't so sure she wanted to tell all—not yet.

How, she wondered, squinting at several huge pieces of machinery standing empty and idle between the house and the barn, did she get herself into these scrapes, anyway? More importantly, **why** did she do it?

It was one thing to be a high-minded disciple of the truth, and quite another to be reckless with it.

"Brace yourself," Tripp warned before he shut off the engine, got out of the truck and came around to offer Hadleigh a hand down.

This time, she accepted his help. "Brace myself for what?" She worried that Jim might be in worse shape than she'd thought, and she schooled her face not to betray shock or, worse yet, pity when she saw him.

"The dog," Tripp answered. "Ridley's mighty enthusiastic when it comes to welcoming company. I put in one of those pet doors for him, so he can come and go as he pleases, and now when he hears a motor, he shoots through the gap like a lead ball fired from a cannon."

Hadleigh smiled. She could handle a canine missile.

Seeing Jim, a strong, proud man broken by his long illness, though—that would have been tough to handle.

They were moving toward the side entrance—it led to the kitchen, if Hadleigh recalled correctly—Tripp with his hand on her elbow again, steering her through the maze of stacked building supplies and all that heavy equipment.

"I heard you were doing some repairs," Hadleigh said, needing to make conversation as her nerves kicked up again, "but from the look of things, you're planning on leveling the house and barn and starting over from the ground up."

Before Tripp could respond, Ridley blasted through the pet door, leaving it to flap wildly in his wake, and streaked toward them, barking his fool head off out of sheer joy. He was no guard dog, that much was clear.

But then, neither was Muggles.

Tripp stepped in front of Hadleigh just as the dog sprang off its hind legs and all but took flight.

Laughing, Tripp caught the animal in midair, holding him in both arms, and Ridley squirmed with delight, frantically licking his master's face and giving little intermittent yelps of delight.

"Weird dog," Tripp said with affection.

Hadleigh found herself envying the animal for a moment, imaging what it would be like to jump and know Tripp would catch her, wrap her in his arms, hold her against his chest—

Even the face licking wouldn't have been such a bad thing.

Since Tripp was occupied with the dog, she had a chance to get her wits about her, and she was grateful, because whatever the man said to the contrary, she was, if not an outright idiot, something of a fool—especially when it came to him.

Soon enough, Ridley began to settle down and, having spotted Hadleigh, who'd moved out from behind Tripp by then, he perked up his ears and wriggled, wanting to be set down.

Tripp complied, but he kept a close watch on Ridley until he was sure the dog would behave himself. Hadleigh leaned down and patted the critter's furry head, telling him he was a good dog.

"Watch out," Tripp joked, "or he might

get conceited."

Hadleigh rolled her eyes, then straightened, feeling both relaxed and anxious. That was when the side door opened and Jim appeared, not as tall as Hadleigh remembered, thinner, too, and kind of unsteady on his feet. His hair had gone from salt-and-pepper to all salt since she'd seen him last, but when he moved into the porch light, she saw the familiar smile.

"Hadleigh Stevens," Jim almost crowed as she and Tripp mounted the two steps onto the small porch. "Is it really you, or do my eyes deceive me?"

Hadleigh smiled and stood on tiptoe to kiss Jim's scruffy cheek before he stepped back to let her and Tripp and the dog inside.

"It's really me," she replied cheerfully, while Jim gazed at her with astonished pleasure.

Tripp took her coat, hung it over the back of one of the kitchen chairs, put his own over it. The cheerful paper she faintly remembered had gone, and now there was only drywall, still smelling of newness. Lightbulbs dangled where there had once been fixtures, and the appliances were all askew, putting Hadleigh in mind of a few confused cattle milling around at the edge of a fast-moving river.

"Good thing I fired up the coffeemaker a little while ago," Jim said, still pleased, apparently, by the unexpected pleasure of a late-night visit from the famous stolen bride of Bliss County.

Was that how she'd be remembered?

Perish the thought.

Tripp, meanwhile, slid another chair back from the table for Hadleigh, and she sat. He made a face at her, and Hadleigh smiled up at him in triumph.

So much for his theory that Jim would be in bed.

Tripp wasn't giving any ground, though. He looked right into her eyes and a powerful jolt passed between them, making Hadleigh fidget. Tripp simply watched her, that wicked grin of his tugging at one side of his mouth.

"You'll be awake half the night if you

start swilling java now," he told his stepfather affably.

Jim merely laughed and sat himself down at the table next to Hadleigh. "Don't you fret about me, son," he said, in the deep, rumbling voice that was as much a part of him as his character and his fine reputation. He didn't even glance at Tripp, focused on Hadleigh the way he was. "Thing is, I'm pretty sure I'm **already** sound asleep and having myself a right nice dream." His eyes twinkled. "Why, I'd swear I'm looking at the prettiest woman this side of yonder, and that means I **have** to be dreaming."

Hadleigh, though she was still smiling back at Jim, felt a few faint pangs of guilt. She knew most of the neighboring ranchers and their wives had stopped by to check on Jim while he was undergoing treatment, the men lending a hand with the chores, the women cooking and cleaning and doing laundry. The people in town had rallied, too, and done as much for Jim as he'd allow, bringing him soup and casseroles and home-baked bread, ferrying letters and catalogs up from the mailbox. In season, when the beans and tomatoes came on, he got so many that he'd called the food bank over in Bliss River and asked them to come and get the overflow.

So why hadn't **she** paid him a single visit?

The most honest answer was also a selfish one. She hadn't driven out to the ranch for one reason—because Jim was Tripp's dad, and she hadn't wanted to spend even a minute in a place where Tripp ought to have been and wasn't. His absence would have been too glaring, as though he'd been torn from the very fabric of the universe. Just like Will.

"I'm so sorry, Jim," she managed. "I should have stopped by, or at least called..."

He patted her hand, shook his head. "There's nothing you need to be sorry about," he said gently. "Folks do what they can, when they can, and that's the way things should be."

Hadleigh swallowed a lump and nodded

her thanks.

Tripp might or might not have seen the exchange, and read it for what it was; if he had, he gave no sign of it. Visibly suppressing a sigh, he rustled up three mugs, filled them at the old-fashioned coffeemaker and brought them to the table.

Needing to get her emotional bearings, Hadleigh looked around at the kitchen. All the cupboards were gone, except for one next to the outdated stove. The brushed-steel refrigerator was surely new, a massive thing with an ice and water dispenser, freezer drawers at the bottom and handles that gleamed fit to blind a person. A pair of dishwashers, still in their wooden crates, waited to be installed.

Having followed her glance, Jim's smile brightened, if that was possible. He sipped some coffee, savored it awhile before he swallowed. Then he said, "My son has some mighty fancy ideas about kitchens. He's fixing to tear out the bathrooms, too, and put in swanky fixtures, and unless I miss my guess, he'll have the whole place rewired to run computers and the like without blowing a fuse every five minutes. Yep, the minute I'm out of his hair, all hell will break loose."

Tripp was looking down at his coffee, a slight smile playing on his mouth, but he didn't offer a comment.

Hadleigh stiffened. "Out of his hair?" she echoed. "You're going somewhere?"

Jim Galloway was legendary for his attachment to the land—**this** land—which had been in his family for generations. The Galloway brand was one of the first to be registered in Wyoming, before it was even a state, and then there was the cemetery, where his wife and several dozen of his ancestors had been laid to rest. All of which made it next to impossible for Hadleigh to imagine him anywhere else.

Unless—

Jim gave a resounding hoot of laughter when he recognized the horrified expression on her face. "Nope, I'm not ready to turn up my toes just yet, young lady. I'm headed north to Alaska, like that old song says. Only I'll be traveling in style, on board one of those cruise ships with twenty-four-hour buffets and ice statues as big as bison."

Tripp smiled at the description but still said nothing.

"Wow," Hadleigh said, as surprised by this dedicated rancher's vacation plans as she'd ever been about anything. She'd have pegged him for the pack-trip type, leading mules along narrow trails, camping out in the wilderness with a few buddies, living off the land, all of them sipping Jack Daniels around a big bonfire at night while they swapped yarns. But a **cruise?** She would never have guessed that one. "That's...great!"

"They dance till dawn on those ships," Jim added after a few more sips of coffee. "There's bingo with fancy prizes, and some kind of stage show every night. I don't know how those people get any rest."

"Speaking of rest," Tripp interjected mildly.

His eyes still sparkling, Jim pushed back

his chair, made a big production of yawning and stretching his arms. When he spoke, it was with exaggerated sincerity. "I **am** a trifle worn-out, come to think of it— it's downright wearying, sitting around watching all those carpenters and electricians and plumbers work every day but Sunday." He closed with another expansive yawn.

"Good **night,** Dad," Tripp said. But he'd stood up when Jim did, out of respect for his stepfather.

Jim ignored him and turned to Hadleigh, executing an elegant bow from the waist, more like a charming courtier than a rancher. He took her hand and kissed it.

"If I were thirty years younger," he whispered loudly, mischief dancing in his eyes, "I'd give Tripp here a run for his money, and that's for sure."

Hadleigh laughed softly and squeezed Jim's calloused fingers in farewell.

He straightened, winked at her and left the room.

Hadleigh was sorry to see him go, and not just because he'd served as a buffer between her and Tripp. "I think I'm in love," she said quietly once they were alone.

"Dad's a charmer, all right," Tripp said with a chuckle.

"He's really going on a cruise to Alaska?"

"He's really going," Tripp confirmed, turning his chair around and sitting down again, this time straddling the seat, his arms folded atop the high back. "The doctor gave him the go-ahead yesterday. His fare's paid and he's even made up his mind to pick up some new clothes for the trip."

"I'm impressed," Hadleigh said, and she meant it.

"You're also stalling," Tripp informed her lightly.

She giggled, more nervous than amused. "That, too."

Tripp caught her gaze and held it. "Something made you skittish, back at Billy's tonight. And it was awful sudden."

Hadleigh gulped, nodded.

He waited, not pushing, not prompting. He'd already stated his terms; if she could look him in the eye and tell him that whatever was bothering her had nothing to do with him, he wouldn't press for answers.

She didn't look away, much as she would have liked to. "I was thinking back. I couldn't help it, with us sitting in the same booth we as did back then and everything."

Tripp took her hand. And waited.

Hadleigh was reassured but no less nervous. "I don't know what you think I'm going to say, but—well—I'll bet it's going to come as a surprise. You might even laugh."

He skimmed his thumb over her knuckles, the same ones he'd brushed with his lips earlier. Hand kissing, it seemed, ran in his family. His eyes were steady when he spoke again, his voice husky. "Never gonna happen," he said. He swept his free hand through his hair, leaving it attractively mussed, and then grimaced. "Look, Hadleigh, you don't have to do this—you know that, right? I shouldn't have pushed you, but the truth is, some of the stuff I'm imagining is just about driving me crazy."

A strange, sweet warmth washed through Hadleigh's heart in that moment, and her eyes scalded. Her throat went tight and she clutched Tripp's hand when he probably would have pulled it away.

She'd known all along that Tripp wouldn't press her for an answer when push came to shove—the same way she'd known, a decade before, that he'd stop her from marrying Oakley.

Maybe it was just for closure but, scared as she was, **embarrassed** as she was, Hadleigh needed to tell Tripp what she'd avoided realizing, what she'd so carefully blocked from her mind for all these years and why. What had been her motive?

The answer left her thunderstruck, and more than a little ashamed.

She'd been able to blame **him** for what was lacking in her life, that was the real reason, releasing herself from having to take responsibility for making her dreams happen.

Well, Hadleigh thought, perhaps she'd been a lackluster participant in the marriage pact, up until now, but after this, she'd be free to move on, let go of the past, get serious about finding a man who truly loved her, one she could love in return, without reservation. Together, she and Mr. Right could make a home together, build a family and **be happy.**

Okay, so it might not be a grand, passionate romance.

Nobody had everything.

"You were right," Hadleigh said. "Back then, I mean. I **was** too young to get married, and I didn't love Oakley any more than he loved me. What I realized tonight— what shook me up—was that I was really just using him."

Tripp raised one eyebrow slightly. "Using Smyth? How?"

Hadleigh drew a breath, let it out slowly and took the plunge. "I was hoping you'd come back before it was too late," she said, biting her lower lip. When he didn't respond, she went on. "I was only eighteen, Tripp. My parents were both dead, I'd lost my brother, and Gram, well, she was a rock, but she aged a lot faster after Will died. I guess I wanted a husband, children, a home—some kind of emotional security."

Tripp looked tired. But surprised? No. That he wasn't.

He was quiet for a long time.

Hadleigh, though somewhat humiliated, felt an old burden fall away, and her spirit soared even as she said, "So I asked you to take me to California with you when you left here—"

"And I told you I was married," he finished for her.

"Yeah." She paused. "I was a dumb kid with stars in her eyes," she continued, letting the hurt rise to the surface, so she could finally release it. "But you were my brother's best friend, Tripp. You grew up in Mustang Creek, and weddings are the kind of thing people talk about in places like this—**a lot.** That being the case, I guess I thought I would have heard about your plans a little sooner."

"I'm sorry, Hadleigh. I could have handled that better."

But she shook her head. "Don't you see? You didn't hurt me. I hurt myself by having all these crazy expectations. You were a grown man, Tripp, with every right to marry whomever you wanted, **do** whatever you wanted. I was the one living in a dreamworld. I was a kid, as you so bluntly pointed out—"

"You were a kid," Tripp confirmed. "A smart, **beautiful** kid with a future. One that was way too good to be wasted on Oakley Smyth."

Just then, Ridley ambled over, rested his muzzle on Hadleigh's right knee and gave a sympathetic whine. She laughed and stroked the dog's gleaming head, touched by his efforts to cheer her up. After a moment, though, she met Tripp's gaze.

"You knew? That I was hoping you'd show up at my wedding, I mean?"

Tripp hesitated a fraction of a second too long, then shook his head. "No," he said, and his voice was so hoarse, he had to clear his throat. "I didn't know—not then."

But he'd figured it out since, obviously.

Hadleigh, exhausted now, decided not

to pursue the subject any further until she'd had time to mull things over.

"I think I'm all talked out—for tonight, anyway," she said, trying to smile.

Tripp nodded, looking both confused and relieved.

"Guess I'd better get you back to town," he told her, "before Melody decides I've kidnapped you for real this time and calls in the FBI."

As Tripp helped her into her coat, Hadleigh suddenly felt light, fatigue notwithstanding, as though a great burden had been lifted from her shoulders, one she hadn't fully realized she was carrying.

Was she ready, at long last, to leave all those worn-out, dusty dreams behind, to stop being haunted by her eighteen-year-old self and get on with her life?

She knew one thing for sure: it was time to make some changes—some **big** changes.

CHAPTER EIGHT

Neither one of them said a word during the drive back to town, and since Tripp wasn't in the mood to chat, that was fine with him. Still, the road would have seemed a lot longer and lonelier than it was if Ridley hadn't come along for the ride and kept him company.

Physically, Hadleigh was right there in the truck with him and the dog.

Mentally, though, it seemed she'd gone off somewhere in her head, where he couldn't follow. Or maybe she was just asleep.

Tripp reminded himself that Hadleigh had told him she didn't want to do any more talking that night, and he could definitely see her point. She'd made her big confession, and it followed that her batteries were low.

The thing was, women didn't usually mean it when they claimed they didn't want to talk, not in his experience, anyway. What they **wanted,** 99.9 percent of the time, was tender and preferably poetic inquiries about their feelings.

Same when there was a domestic shit storm brewing on the horizon—they'd get suspiciously quiet and radiate hostility, but ask them what was wrong, and they'd inevitably say, "Nothing."

A man couldn't win for losing when it came to getting a straight answer out of a pissed-off female, but he'd damned well better keep trying anyhow, no matter how hopeless the effort seemed, if he knew what was good for him.

With all these thoughts roiling in his head, Tripp glanced over at Hadleigh. She was as beautiful in profile as she was from the front, and the rear view wasn't bad, either.

Maybe she was playing possum or she'd actually dozed off; he couldn't tell. The sweet and slightly wicked little smile resting on her mouth both intrigued and troubled him. If Hadleigh **was** asleep, she was having a dream that pleased her. And if she was awake, she was thinking some pretty happy, even sensual, thoughts.

What was going on in that brain of hers, waking or sleeping?

Right around then, Tripp would have given just about anything to know that he figured into this particular equation somewhere, because if that smile meant she had a man on her mind, he damn well wanted it to be **him.**

Tripp had kept one eye on the road while he was checking Hadleigh out, but the next time he risked a glance in her direction, it wasn't her dreamy expression that caught his attention. It was her breasts.

Damn, but Hadleigh had herself a fine pair of breasts, perfect ones, in fact, and the way that clingy pink top emphasized their contours made Tripp's heart go skittering like a bucking bronco on a patch of ice. And the need to free those breasts from the confines of Hadleigh's shirt and bra, look at them, cup them in his palms, was like a swift, sharp stab.

He damn near went off the road.

Muttering a swear word, he turned the wheel just in time and kept his gaze straight ahead, but even then, Tripp could see her at the periphery of his vision, and clearly.

Hadleigh's breasts, he reflected miserably, were neither too big nor too small, but just right—anything more than a handful being a waste, as the old saying went.

Tripp groaned inwardly. Why had he thought taking Hadleigh out on what, by Mustang Creek standards, constituted a date, was such a good idea?

The answer surfaced almost immediately, and it wasn't flattering. He'd believed, arrogantly enough, that if the two of them could spend an evening together, share a meal in the least romantic place available—that being Billy's—he'd be able to win Hadleigh over, find his way around all those booby traps and barriers she'd spent a decade building around herself.

As if.

Thinking back over the early part of the evening, he knew all those genial interruptions hadn't helped, but these were old friends and longtime neighbors, along with a few well-meaning acquaintances stopping by to say hello and ask about his dad. Sure, they'd been curious, but they genuinely cared about Jim and wanted to make sure Tripp felt welcome. They were good people, people he couldn't and **wouldn't** have brushed off for anything, not if he wanted to look in the mirror ever again.

Years away from home—college, and then air combat in Afghanistan, followed by a job he loved captaining 787s for a major airline and building his own company after that, hadn't changed who or what he was: a Wyoming wrangler who was happier on the open range than anywhere else. Early on, he'd believed he wanted to get away from the hard work and frequent difficulties any rancher or farmer had to deal with, day after day, year after year. Now, looking back, Tripp wondered if he hadn't done all that just so he **could** come home for good, when the time was right, and not spend the rest of his life wondering if he could have made it in the outside world.

If he'd stayed on the ranch, he figured, he would have been happy enough. But he might have spent more than a few restless nights staring up at the bedroom ceiling and asking himself what he'd missed out on, what he could have accomplished if he'd only taken the risks.

No, Tripp had no real regrets about the choices he'd made, with the possible exception of marrying Danielle instead of just sleeping with her for a while. That way, they could have gotten each other out of their systems and maybe even parted as friends.

Grimly, Tripp put all that out of his mind, believing as he did that what's done is done and hashing it over wasn't going to change a damn thing. And anyway, right here and right now wasn't such a bad place to be, for all the sudden and completely unfamiliar things going on in his heart as well as his brain.

He wanted Hadleigh, he knew that now, for sure and certain, not just in his bed, but in the whole of his life. He was intoxicated by the spicy-floral scent of her skin, the silken shine of her hair, the ripe curves of her body—the whole package.

And his gut told him it wasn't going to be easy.

Tripp couldn't have said how he knew, but he was convinced Hadleigh had gone through some changes that night, and the road she was headed down might well lead her **away** from him for good.

The irony of that might have amused him if it hadn't struck his middle like the blow of a sledgehammer.

And what about that kiss he'd laid on her, right there in the middle of Billy's place, with practically the whole town looking on? What the hell had he been trying to prove?

Okay, so Hadleigh hadn't hauled off and punched him for it or walked out or done any of a million other things she would have been justified in doing. In fact, she'd kissed him back.

It had been a stupid move on his part, just the same, Tripp thought, and damned arrogant, too.

Same with that caveman crap he'd pulled next, hustling Hadleigh out to the truck and then not taking her home, as she'd asked him to, but out to the ranch.

True, if Hadleigh hadn't **wanted** to go with him, she wouldn't have, but that didn't justify what he'd done. He owed her an apology at the very least.

Yet she'd seemed happy enough when they got to his place, and when Jim showed up on the side porch, she'd been so kind, so engaging, that within a few moments, the old man was lit from within, glowing like a happy jack-o'-lantern with hair.

Finally, when Jim had gone to bed and Tripp and Hadleigh had the kitchen to themselves, she'd overridden her con-siderable pride to say she'd realized that she'd never wanted to marry Oakley Smyth, that she'd been hoping all along that he, Tripp, would swing into the church like Tarzan on a vine and carry her off.

A crazy idea, yes—but Hadleigh had been **eighteen** at the time, and a very sheltered eighteen at that, since Will had run almost constant interference between his kid sister and the big, bad world after their parents had died, and so had their grandmother. Alice, down to one chick in the nest after Will's death, and probably figuring her granddaughter had already endured enough reality for one lifetime, might as well have swathed the girl in cotton batting or locked her up in an ivory tower with nothing to do but read fairy tales and watch animated movies filled with princes, princesses and singing bluebirds.

Now, as the town limits of Mustang Creek twinkled into view, Tripp concluded sadly that Hadleigh must have met with considerably more opposition that he'd thought once she'd taken up with Oakley Smyth.

Alice surely hadn't approved of the match—no sensible person would have, knowing anything at all about the potential bridegroom—and the woman must have said and done just about everything she could to stop Hadleigh from seeing Smyth, let alone **marrying** him.

No easy matter, considering that her grandmother had been the only blood kin Hadleigh had left, and her approval would have meant a great deal, especially to a girl fresh out of high school. Still, Hadleigh had been brave enough to bust out and take a chance. She'd mapped out a game plan, however misguided it might have been, and she'd followed through, wagering everything on a chance at happiness, on the hope of a family of her own.

Finally, if all that wasn't enough, Hadleigh had innocently handed her heart over to Tripp, that day at Billy's, all a-froth in her wedding dress. **Take me with you,** she'd said.

What had **that** request cost her?

And how had he responded? He'd handed Hadleigh's fragile heart right back to her—after fracturing it first.

Tripp thrust out an angry sigh, remembering. He hadn't meant to be callous—he'd wanted to **help**—and while he didn't know what he could have done differently under the circumstances, he wished he'd been kinder, gentler and a whole lot less blunt.

He stopped for a red light, as furious with himself as he'd ever been with anybody. Hindsight might be 20/20, but damn, it still sucked. Even after he'd cavalierly dismissed Hadleigh with the news that he had a wife, she'd loved him. He realized that now—and a fat lot of good it did this late in the game.

Okay, a case could have been made for what he'd done that day, but if he'd given the matter any real thought, he would've been kinder about it, taken the time to be sure she understood, even stuck around to lend moral support until the worst of the gossip died down.

Instead, he'd simply dropped Hadleigh off at home, once he knew Alice was there to pick up the pieces, and gone right back to his own well-ordered, big-city life. Thereafter, when he did think about Hadleigh, he'd smile, remembering her not as a woman, but as his best friend's spirited kid sister—painfully young, vulnerable and, therefore, strictly off-limits.

In the interim, naturally, she'd grown up. Hadleigh was not only beautiful, she was smart and sexy, too. Some lucky bastard was bound to snatch her up, and this time around, she wouldn't need—or want—rescuing. Nope, Hadleigh would find a good man, marry him, bear his children and make him glad to be alive every day of his life.

Tripp wanted Hadleigh to be happy, no question about it.

However, just the idea of her sharing someone else's bed, giving birth to somebody else's babies, was almost more than he could take.

Still, if his hunch was correct and Hadleigh was finally through waiting for him, finally ready to move on, there wouldn't be much he could do about it, would there?

Just as Tripp came to that dismal conclusion, Hadleigh woke up, if she'd been asleep in the first place, sitting up straight, blinking, looking over at him with an expression that faintly resembled surprise.

To lend a little comic relief, Ridley chose that moment to stick his floppy-eared head through the gap between the front seats and run his wet, sloppy tongue the length of Hadleigh's left cheek.

Startled, she laughed, wiped away the dog spit with a quick motion of one pink-sleeved arm and reached back to tug gently at Ridley's ears. "Goofball," she said, with a note of such tenderness in her voice that, on top of everything else, Tripp found himself envying his own four-legged sidekick.

"We'll be at your place in a minute or so," he told Hadleigh, and his own voice sounded, to him anyway, as though it were being piped in from somewhere far away.

Brilliant, he thought. As if Hadleigh wouldn't know that already, having lived in Mustang Creek her whole life, except during college.

"That's good," she replied distractedly,

still focused on Ridley. She was stroking the critter's head, bathing the mutt in the sunny glow of her smile.

In that moment, the hackneyed term "lucky dog" took on a whole new significance for Tripp.

He couldn't think of anything to say, nothing that would raise his rapidly dropping stock with Hadleigh, so he just drove, and, pretty soon, they were pulling up at the curb in front of her house.

Most of the lights were on, and Melody's car was still parked outside, though she'd at least had the courtesy to move the thing so it wasn't blocking Hadleigh's station wagon in the driveway the way it had earlier in the evening.

Tripp parked the truck, shut off the engine and left the dog in the backseat when he got out. He walked around and grabbed the door handle on Hadleigh's side about a second before she shoved it open with so much force that she practically knocked him over. Yep, if Tripp hadn't been quick on his feet, he figured, she'd have body-slammed him to the sidewalk.

"Oops," she said with a tired smile.

In an alternate universe, Tripp thought glumly, Hadleigh would invite him in, and Ridley, too. At that point in the fantasy, her dog **and** his conveniently disappeared into another dimension—only temporarily, of course—and after some sweet talk, perhaps in front of a crackling fire, and maybe a few glasses of wine, Hadleigh, smiling a come-hither smile, would take Tripp by the hand and lead him into her bedroom—

Tripp brought himself up short. **Yeah, right.**

Ridley, meanwhile, being stuck in the backseat, began to whine and trot back and forth, clearly unhappy that he'd been left behind instead of gallantly walking Hadleigh to her door and looking on with canine approval while Tripp kissed her good-night.

Get a grip, Tripp muttered to himself.

He'd walk Hadleigh to the house, though, and wait on the porch until she'd gone inside and shut the door.

Kissing her would have been nice, but even the dog probably knew **that** was out of the question, at least for tonight.

"I'll be fine," she protested, obviously flustered when Tripp opened the gate and gestured for Hadleigh to precede him. "Really. You don't need to—"

Before she could finish her sentence, the front door flew open, and Melody stood in the chasm, peering out at them. The retriever—Muggles, wasn't it? Or some other Harry Potter–type name?— seemed glued to Melody's side, glistening black schnoz pressed against the screen in the outer door.

Great. An audience.

Not that he was exactly surprised.

He leveled an eloquent look at Melody, and she responded by wrinkling her nose as if to say "gotcha."

Hadleigh seemed blissfully unaware of the exchange, and that was probably a good thing. "You see?" she asked Tripp brightly, goddess-beautiful in the light of the moon. "I'm perfectly safe, so you can go now. Thanks for dinner and—

everything."

Everything? Tripp was mystified. He'd bought her a salad and some iced tea, and she'd barely touched either one, and then he'd abducted her, behaving like a nutcase in one of those true-crime shows on TV.

He should have dressed for the part, he thought ruefully. Worn camouflage and maybe a ski mask. Scoured his finger-tips with sandpaper so he wouldn't leave prints.

"Uh, you're welcome," he said, several beats late and with all the urbanity of a turnip.

"It was nice," Hadleigh said, quietly generous. She raised herself onto her toes and kissed him on the cheek, the way women did when they were bussing Great-Grampa goodbye, once visitors' hours were over at the old folks' home.

Melody remained in the doorway, and so did the dog—Hermione? Hortense? Whatever. What was this, anyway, some kind of sideshow?

Tripp, speechless for once in his life of

free-flowing bullshit, opened his mouth and, when nothing came out, closed it again.

Hadleigh, meanwhile, turned and strolled toward the porch steps. Looking back over one silky pink shoulder, she waggled her fingers in a goodbye wave and then left him standing there, in the middle of her front walk, like a bad prom date.

He didn't move until Hadleigh had gone into the house and closed the door behind her.

He didn't hear the lock click, which was what he'd expected, but maybe Melody was leaving right away.

Tripp sighed once and headed for the truck.

At his approach, Ridley began to bark again, this time yapping like a teacup poodle. He didn't like being kept out of the action—such as it was—or maybe he just objected to letting Hadleigh out of his sight.

Join the club, dog.

At least there was one good thing he

could say about tonight. It was **over.**

And tomorrow was a new day.

Melody, who had changed out of her own clothes and into Hadleigh's red sweatpants and a worn-out concert T-shirt at some point in the evening, stood impatiently in the entry, shifting from one foot to the other like a kid waiting for a turn at hopscotch on the playground.

"I see you're planning on spending the night," Hadleigh observed casually, bending to pet Muggles, who was frantic with joy at her return. That was the great thing about dogs, she thought—they were so unabashedly glad to see their people again, whether the separation had lasted five minutes or five months.

"You're stalling," Melody accused her. Besides the sweatpants and T-shirt, she'd helped herself to another carton of yogurt at some point, and now she was waving the spoon at Hadleigh like an orchestra conductor's baton. "Tell me what happened!"

Hadleigh smiled. "Okay," she said

agreeably.   "**Nothing.**   That's   what happened."

Melody narrowed her eyes. "Are you kidding me? I checked the social media sites, my friend, and what do I see? They're absolutely **peppered,** all of them, with pictures of you and Tripp—kissing!"

"I hope you made yourself at home when I was away," Hadleigh said, her tone sweet as she took off her coat, hung it on its customary hook on the coat-tree. All the while, she had one ear trained on the sound of Tripp's retreating truck, but Melody didn't need to know that. "I mean," she went on merrily, "like logging on to my computer—maybe peeking into my medicine cabinet and, if you really got bored, checking the expiration dates on the stuff in my fridge—"

Melody squared her shoulders and tried to come off as indignant. "You know very well," she said archly, "that I didn't **need** a computer to check up on you. I used my phone. Furthermore, I most definitely did **not** 'peek into your medicine cabinet,' but if I had, I might have wondered when you plan to look into **birth control.** As for your fridge, I probably saved your life. There were things in there that your grandmother must have bought during the first Bush administration—but not to worry. I tossed everything that bubbled or shouldn't have been green so you wouldn't poison yourself."

Hadleigh laughed, shaking her head. "And those clothes?" she asked, indicating the purloined sweatpants and T-shirt.

"They were in the **drier,** for pity's sake," Melody said. "I was at loose ends and there was absolutely nothing on TV, so I decided to fold the laundry. Then I figured this outfit looked pretty comfortable and it was still nice and warm, so I changed into it. Sue me."

"You're impossible," Hadleigh said, still smiling. Tripp would be well on his way home by then, heading back through town, out into the countryside, the sky popping with stars and the moon shining, even at half strength, as brightly as if it could barely contain all that light and might burst at any second.

A pang of something—yearning?— struck her, the way homesickness used to, just at twilight, when she was very young and away from home for a slumber party or a sleepover at a friend's house. Most likely, what she felt was clearly visible in her face, but she'd already gone past Melody at that point, on her walk to the kitchen. She wanted to let Muggles out in the backyard for a few minutes and brew a cup of herbal tea in the vain hope she'd be able to sleep that night.

"That's all you've got to say? That I'm impossible?" Melody ranted gleefully, curious beyond all endurance, trailing through the house in Hadleigh's wake, right along with the dog. "The man **kissed** you in the middle of a busy restaurant— hell, Tripp didn't just kiss you, he just about **swallowed** you, and it didn't look like **you** were putting up any resistance—"

Hadleigh sighed as she moved through the archway between the dining room and kitchen and flipped on the lights. Although she knew better, she cherished a faint hope that, if she didn't spill the whole story of that night's nondate, Melody might drop the subject, at least for tonight, then either go home or crash in the guest room.

No such luck.

When Hadleigh opened the back door to let Muggles out, Melody started waving her smartphone around and challenged, "You don't believe me? I can show you the pictures—"

Hadleigh followed the dog across the screened-in porch, opened the outer door and stood on the steps, hugging herself against the chill. "Of course I believe you," she told Melody in her own good time. "And I don't need to see the pictures because, well, actually, I was **there.** An eyewitness—didn't miss a thing."

Melody, standing in the inner doorway, heaved a dramatic sigh. "Why are you doing this to me?" she asked pitifully. "Damn it, Hadleigh, I'm your **friend.** We made a pact, you and me and Bex, that we were all in this husband-finding pact together. Now, all of a sudden, you're being swept off your feet and you're not giving up a single detail? Honestly, I'm hurt."

"You're not hurt—you're nosy," Hadleigh replied, glancing back at Melody while she waited for Muggles to finish the yard tour and come inside. She smiled then. "But you're a best bud and I know you mean well."

"If I'm a 'best bud,' why not put me out of my misery and just **tell me what happened.**"

"The kiss happened," Hadleigh said softly, even a little sadly. "Oh, and I told Tripp something I probably should have kept to myself." At the look of concern and sympathy on Melody's face, she worked up another smile, albeit a flimsy one, and raised her shoulder in a shrug. "Other than that, there's nothing much to tell."

Melody squinted in the dim light flowing onto the porch through the window over the kitchen sink. "Are you all right?" she asked in a near whisper. So much for the wronged-friend diatribe.

"I will be," Hadleigh said very softly but

with a note of conviction. "What if we talk about this tomorrow, Mel? Bex is due back sometime in the afternoon, isn't she? If we wait until she's home, I won't have to tell the whole story twice."

Melody nodded her assent, if somewhat reluctantly, and crossed to where Hadleigh stood on the chilly threshold, laying a gentle hand on her shoulder. "Fair enough," she said. "But you're okay, right?"

"I'm okay. Go home and get some rest." Hadleigh managed a raw chuckle as Muggles bounded up the porch steps toward them, and her voice was steady when she teased, "The stress of all this is starting to take a toll on you, Melody. You look terrible."

Finally, Melody laughed, though her eyes were moist with tears. "Gee, thanks," she said with a loud sniffle.

Once they were back in the kitchen, Hadleigh filled the teakettle at the sink and Muggles consumed the last few bits of kibble in her bowl. Melody stood with her back to the counter, watching Hadleigh for signs of God knew what and gnawing away at her lower lip.

"Stay and have some tea," Hadleigh said. After all, Melody was one of her two BFFs, and it had been kind of her to stay with Muggles all evening—ulterior motives notwithstanding. Her heart was definitely in the right place, and she definitely didn't deserve to get the bum's rush.

But Melody shook her head and launched herself away from the counter, only in slow motion. "I'd better go home," she replied. "Cats are independent, and mine have plenty of food and water, but they've probably been waiting for me. Can't have them thinking I'm dead or something."

Hadleigh switched on the burner under the teakettle, crossed the room and gave her friend a quick hug. "Another half hour won't matter, will it?" she reasoned. "Stick around for one cup of tea?"

Melody had made up her mind to go, however, and once she decided on a course of action, large or small, she invariably followed through. She was already headed for the front door as

Hadleigh spoke, in fact, picking up her purse on the way, taking her coat from the brass tree in the entry.

Hadleigh hurried after her. "I'll walk you to your car," she said.

Melody grinned wearily. "This is Mustang Creek, Wyoming," she reminded her friend. "Not the mean streets of Gotham City. I'll be perfectly fine."

Déjà vu, Hadleigh reflected. She'd said something similar to Tripp when he brought her home and insisted on waiting around until she was safely inside the house. Protesting had done her about as much good then as it would do Melody now.

Her friend wasn't the only stubborn woman around, after all.

"I'll just stand on the porch and keep an eye on you until you get in your car and drive away," Hadleigh insisted.

"Whatever," Melody said, spreading her hands in a gesture of tolerant exasperation. She went down the steps, turned at the bottom and looked back at Hadleigh, holding up her keys and jingling them for emphasis.

Hadleigh knew that was her cue to go inside, but she stayed put. Even though there was a definite nip in the air—winter was still a couple of months off, but it was on its way for sure—she wasn't about to move, so she wrapped both arms around herself to keep from shivering and waited.

Melody slowly lowered the keys, and her expression, rimmed in the glow of the porch light, had gone solemn. "Was it bad, Hadleigh?" she asked, so softly it was a strain to hear her. "Is that why you don't want to talk about tonight?"

"Not bad," Hadleigh hastened to say, touched at the worry she saw not only in Melody's face, but in her bearing. "Just—I don't know—like being in one place as far back as you can remember, then suddenly finding yourself somewhere else."

Melody's brow furrowed. **"That's** cryptic," she said. Then, "If Tripp took you tonight just to spring another wife on you," she vowed, "I may have to shoot him." She brightened, but only a little. "And Bex will be delighted to help me hide the body."

Hadleigh heard the teakettle beginning to whistle, way back in the kitchen. It had been Gram's, that kettle, and it had a small bird on the spout that breathed steam and "sang" loud and shrill when the water came to a full boil. She'd always hated the darn thing, thought for sure it would split her eardrums wide-open one of these days.

For now, though, she ignored it.

"If there's another wife," she told Melody, "Tripp didn't mention her. Now, will you please either agree to stay the night or get in your car and go home before I freeze to death?"

Melody hesitated for a fraction of a second, but then she grinned again, turned and practically sprinted down the walk. "I'm going, I'm going," she called back when she reached the gate.

Hadleigh laughed, and it felt good this time, not forced, not manufactured, but natural and real.

Melody unlocked her car, got in and waited to close the door, so the interior lights would stay on, thus making her glaringly visible. She mugged, raising both eyebrows, and waved with comical enthusiasm—**See, no ax murderer hiding in here**—and Hadleigh waved back, sending a nonverbal message of her own. **If I have to stand here all night, waiting for you to shut your door and drive away, I'll do it.**

When Melody finally fired up the engine, tooted her horn and drove away, Hadleigh counted it as a victory, however small, and went inside to silence the teakettle.

CHAPTER NINE

He'd mark the days off on a calendar if he had to, Tripp promised himself the chilly, dark morning after his big night out with Hadleigh, but one thing was for **damn** sure: he wasn't going near the woman again for at least a week, not on purpose, anyhow.

Tripp was 100 percent positive that if he didn't keep his distance long enough to get his bearings, he'd do—or say—something **really** stupid again. Moreover, if Hadleigh happened to be looking drop-dead sexy at their next encounter, like she had in the black jeans and second-skin pink shirt she'd worn last night, well, that would probably double the odds that he'd make a damn fool of himself.

On top of that, he wondered where it had come from, this totally unfamiliar yahoo, hyped-up version of himself, walking around in his body, wearing his face and called by his name.

Would the **real** Tripp Galloway please stand up?

Because, damn it, this wasn't him.

He'd been a combat pilot, for God's sake, and he'd seen plenty of action. Once he was out of the service and flying jumbo jets for a major airline, he'd been responsible for the lives of literally thousands of passengers, as well as crew, and he'd never broken a sweat, even in some of the tough situations every pilot eventually runs into.

Later, while starting and building his charter-jet operation, he'd flown smaller, sleeker crafts a lot, especially in the beginning, when he was still getting established and couldn't afford to hire more pilots. Over time, Tripp had coped with wind shears, ice on the wings, instrument failures, in-flight engine blow-outs, some rodeo-worthy turbulence, flocks of birds, along with a few unscheduled nosedives just to make things interesting. And not once—**not once** in all that time—had he lost his cool. He'd simply handled it, whatever **it** happened to be, as he'd been trained to do.

And what all of that came down to was one outstanding fact: Tripp had never had any call to think of himself as the jumpy type. Hell, he hadn't even known **how** to be anything but his normal, competent, unflappable self.

Now, because of one night, with one woman, he was a nervous wreck.

Even ranch work didn't help calm him. He'd already fed the little band of basically useless horses out there in Jim's sway-roofed barn, lugging hay to the stalls, filling the troughs with the garden hose, brushing the critters down.

And all he'd been able to think about, the whole blessed time, was Hadleigh—the way she looked, the way she smelled of soap and flowers, the way her whiskey-brown eyes turned almost amber when she felt strongly about something.

Which was pretty much all the time, because even when she was a little kid,

Hadleigh had been opinionated and stubborn. And she hadn't changed, at least in that respect, over the intervening years, as far as Tripp could tell.

In short, he felt as if he'd jump right out of his skin if he didn't find manage to put her out of his mind for a while.

Tripp sighed, which he'd been doing a lot over the past twelve hours or so. The sun wasn't even up yet as he stood there in the torn-up kitchen, alone except for Ridley, who had condescended to go out to the barn with him earlier, instead of hanging around in the house the way he'd been doing lately.

Presently, the dog was munching away on his morning ration of kibble with as much greedy vigor as he might have if he'd put in a hard day's work rounding up strays instead of just moseying around behind Tripp, sniffing the dirt floor and wagging his tail in indolent, halfhearted swipes, like a windshield wiper slowed down by heavy slush.

Tripp made up his mind to stop ruminating—easier said than done—

flipped the switch on the outdated coffeemaker and yawned broadly as he waited for the java to start flowing. With luck, he'd feel semihuman again as soon as the first swallow hit his bloodstream.

He'd caught an hour or two of sleep, max, and forget REM and all the stages that were so vital to a functioning brain; when he **had** dropped off, he hadn't gone deep enough to get any real rest. Instead, he'd hovered just beneath the surface of consciousness, as fitfully active as if he'd gotten trapped under an iced-over lake, left to search wildly for a way out—all without finding so much as an air pocket.

The drip machine on the counter chugged and chortled, working hard but making no discernible progress. Tripp wasn't into consumerism—the new appliances, the flooring and the lighting and plumbing fixtures being installed had been carefully chosen to fill a particular purpose and stand up to heavy use over the long haul, and all the renovations were being done for practical reasons rather than aesthetics. But despite all that, he meant to junk that piece-of-crap coffeemaker before the day was out, replace it with one made in the current century. He should have brought the steel-clad, state-of-the-art one-cup wonder he'd used in his Seattle condo, he supposed, but since he'd donated the thing to charity, along with all the other items he'd considered extraneous—that being nearly everything he owned, as it turned out—there was no point in stewing over it now.

He was facing the counter, leaning in with both hands braced against the edge and **willing** that coffee to brew already, when he heard his dad shuffle into the kitchen. The sound was accounted for by Jim's newfound tendency to walk around in slippers for half the morning. Back in the day, the man wouldn't have left his bedroom without being fully clothed, right down to the pair of boots on his feet.

His chuckle was low and raspy, just as it had always been, and that was a comfort to Tripp.

"I reckon staring at that coffeemaker like you're trying to set fire to it is akin to the old saying as how a watched pot never boils," Jim drawled.

Tripp glanced back over one shoulder, didn't smile. He wasn't exactly at his sweet-tempered best without coffee, especially after a restless night. Then there was the whole Hadleigh situation. "This thing's a relic," he grumbled, indicating the antiquated gizmo with a slight motion of his head. "Should have been tossed out years ago."

Jim stood just inside the kitchen, still in his plaid flannel robe, which was probably even older than the coffeemaker, cinching the tie-belt a little tighter around his skinny middle. His thick gray hair stood out from his head every which way, and his beard had grown in, coarse enough to sand concrete glass smooth. Sure enough, Jim's big ugly feet were overflowing a pair of leather slippers that had seen better days.

On top of that, dear old Dad was grinning from ear to ear. He narrowed his eyes, as if he might be trying to pick Tripp out of a lineup of dead ringers and wasn't sure which was which. "Now why would I do a damn fool thing like that?" he retorted cheerfully. "That's a perfectly good coffeemaker, first off, and **second** off, you gave it to your mother and me for Christmas the year you turned fourteen, and that means it has sentimental value. You'd shoveled a lot of snow and mucked out a lot of stalls to buy that thing, and you were proud as all get-out, too."

That long-ago Christmas seared itself into Tripp's mind with the clarity of a flashback in a sentimental holiday movie. His mom had still been with them then, of course, full of life and laughter, none of them even dreaming how soon Ellie would be gone. And she'd been so delighted with that modern coffee-making device, as she sat perched on the edge of the living room couch in her pink chenille robe and fluffy slippers to match, ribbons and wrapping paper at her feet, her face shining more brightly than the gleaming multicolored lights on the tree.

Tripp closed his eyes for a moment, dealing with the aftershock of a memory that was both vivid and poignant, and when he opened them again, a second or two later, his dad was standing right next to him, one fatherly hand resting on his shoulder.

"I miss her, too, son," Jim said. "I miss her, too."

Tripp pushed away from the counter, straightened and gave another sigh. The coffee still wasn't ready, so he decided to settle for the strong beginnings already pooling in the bottom of the carafe, dark and bitter-smelling, looking like some kind of toxic waste and probably tasting about the same, and sloshed some into a mug.

Still unsteady, and therefore not trusting himself to speak yet, he took a big swig of the brew—it tasted just as he'd expected it would—and scalded his tongue in the bargain.

He grimaced.

Jim chuckled again, shaking his head.

Ridley, having inhaled his breakfast by now, lapped up the contents of his water bowl, went to the door and proceeded to whine, asking to be let out.

Both Jim and Tripp waited for the dog to remember the recently installed pet door. When he did, he low-crawled through it, leaving the flap swinging behind him like the saloon doors in an old Western movie.

"Don't go expecting too much of the critter," Jim quipped. "After all, he's new here."

Avoiding his dad's gaze as best he could, and in no hurry to make small talk, Tripp toned down his coffee with a little tap water and took a cautious sip.

Jim was in the mood for conversation, it seemed. "Let me hazard a wild guess," he said drily. "Last night didn't go well for you and Hadleigh."

"It went fine for Hadleigh," Tripp allowed, still grouchy and still taking care not to look directly at his dad. But out of the corner of his eye, he saw Jim approach the table, draw back a chair and sit down heavily, as though the short walk from his room had used up his last reserves of energy.

"If you don't want to tell me about it," Jim replied, quietly magnanimous, "that's certainly your choice. You might feel—and act—a little less like a scalded tomcat if you blew off some steam, though."

Tripp turned and met his father's steady gaze, if only to prove he could. "I'm sorry," he said hoarsely. "None of this is your fault, and I shouldn't have taken it out on you. Guess I'm too used to living alone."

Jim, though watchful and no longer smiling, seemed inappropriately cheerful. He rolled his thin shoulders in a move that resembled a shrug but wasn't. "Aren't we all?" he asked. "Anyway, no offense taken, son. Fact is, you never were all that easy to get along with in the morning. Getting you to roll out of the sack, pull some clothes on and help me with the chores was no simple matter, as I recall. You may remember that when your mother woke you up on schooldays, she used to stand as far from your bed as she could, lean in and poke at you with the end of the broom handle until you came out of hibernation. You were downright surly soon as you opened your eyes, and for a good while afterward, too."

Tripp couldn't help grinning, if a mite wanly, at the recollection of his petite, determined mother, prodding him with that damn broomstick of hers, warning him that if he didn't **get up,** he'd not only miss out on breakfast, but get left behind by the school bus. And he'd better not go thinking for one moment that he could get out of doing all his usual chores, either. Plus, Ellie had said, sounding remarkably chipper for that ungodly hour, it would be a long walk to school, because nobody was going to drive him all the way into town just because he was too lazy to get out of bed on time.

"I remember," he said, crossing to the sink, dumping the noxious contents of his mug. The coffeemaker had finally completed its mission, and he poured some, took a sip and found the brew slightly—and **only** slightly—more palatable than it had been the first time around. "Want a cup of this…stuff?" he asked Jim.

"I can get my own," Jim said, setting his jawbone in that obstinate way he had. "Never have needed waiting on like some high-and-mighty potentate, and I'm not inclined to change now."

Tripp laughed, ignored his dad's response and fixed a second cup of coffee, which he set down squarely in front of Jim—all while the old man was still gathering his forces to rise from his chair.

Ridley, meanwhile, zipped back in through the pet door, crawling on his belly again, like a soldier slithering along the ground under a steady strafe of enemy machine-gun fire.

Jim frowned at the coffee, grumbled a thank-you and gingerly drank some of it.

Tripp slapped his dad on the shoulder, but not too hard. They'd roughhoused in the old days, the two of them, but Jim had been leather-tough back then, digging postholes, stacking bales of hay in the barn or hurling them off a flatbed truck for the range stock. He'd done it all, Jim had— wrestling cattle to the ground at branding time, castrating bulls, delivering calves and foals when there was some kind of hitch in the process and the vet was too busy elsewhere to come around. He'd trained horses to the saddle and trimmed their hooves and shoed them. Not to mention splitting wood for the fire and braving the weather to chain up some old rig held together by chicken wire, high hopes and spit, or just get the damn thing to start up and run.

This new, more fragile Jim would take some getting used to, prickly attitude, threadbare bathrobe, sorry-ass slippers and all.

"Are you gonna try to tell me Mom didn't wait on your hand and foot?" Tripp teased, hoping to lighten the mood now that the caffeine was kicking in. "If so, save it, because I was here, remember, and she couldn't pour your coffee or iron your shirt or rustle up your supper fast enough."

Jim made a sound that fell somewhere between a huff and a grunt, but his mouth was twitching almost imperceptibly at the corners, and when Ridley ambled on over to rest his muzzle on one of his bony knees, Jim chuckled and jostled the dog's ears. When his dad looked up and met Tripp's gaze, Tripp saw both strength and sorrow in his eyes.

"You make Ellie sound like some downtrodden, unappreciated **hausfrau**," Jim said straight out. He spoke quietly and evenly, in no way defensive, just sure of himself. "But since your memory is so damn clear, son, then maybe you recall how strong-minded your mama was—and how anybody looking to push her in any direction she didn't want to go would have needed a bulldozer to budge her an inch. Ellie enjoyed being my wife, and she enjoyed being your mom. Making a nice home for all three of us was mighty important to her."

"I know that, Dad," Tripp said just as quietly. He paused, drank a few more swallows of coffee before going on. "You up to this big trip you've got planned? We could always postpone it for a while. Say, till spring…"

Jim scowled. "Well, I'll be damned," he said testily. "You've been on my neck from the minute you got back, telling me I need to get off this place and do something different, kick up my heels a little. Now, all of a sudden, you're singing a whole different tune."

"I'm just concerned about you, that's all," Tripp told him. "No need to take my head off."

"You're a fine one to talk," the old man retorted. "When I came in here, you looked like you might just unplug that old coffeemaker, open the back door and hurl the works halfway to the barn."

Tripp shoved a hand through his hair, clamped his molars together for a moment, then forcibly relaxed his jaw muscles. "Okay," he said, drawing the word out to twice its normal length.

Jim thumped at the tabletop with his right index finger, the way he'd always done when he was adamant about making his point. "Ellie was **happy,** damn it, tending this house. She could have gotten a job in town if she'd wanted to—she had secretarial skills, you know. Supported herself and you both before we met and got married. But she liked being right here, doing what she was doing, being who she was."

"I wasn't saying different, Dad," Tripp pointed out diplomatically.

The dog, seated a few feet away, perked up his ears a little and looked from Tripp to Jim and back again, like a fascinated spectator at a badminton game.

Jim's sigh came from somewhere deep within him. "I realize that, son," he said after a few minutes. "I reckon I just get to fighting my own head sometimes when it comes to Ellie. Except for not having any more kids—she was sad about that and so was I—I always figured she was pretty content with the lot of a mom and a rancher's wife. I tend to get my hackles up if anybody suggests otherwise, maybe because there's a part of me that'll always wonder if she ever regretted throwing in with the likes of me."

"She was happy," Tripp said, and he knew it was true. He could still see the light in his mother's eyes when Jim was due back at the house after a full workday. By then, having finished his after-school chores, Tripp was usually parked at the kitchen table—this very one, in fact—

doing homework. Ellie, busy fixing supper, would glance at the wall clock often. She'd hum under her breath and when she heard the roar of Jim's truck pulling in, she'd dash into the bathroom to fuss with her hair and put on lipstick and come out wearing a fresh apron.

Ellie had a thing about aprons, even though they hadn't even been in style, and she whipped them up herself, on her trusty sewing machine, always choosing bright fabrics with polka dots or stripes or splashy floral prints, adding ruffles and rickrack trim, and she must have had at least two dozen of them. Once one of these creations was stained, or began to look a little shabby, she'd toss it into the ragbag and make a replacement, pronto. She'd starched and ironed them, too; that was Ellie Galloway, retro when retro wasn't cool.

At the time, Tripp reflected, thinking back over the years, he'd found it funny, the fussy aprons and all that carrying on with her hair and her lipstick, just because Jim was about to walk through the door, same as he did every night, covered from head to foot in dust or mud. There'd be a sweaty ring pressed into his hair and circling his head, showing where his hat had rested. He'd give Ellie a quick once-over and say he was surely the luckiest SOB ever to have a wife like her, and she'd blush like a cheerleader after a couple of good cartwheels. Tripp, meanwhile, rolled his eyes.

Ellie would pretend to pout when Jim refused to kiss her until after he'd taken a shower, and sometimes she'd tell Tripp to keep an eye on the potatoes or the creamed peas or the chicken roasting in the oven for a while, and she'd disappear.

None the wiser, Tripp would do as he was told and make sure supper didn't burn until she eventually turned up again, with Jim right on her heels, half an hour or so later, bright-eyed and smiling in a very different way than usual.

Why, he wondered now, with a pang, hadn't he realized what a good thing it was to grow up in a home like that, with parents who loved each other, who loved **him?** Okay, he'd been a kid, and pretty clueless when it came to anything other than rodeo, football, horses and girls. Still, he'd had plenty of friends at school who came from broken homes and lived with one parent or the other—or, like Will and Hadleigh, didn't have either. Their grandmother had loved and looked after them, but it wasn't the same.

Tripp couldn't help knowing how badly Will missed his and Hadleigh's folks, because there wasn't much the two of them didn't talk about. The deepest confidences traveled between their two bunk beds, after the lights were out.

He'd known Will envied him a little— maybe a lot—because Tripp's mom nagged him to study and clean up his room, not in spite of it, and because he had rules to follow and chores to do. Jim had never once laid a hand on Tripp, but he'd been strict just the same, and even come to town looking for him a time or two when he'd stayed out past the agreed-on curfew. Tripp had been mighty embarrassed when that happened, especially given that most of his friends were around, and Jim's voice would be real quiet when he said, "Get in the truck."

The old man rarely said much during the drive back to the ranch, beyond a grim, "Your mother's been worrying." This, to Jim's mind, was a near-felonious infraction, and Tripp would feel so guilty about it, he'd start wishing his dad would yell at him the whole way.

It would have been better than that tight-jawed silence.

"Thanks," he said now.

Jim looked puzzled, sitting there with his wild gray-white hair and his bathrobe and those god-awful slippers, his coffee half-finished on the table in front of him. "For what, exactly?" he asked.

Tripp chuckled hoarsely. "For giving my mom a good life and treating the kid she brought along with her like your own son."

Jim's eyes misted over for a moment; he sniffled and looked away briefly. "You **are** my son," he said, gravel-voiced even after clearing his throat a couple of times. "Your last name is Galloway, isn't it?"

Tripp folded his arms, his head tilted

slightly to one side as he studied his dad's gaunt face. "Come on," he said. "Mom was pretty and smart and funny, and a whole lot of other things, too. But you must have had a few misgivings where I was concerned, in the beginning at least."

"Your mother was **beautiful,** not just pretty," Jim clarified, and though the mist had disappeared, his eyes were faraway, with a hint of a smile in them now, soft as a twilight shadow. "You were three years old and cuter than any kid has a right to be. Smart as a whip, too—you could already read a little and count to twenty without a misstep. It was clear from the first that you and your mom were a package deal, and I figured that just made me twice as lucky as I already was for catching Ellie's eye—**me,** a lunkheaded bachelor cowboy with a run-down ranch and not much else, and suddenly, after a lot of lonely years, I got myself a **family.** And this old place wasn't just a house anymore, either—it was a home." He paused, cleared his throat again and looked Tripp square in the eyes. "Now," he went on with resolute cheer, "shall I scramble us some eggs and burn a few slices of toast, or are we just going to sit here and blubber over the past until we waste away from hunger?"

Tripp laughed, shook his head. "Get yourself dressed," he said, "and we'll drive to town—get ourselves some breakfast and buy you some new duds for that fancy cruise of yours."

"What about all those construction fellas?" Jim fretted. "They'll be here pretty soon. And then there's the dog. And the chores."

"I fed the horses, Ridley can wait in the truck and the construction crews will be fine even if you're not here to breathe down their necks and ask them a dozen times an hour if they're sure they know what they're doing." He smiled at the consternation he saw in Jim's face. "Plus," he finished up, "I'll be able to get a halfway decent cup of coffee."

Hadleigh, Bex and Melody gathered around an old table in the center of

Melody's spacious studio, where she drew up jewelry designs, soldered and drilled and repeatedly soaked various metals in a stinky Crock-Pot concoction with the unappealing name of liver of sulfur, though Melody called it pickle juice. Her three cats, Ralph, Waldo and Emerson, a ragtag calico crew of indeterminate breed, were lined up along the top of a nearby bookshelf like china figurines, inscrutable and unblinking, but keeping a close eye on Muggles, who apparently hadn't noticed their presence at all, let alone felt any inclination to chase them.

"You promised to tell all," Melody reminded Hadleigh, propping her elbows on the table, propping her chin in her palms and leaning in a little.

"I could hardly wait to get over here," Bex added, wide-eyed.

Hadleigh figured they'd be pretty disappointed once she'd spilled the proverbial beans, but she launched in anyway, if only to get it over with, so they could talk about other things.

"I'm free," she blurted, perhaps overzealously, and watched as Bex and Melody's mouths fell open simultaneously. "It's over," Hadleigh went on, picking up speed. "I can finally leave the whole Tripp Galloway obsession behind for good and get on with my life."

Melody blinked, then belatedly closed her mouth.

Bex gazed at Hadleigh with narrowed eyes. "**What's** over?" she asked.

Melody had recovered enough to comment drily, "If anything ever actually **started** between the two of you, I must have been looking the other way at the time, because I definitely missed it."

Hadleigh glanced down at a sleeping Muggles, whose muzzle rested companionably on top of her right foot, and a rush of affection went through her, so intense it bordered on pain. **Love.**

Scary business indeed.

Her cheeks felt warm when she met her friends' eyes and continued, speaking slowly and precisely, in the vain hope of avoiding misunderstandings. "Tripp and I had something to eat over at Billy's," she recounted, her tone dutiful. "And while we were sitting there, a...thought occurred to me." When she paused, Melody made a rolling motion with both hands, urging Hadleigh to explain and be quick about it.

So Hadleigh went on, conveniently leaving out that scandalous kiss. Melody had, no doubt, showed the photos to Bex by now.

"I—I had a sort of...epiphany, I guess you'd call it—about the wedding." On the shelf above Melody's unlighted Franklin stove, her great-grandmother's sturdy mantel clock ticked ponderously, as if marking off Hadleigh's slow, thudding heartbeats, one by one. She took a deep breath and resumed. "I realized that I'd never really wanted to marry Oakley in the first place, although I wasn't actually conscious of that at the time of the wedding, you understand. The embarrassing truth is, I'm almost positive I was counting on Tripp showing up like a knight in shining armor, stopping the ceremony and—here's the part that makes me wince—declaring his undying love for me, right there in front of everybody. Insisting that he and I belonged together." Hadleigh paused and rolled her eyes in self-deprecating amusement. "What an idiot I must have been."

Neither Bex nor Melody looked particularly surprised by Hadleigh's admission that she'd loved Tripp the whole time. Nor did they correct her for referring to herself as an idiot.

Of course they'd guessed the truth, probably from the very first. The miracle was that after trying to talk her out of marrying Oakley and getting nowhere, they'd gone along with the idea.

"Please say you didn't tell Tripp that," Melody said.

Hadleigh bit her lower lip. "I wish I could," she answered softly. "For whatever reason, I couldn't hold it in—I did try at first, though. We went out to his ranch, and Jim was around, so we talked for a while, the three of us—mostly Jim and me. Then, when Tripp and I were alone, I told him."

"**Why?**" Melody and Bex chorused, in pained and perfect unison.

"Because it's the truth?" Hadleigh ventured, with less conviction than before. "Anyway, I think he already knew, because he didn't seem very surprised."

"Oh, Lord," Bex commiserated, whacking her forehead with the heel of one palm. Then, hastily and with a flash of anger in her eyes, she demanded, "What happened then? Did Tripp brush you off like he did before? Make that same speech about how you were still young, with your whole life ahead of you, and the right man would come along someday?"

Hadleigh relaxed a little. "No," she replied. "He didn't. But then **another** really peculiar thing happened. Something—something **shifted** inside me all of a sudden and that's when I knew."

Melody and Bex were both visibly holding their breath, and their eyes were huge with suspense.

Enjoying the drama of it all the tiniest bit, Hadleigh spread her hands for emphasis. "I'd just fallen **out** of love with Tripp—which came as a shock, since I never thought I was **in** love with him to begin with."

Melody blinked again. Bex just stared.

"You fell **out** of love?" Melody almost whispered once she'd recovered some of her composure. She sucked in a breath, let it out slowly and audibly. "And you think that's a **good** thing?"

"How could you not have known how you felt about Tripp?" Bex asked fretfully. "**Everybody** knew, except maybe for Oakley. And if you **did** know, on any level, why go through with the wedding for heaven's sake? What if Tripp hadn't fallen in with your crazy plan and hauled you out of there, Hadleigh? Would you still have married Oakley?"

Melody gave a shudder at the thought, though she kept her opinion to herself. For the moment, that is.

"I don't know what I would have done," Hadleigh admitted, feeling stupid and, at the same time, thinking she could have used a little more understanding and sup-port from her dearest friends. "Obviously, I wasn't exactly in touch with my authentic self." She lent just the faintest note of mockery to the term **authentic self,** not sure she possessed any such thing.

"I can't believe you told him," Melody reiterated.

"Were you listening before, Melody, when I said it seemed to me that Tripp already knew the truth anyhow?" Hadleigh retorted, turning snappish now. Both Melody and Bex were making her feel like a witness in a courtroom, testifying against herself.

"I really wish you hadn't said anything," Melody moaned.

Bex shifted her attention from Hadleigh to Melody. "Breathe," she commanded. "It's not as if the world is ending." She took a moment to do some breathing of her own. "Besides, what does any of it matter now? Hadleigh's **over** Tripp—she just said so. She's ready to move on. And that **is** a good thing. Isn't it?"

Melody sat up very straight and her eyes shot blue-green fire as she glared at her friends. "It would be **very** good," she said pointedly, "if our scorned bride here hadn't just crowned herself the new Queen of

Denial."

"I beg your pardon?" Hadleigh countered, out-and-out indignant now.

"You're doing it again!" Melody wailed, waving her hands wide as she spoke. Startled, the three cats shot off the bookshelf like furry bullets, headed in all different directions, and Muggles, finally surfacing from dreamland, gave a whimper of concern.

Chagrined, Melody had the belated good grace to lower her voice. "Hadleigh, **don't you see?** You're fooling yourself again—you're **not** over Tripp. You're scared as hell, and you're hoping if you pretend you don't care about him anymore, this whole thing will go away and you won't get hurt."

Hadleigh rose to her feet, trembling a little. "Don't you think you're assuming an awful lot?" she asked very quietly. "Do you actually believe you know me better than I know myself?"

Melody sighed, and she seemed to deflate before their eyes. "No," she said, her voice a sad whisper, her expressive eyes reflecting a deep sadness. "I don't think I'm assuming anything, Hadleigh. And, **yes,** I **do** know you better than you know yourself, at least right now, in this moment. You've lost so much in your young life, my friend—your parents, your grandmother, your brother—and it's perfectly natural that you wouldn't want to risk losing still another person you love."

"Hey, you two," Bex inserted, alarmed "let's not—"

On a rational level, Hadleigh knew, of course, that Melody meant well, and that she was as true a friend as she'd ever been. Hell, she might even have a point— to a degree. But sometimes her blunt statements and firm conviction that she was always right were difficult, if not impossible, to take—and this was one of those times.

"We all need some space," Hadleigh said instead of goodbye, snatching up her shoulder bag and scrambling awkwardly into her coat, in a major hurry to get out of there before she burst into tears of frustration and sorrow and heaven knew what other mixed-up emotions.

Muggles watched her curiously.

"Hadleigh, **wait,**" Bex protested when Hadleigh turned on her heel and marched across the studio toward the outside door, Muggles trotting behind her. "Hadleigh, please don't—"

"Let her go," Hadleigh heard Melody say, sounding defeated.

Because she didn't want Muggles to be any more alarmed than she probably already was, poor dog, Hadleigh denied herself the zing of pure satisfaction she would have gotten from slamming the studio door so hard it rattled on its hinges.

She stormed around the side of the house, through the gate and onto the sidewalk, fists bunched in the pockets of her coat. Muggles, though oddly hesitant, kept pace with her long strides.

Steaming like a boiler on overload, Hadleigh got all the way back to her place before she remembered her car was still parked in Melody's driveway.

For now, she decided, it could just stay where it was.

CHAPTER TEN

For the next week, Tripp made good on his decision to steer clear of Hadleigh Stevens at all costs, but the urge to see her—hell, to do a lot more than that—only got stronger, more primal. He did everything he could think of to distract himself, starting with an all-night poker game in Spence Hogan's basement and progressing to marathon episodes of **Pawn Stars** viewed on his laptop, arguments with Jim over everything from the best way to scramble eggs to the current political situation and reading every word of every piece of junk mail as it arrived.

No doubt about it, Tripp was forced to conclude, he was falling apart, and his next career—as a stalker—seemed likely to commence at any moment.

At night, he slept in fits and starts, when he slept at all, and tossed and turned the rest of the time. Come the next morning, even coffee, buckets of the stuff, made in the fancy steel-clad megabrewer he'd bought online—following his discovery that all the merchants in town had to offer were updated versions of the one Jim already owned—failed to ratchet up his mood by so much as one notch on his inner pissed-off-ometer.

It would have represented real progress just to go from bone mean to reasonably civil, but that seemed beyond him. Jim declared him about as companionable as a bee-stung grizzly with a bad tooth, grumbled that it would take a NASA engineer to operate that miserable excuse for a so-called coffeepot Tripp had paid the earth for, and that was before the cost of overnight shipping was added on.

In the end, father and son, both of them testy as hell, managed to work out a grudging compromise. Jim's machine reappeared in the kitchen, having been rescued from a dusty shelf in the cellar, but Tripp's ultramodern number with the chrome spouts and the built-in grinder stayed, too.

That trip into town for breakfast had gone pretty well, since they were both hungry, but things started going downhill when they left the café and headed out to shop for what the old man snidely referred to as "cruise-wear," having decided that his usual jeans and Western-cut shirts and boots would do just fine, and it was a waste of good money to buy a bunch of duds he'd never wear again.

By the time the dust settled, their haul from the shopping jaunt amounted to some toiletries, a modest supply of underwear and socks, dress slacks in black, gray and navy blue, one pair of lace-up shoes, which Jim claimed he didn't need, and wouldn't be caught dead in, any place he might run into somebody he knew.

And what the deuce was wrong with the boots he only wore for special occasions and could still polish to a respectable shine, he'd like to know?

A few presentable shirts, with buttons instead of snaps, two clip-on ties and a single dark suit jacket completed the travel wardrobe.

On the way to the checkout aisles Tripp suggested springing for a nice set of luggage, but Jim glowered and shook his head. There wasn't a damn thing wrong with the suitcase he'd bought for his and Ellie's honeymoon up at Yellowstone, and he could use that.

They'd bickered, matching each other stubborn for stubborn, during the whole drive back to the ranch, exchanged scowls and very few words through lunch and then supper, and they both did some door slamming, too.

Frankly, it had been a weight off Tripp's mind, dropping the old man off at the airport in Cheyenne a few days back so he could catch a flight to Idaho Falls. From there, he'd made his connection to Seattle, spent the night there and finally boarded his Alaska-bound cruise ship first thing the following morning.

The cruise would take ten days, and

Tripp sure was ready for that much peace and quiet. If not more…

It would be just him and the dog, the horses and a few cattle, none of which would give him backtalk or criticize his taste in coffeemakers.

The ever-present construction crews had slipped his mind in the beginning, but he'd soon figured out that he could stay out of their way most of the time by saddling up and heading out to the range.

Problem was, there were **more** crews there, replacing fences, putting up the new hayshed.

There was no rest for the wicked in the house or the barn, either, because the carpenters hammered and power-sawed and drilled holes all over both places, calling out to each other, asking questions or swapping jokes, all of which were unintelligible because every man there seemed to have a row of nails pressed between his lips from daybreak till quitting time.

When he couldn't take it anymore, Tripp surfed the internet until he found an ad for a private livestock sale, over in the next county, loaded Ridley into the passenger seat of the truck and drove almost a hundred miles to a ranch called the Double-Sorry.

Hell of a name, he thought, pulling onto a driveway as long and rutted as the one back at Jim's place. The field closest to the barn was lined with cars and farm trucks and a few horse trailers, but at least there weren't any foreclosure notices posted, as far as Tripp could tell.

In fact, the house and barn looked sturdy and well maintained, and the fences seemed to be in good shape, too.

All of which was encouraging. As badly as Tripp wanted to buy cattle, and plenty of them, along with a string of decent horses, he certainly didn't relish the idea of taking advantage of somebody else's misfortune, financial or otherwise.

After giving Ridley a chance to get out and stretch his legs, Tripp put the dog back in the truck, rolled the windows partway down so the air could circulate and headed toward the weathered fruit stand near the barn, intending to sign up for a bidder's card. A ruddy-cheeked woman greeted him jovially, her eyes twinkling as she handed him a clipboard with a simple form attached, along with a pen that had bite marks on the shaft.

The auctioneer was already hitting his verbal stride somewhere inside the barn, and the spectators overflowed through the gaping doorway, some of them craning their necks in an effort to watch the ongoing sale. Others stood around chatting amiably, paying no more attention to the goings-on than if they'd met up in front of the post office, instead of an auction out in the countryside.

"Don't you worry," the bright-eyed woman said, when Tripp handed back the clipboard and the pen. He **hadn't** been worrying, actually, but an explanation wasn't required, so he didn't correct her. "There's a lot of folks lookin' today, but not all that many buyin'." That said, she turned halfway around on her stool and shouted, "Charlie, Roy, Beanie—kindly get yourselves out of the way and let this fella through!"

Tripp smiled to himself. Evidently, he was a hot prospect, somebody with money to spend and a serious interest in acquiring some horses and cattle. Which, of course, he was, although he hadn't made any attempt to advertise the fact.

"Thanks," he said, but he was thinking, **Beanie?**

"My name's Chessie," the woman said, extending a hand reddened by hard work and passing years.

Tripp shook Chessie's hand and found that she had a grip like a longshoreman's. "Tripp Galloway," he said, even though the information was right there on the form he'd just filled in.

Chessie studied him thoughtfully. "You any relation to Jim Galloway, over by Mustang Creek?"

"He's my dad," Tripp replied. He and the old man had gotten on each other's nerves plenty of times lately, but the quiet pride he took in who Jim was and what he stood for hadn't lessened one iota.

"He's a good man." Chessie smiled

widely again, showing her dentures. "You tell him Chessie and Bert Anderson said howdy."

"I'll do that," Tripp promised, ready to start for the barn where, thanks to Chessie's brisk but kindly command, a gap had opened in the doorway.

"You don't look a thing like him," Chessie remarked, obviously in no rush to add another buyer to the mix, even after clearing the way for him. "Jim, that is."

Tripp chuckled. "I get that a lot," he said.

Chessie nodded, as though some long-held and cherished conviction of hers had just been verified. "Well," she said, "I guess I'd best stop bending your ear and let you get in there for a look at the livestock. Bert and me, we decided we can't take one more Wyomin' winter, and it's time we retired anyway. Don't have any kids to pass the outfit down to, and we sure can't take all these critters along with us when we leave." She paused, drew a catchy breath, let it out again. "I don't mind telling you, I'll miss these four-legged hay-burners, though, and this place, too, once we've been wherever we're going for a while and the novelty's worn off."

Tripp nodded in response. He waited, in case Chessie had more she wanted to say. Sometimes, he thought, with a pang of sympathy, it was easier to confide in a stranger than a friend, and it appeared that was the case here.

But Chessie really was through talking. She smiled and made a shooing motion with one hand. "You go on now," she said. "I've kept you long enough."

Tripp took the woman at her word, smiled a goodbye and headed for the action. Turned out, the barn was considerably bigger than it looked from outside, and that was a good thing, because the place was packed to the walls.

A space had been cleared in front to show the livestock up for sale, and the auctioneer, a small man with a big voice, stood on a bale of hay, wearing a headset and chiding some onlooker, albeit humorously, for expecting to get something for nothing.

Tripp smiled again. He'd never been to Chessie and Bert's ranch before, but it was familiar territory just the same. As a boy, he'd tagged along with Jim to farm sales much like this one, and he'd learned, primarily because of the example his dad had set, to listen a lot and say very little, to check out the calves or bulls or cow ponies or whatever else was on the block very carefully, decide how much he was willing to pay and stick to that decision, no matter what. "Look these people straight in the eye, boy, and show respect," he'd counseled, early on, as the two of them bumped over country roads like the ones Tripp had just traveled. "They're not necessarily glad to be selling off their land or their horses and cattle or their hogs or equipment or whatever else. Some don't have a choice, and leaving behind the place they've worked and struggled and prayed to hold on to, come hell or high water—like their parents and grandparents before them, often as not—well, that kind of thing's not just hard on a person's pride, having to be the one who finally had to let go. That kind of sorrow runs so deep, it becomes part of a man or a woman."

Now, glancing around the shadowy, hay-and-manure-scented barn, Tripp felt a brief but keen pang of pure sorrow because Jim wasn't standing beside him, arms folded, watching the proceedings from under the brim of whatever hat he was wearing out at the time.

For a second, Tripp's throat constricted and his eyes burned, and he missed his dad as surely and deeply as if Jim had died instead of sailing out to look at totem poles and glaciers and vast expanses of tundra for a week and a half.

A man led a black-and-white gelding up to the front, the horse turned its head to look right at him, and Tripp felt a subtle tug, followed by a swift wrench and the silent, instinctive certainty that he and this horse had established some inexplicable and unbreakable connection.

He kept his expression passive; like the man who had raised him, Tripp knew better than to let himself show anything beyond a mild interest, never mind the eagerness he actually felt. He waited for the bidding to begin, stayed silent as the auctioneer extracted a few tentative offers from the bystanders, but the blood was pounding in his ears and it was all he could do not to wave his bidder's card like a flag.

"This is a fine cutting horse," the auctioneer reminded the crowd in a tone of aggrieved surprise, implying that these folks, of all people, ought to know excellent horseflesh when they saw it. He sighed as he consulted the stack of index cards in his left hand, as though refreshing his memory, though Tripp would have bet he knew all about that paint, right down to the creature's bloodline and the number of teeth in his mouth. A few beats passed before the man looked up. "Apache—" he put a slight emphasis on the name, as if he'd just made an interesting discovery "—Apache here can practically herd cattle all by himself. He's just five years old, according to Bert, and he's as sound as they come." A beleaguered pause. "Now, who'll give me—?"

The number he mentioned next got no response at all.

The auctioneer lowered the suggested price.

There was some foot shuffling and a few murmurs, but no one bid.

As much as he wanted to jump in, Tripp held his tongue. The price didn't matter to him—he could afford to pay many times what the auctioneer was asking and was prepared to do that—but in some ways, buying at auction was like a sport, and there were some unspoken but time-honored rules, the first and foremost of which was **never seem eager.**

So he waited, a little amused to realize how hard that was to do.

By now, the auctioneer was practically pleading.

Someone in the crowd finally took the bait, and the bidding picked up after that. When the moment was right, Tripp touched the brim of his hat.

The auctioneer saw him, shouted in recognition of the bid, jabbing an index finger in Tripp's direction. Then, naturally, he asked for more.

Tripp was in no hurry—he could do this all day, he thought, provided he went back to the truck every so often to let the dog out for a few minutes—but it **was** surprisingly difficult not to bring the bidding to a close by doubling or even tripling the current offer.

More foot shuffling ensued, along with more murmuring.

But no one topped Tripp's bid.

The auctioneer tried again, but nobody moved or spoke. Finally the man shouted, with all the excitement of a tent-show preacher selling salvation, "**Sold** to the gentleman cowboy in the custom-made boots!"

The good-natured gibe made Tripp grin, since he'd made a point of wearing the regulation brand of jeans and a cotton shirt purloined from Jim's closet, but the boots—which were indeed custom-made—couldn't be helped. He'd only brought the one pair with him from Seattle, and none of his dad's well-broken-in shit-kickers would have fit him.

None of this mattered to Tripp anyhow; what counted was the simple fact that he owned a horse again.

It had been too damn long.

Growing up on a ranch, he'd always had at least one hay-burner to feed, water, groom, clean up after and finally ride, but when his favorite gelding, Partner, had died unexpectedly during Tripp's first year of college, the loss had hit him hard. To his way of thinking, he should have been there, had the chance to say thanks for all the good times they'd had together, he and Partner, and say his farewells. But it hadn't gone down like that, and Jim's quiet assurance that the horse hadn't suffered, while comforting, didn't take the ache out of the experience.

If asked why a cowboy, born and bred, didn't have a horse, Tripp would have responded in easy practicalities—in college, he hadn't had the time or the money to board one. After graduation, having qualified for flight school, he'd joined the air force, undergone extensive training and then gone to war.

After his discharge, he would've explained, he'd flown commercial jets all over the world and was often away from home for days at a time. Besides, keeping a horse in Los Angeles—or Seattle, either—didn't make sense to a man raised in the country.

Yep, he'd have said all those things, and they were true enough, but now, having just filled an emotional gap he hadn't let himself dwell on over the years, Tripp knew he'd had another reason, too.

He'd been scared to care for another living creature the way he had for Partner.

Ridley represented the first real chink in his armor. Tripp had bought the pup, the last guy to be picked for the team, from some jerk selling the most recent litter from the back of a beat-up truck. And never mind that just about the last damn thing he needed was a house pet. He'd made the purchase anyway—twenty dollars, marked down from fifty, according to the sales pitch—planning to find the dog a good home.

Instead, he'd wound up giving the animal

a temporary name, and that was the deciding factor. Tripp Galloway learned an important fact about himself right then: naming something—especially when that something came equipped with a pair of hopeful brown eyes, four feet and a heartbeat—meant forging a bond that couldn't be broken.

All these thoughts ran through Tripp's head as he stood there in the Andersons' barn, watching as Apache was led away to make room for another horse.

He bought that one, too—a neatly put together little buckskin mare he could imagine Hadleigh riding—and the sturdy chestnut gelding that was offered next.

Tripp knew he'd need more than three horses, since Jim's were all just about ready to be put out to pasture. Not to mention fifty to a hundred head of cattle, if the homeplace was going to live up to being called a ranch. But this was a start.

And, damn, it felt good.

Outside, in the chilly dazzle of the afternoon sun, he paid and took one of Chessie's neighbors up on his offer to haul the two geldings and the mare over to Tripp's place in his trailer in return for a modest fee.

The two men shook hands on the deal and, after giving Ridley another airing, Tripp and his dog headed for home.

They stopped at Bad Billy's drive-through for a couple of cheeseburgers, one for each of them, along with a large order of curly fries to share, and Tripp, suddenly starving, wolfed his food down with only a little more restraint than Ridley did.

It was already starting to get dark when they reached the ranch. Tripp felt lonely, for a moment, knowing the house was empty. He was glad Jim had actually taken a vacation for once in his life, but he'd been missing the old coot.

Fortunately, there was work to do, with three of the four empty stalls in the barn to prepare for immediate occupancy. The current collection lined the pasture fence, waiting to go inside to be fed, watered and put up for the night.

When the other truck arrived, headlights

piercing the darkness, pulling a dented horse trailer, Tripp was ready to unload the newcomers and get them settled in with the others. Ridley, sensing big doings, was practically beside himself with excitement, running in circles and barking his fool head off.

Tripp finally had to shut the dog in the tack room for a good fifteen minutes, just to keep him from getting trampled.

Once he'd paid the owner of the trailer and watched him drive off, and all the horses were safely in the stalls, he turned Ridley loose again, and the two of them ambled over to the house, ready to call it a day.

"No getting around it," Hadleigh told Muggles ruefully, when they'd been back home for about fifteen minutes. "I owe Melody an apology."

Muggles, seated on her favorite hooked rug in the corner of the kitchen, tilted her golden head to one side and perked up her ears, looking for all the world as if she not only understood but completely agreed with the statement Hadleigh had just made.

She even whimpered sympathetically.

"You are absolutely right," Hadleigh answered, shaking her head as she surveyed the stacks of mismatched pots and pans, skillets and kettles she'd pulled from their customary cupboard and piled on the counter practically the moment she and Muggles came through the door. When she was upset, she had to be **doing** something, preferably constructive, and she'd been feeling a rising need to sort out her possessions, to clear the board, so to speak, and start over.

It was a worthy goal, and the kitchen cupboards were as good a place to begin as any, but the argument she'd had with Melody weighed so heavily on her mind, and her heart, as well, that she wasn't going to get anywhere. This was just busywork. Avoidance, basically.

First things first. The slogan had been one of Gram's favorites, and she'd said it so often that the words were probably imprinted in Hadleigh's DNA, a fact that could be considered a blessing or a curse, depending on a person's viewpoint.

Hadleigh had accomplished a great deal in her professional life—designing quilts, teaching her techniques online and in classes at home and all around the country—and she loved everything about her work, On the other hand, following Gram's well-intentioned dictum had also turned her into a card-carrying perfectionist, an often driven perfectionist, with a distinct tendency to steamroll past or **over** any obstacle or opposition she happened to encounter.

But Melody wasn't an obstacle or an opponent; she was one of Hadleigh's two dearest friends. In spite of many ups and downs over the years, she and Bex and Melody had been closer than most sisters.

Okay, so Melody **was** outspoken and sometimes infuriatingly blunt.

She was also loyal to the death, generous, funny and a million other good things.

"Coming with me?" Hadleigh asked, her hand on the back door's knob.

Muggles, possibly on drama overload, yawned expansively, flopped onto her belly and rested her muzzle on her outstretched forelegs, rolling gentle brown eyes at Hadleigh. All of this combined to form a nonverbal reply. **Not unless you insist.**

"I don't blame you one bit," Hadleigh said. "You can stay here and hold down the fort. I'll· be back after I've said 'sorry' and eaten my share of crow."

Muggles sighed expressively, closed her eyes and promptly fell asleep.

As Hadleigh ducked out, smiling in spite of the butterfly convention warming up in her stomach, the dog gave a single snuffling snore.

Five minutes later, Hadleigh drew a deep breath, straightened her spine and knocked firmly on the outside door of Melody's studio.

Melody's eyes were red-rimmed and a little puffy.

"I'm sorry," the two women said at the same time.

In the next moment, they were hugging,

both of them blinking back tears.

"Me and my big mouth—" Melody lamented when the hug ended.

Hadleigh's words tumbled over her friend's. "I shouldn't have lost my temper—it was childish."

"You're both right," said Bex, who always served as referee when the need arose. "Melody, you don't have to blurt out any opinion that comes to mind, and Hadleigh, **you** don't have to take yourself and everything else so seriously."

Both Hadleigh and Melody laughed.

Hadleigh shut the door behind her and slipped out of her coat.

"I'll make us some tea," Bex announced cheerfully. "Herbal, of course, since neither one of you needs caffeine."

Melody nodded, smiling now, and took Hadleigh's coat from her, hanging it on one of the pegs next to the door.

"And," Bex added, on her way to the kitchen, which adjoined Melody's studio, "I think this would be a good time to show Hadleigh what you've been working on, don't you?"

"Yes," Melody agreed with a glance in the direction of her drafting table, where a small sheet of canvas covered her latest project.

"But wait until I get back!" Bex called from the kitchen.

Melody spoke in an exaggerated whisper, meant to carry. "I wanted to keep this a secret—until Christmas, anyway—but Bex is such a snoop I couldn't pull it off."

"I **heard** that!" Bex sang out.

Hadleigh and Melody exchanged amused smiles.

"I really am sorry I acted like such a prima donna," Hadleigh said softly.

"And **I'm** really sorry I didn't keep my thoughts to myself," Melody responded, giving Hadleigh's hand a brief squeeze.

Hadleigh lifted one eyebrow. "So you meant what you said? About me being in love with Tripp all this time? Without really knowing it, I mean?"

Melody huffed out a breath, looking dejected again and a little tense. "Yes," she admitted. "I meant what I said, Hadleigh. I think what I think, and I can't pretend otherwise—but I didn't have to **say** what I did."

Hadleigh pretended to ponder Melody's reply, but the truth was, her friend's sometimes brutal honesty was so much a part of her that she couldn't always rein it in. The miracle was that Melody **ever** held back an opinion, whether it was good, bad or indifferent.

"Fair enough," Hadleigh finally said. "Which isn't to say I'm prepared to agree."

"Right." Melody's smile was bright with relief and with humor.

"What are you two talking about in there?" Bex called over the shrill whistle of the teakettle.

Again, Melody and Hadleigh laughed in unison.

"Wouldn't you like to know?" Melody called back.

Bex didn't answer, but she looked grimly determined, not to mention hopeful, when she came in, carrying Melody's grandmother's china teapot, three matching cups and saucers, sugar, milk, artificial sweetener, cloth napkins and silver spoons, all carefully arranged on a basket-weave tray.

"Friends again?" she asked.

Melody placed an arm around Hadleigh's shoulders and squeezed, and Hadleigh returned the favor.

"Friends again," they confirmed.

CHAPTER ELEVEN

Once Melody, Hadleigh and Bex had seated themselves, and Bex had graciously poured tea for one and all, an expectant air settled over the small gathering.

"Let's agree," Bex said, primly and carefully, "not to discuss Tripp Galloway."

"Good idea," Hadleigh said quickly. By then, she'd begun to come to terms with an unsettling thought. If she **wasn't** wildly, hopelessly and permanently in love with Tripp, why had she reacted to Melody's earlier remarks so strenuously? It wasn't like her to fly off the handle the way she had, let alone storm off in high dudgeon.

"For now," Melody said mildly, before taking a sip of tea.

Something mischievous but wholly benign rose up in Hadleigh then, some instinct she couldn't define, even to herself. "Of course," she offered in dulcet tones, "we **could** discuss a certain police chief. Namely, Spencer Hogan."

Melody flushed crimson.

"Stop," Bex interjected in a stern voice. **"Now."**

"Sorry," Hadleigh muttered, smiling into her own fragrant cup of steaming tea.

Melody shot her a warning look.

"Melody," Bex said immediately. "Tell us all about your project."

Melody sighed, visibly banking her fiery temper. "You mean the one you discovered by peeking at my designs while I was out of the room?" she retorted, staring pointedly at Bex.

Bex was undaunted. "That's the one," she said.

Again, Melody sighed. It was dramatic, that sigh, and Hadleigh recalled with amusement how active Melody had been in both her high school and college theater arts classes. Back then, she'd planned to become a trial attorney, not an artist, and she'd been convinced that training as an actress would improve her "presence in court."

"Would you mind if I finished my tea first?" Melody inquired, with acid sweetness, glaring at Bex.

"You're stalling," Bex said. "But go ahead—finish your tea. We'll wait."

Melody set her cup and saucer down with a clink of bone china and sterling silver. "Oh, **all right,**" she capitulated. "Anything to keep the peace."

Bex merely smiled.

Hadleigh didn't dare do that, so she hid her mouth behind her cup, well aware that the laughter undoubtedly dancing in her eyes might still give her away.

Melody rose from her chair, stalked over to her drafting table and, instead of throwing back the canvas that covered whatever design she'd been working on, opened one of the drawers. She removed a simple but elegant black velvet box, the hinged kind she bought in quantity and used to display her jewelry creations.

After returning to her chair, she flipped open the box.

Hadleigh used all her self-control not to crane her neck for a look at the contents.

Melody lifted three gold bracelets, each composed of a series of graceful links, from the box. She held them, suspended, from the tip of her right index finger. "I made one of these for each of us," she said. "As a sort of—well, a sort of symbol."

Hadleigh didn't even pretend to catch Melody's drift.

"They're charm bracelets," Bex explained.

Melody extended one bracelet to Bex, and one to Hadleigh and then fastened the third on her own wrist.

"What—" Hadleigh began, but she was strangely choked up, and the sentence she'd been about to voice fell away, uncompleted.

"Tell her," Bex prompted gently, opening the clasp on her own bracelet and putting it on. It glittered beautifully on her left wrist.

"Give me a chance," Melody said, her tone a little on the snippy side, her color high.

Bex just shrugged.

Hadleigh looked down at the golden glow encompassing her wrist, feeling moved but unable to define the reasons. Jewelry was jewelry, after all, and Melody had presented both her and Bex with many pieces over recent years—pendants, rings, even bracelets. And, yet, she knew this one was special.

"It represents our covenant," Melody said, almost shyly. "The marriage pact, I mean."

"Okay—" Hadleigh said. "It's beautiful, Mel, but—"

"Let her finish," Bex interrupted, though not unkindly.

"Here's the plan," Melody went on, after drawing a deep breath and releasing it slowly. "We wear the bracelets, the three of us, and as we find true love, I'll make a special charm, in triplicate, something symbolic. You know, a different design to represent each of our romances." Hadleigh's throat constricted, and tears scalded her eyes. "Oh, Melody—" she began, but again she couldn't go on.

"It's a beautiful idea, isn't it?" Bex put

in.

"The point," Melody explained, clearly moved to tears herself and yet doggedly pressing on, "is shared purpose. We **believe** for each other. We honor each other's intentions, and we keep going, no matter what. Finally, we celebrate each other's success." A sniffly pause. "Essentially, it's one for all and all for one. Nobody is really home free until everyone is."

"Wow," Hadleigh breathed, almost overcome.

"Yeah," Bex agreed. "The marriage pact is more than just a common goal. It's a sacred **covenant,** like Melody said."

"But it's no good," Melody added, somewhat breathlessly, "unless all three of us are in this for the duration."

Hadleigh felt a jolt of genuine commitment, of a promise, a vow. "Let's make it happen," she said.

"Me, too." Bex nodded, her eyes shining with tears.

"Then it's settled," Melody said. "As we find true love, whether it's all at the same time or at different times, I'll make matching charms for all three of us, designed to commemorate each romance and marriage. Nobody gives up—that's the agreement—until we **all** have three charms on our bracelets."

"That's beautiful," Hadleigh whispered.

"Yes," Bex agreed, examining the bracelet twinkling on her wrist with quiet pride.

"What happens next?" Hadleigh heard herself ask.

"That's up to the fates," Melody said, looking intently at Hadleigh and then at Bex. "Our part is to decide—and then stand by our decision." She paused. "So," she went on. "Are we in or out?"

"I'm in," Hadleigh said firmly. Inside, she was trembling a little, because on some level, she understood that this was no lark; it was some kind of serious cosmic business.

"Me, too," Bex repeated.

Melody thrust out her upraised hand, the one sporting the glimmering gold bracelet. Bex clasped Melody's hand, and Hadleigh grasped both.

Heaven knew what the results of this odd ritual would be, Hadleigh thought, but one thing was absolutely clear: there was no going back.

One day, out of the blue, Jim—still aboard ship—called home, ebullient, and considering his habit of silence, incredibly talkative. "I've met somebody," he announced, before Tripp had had a chance to process his stepdad's unusually jubilant mood.

Tripp, standing in the ranch-house kitchen with the landline receiver pressed to his ear—God forbid Jim should call him on his cell phone, like anybody else would have—was a few beats behind the action. "You've—what—?" he asked stupidly. At least they could have a private conversation, since the construction crews were all on their lunch breaks.

Jim had been gone for five days by then, and all that time Tripp had been awaiting news that he'd successfully boarded the Alaska-bound cruise ship. Not a word out of him. Now, to Tripp's shock, his taciturn and patently unfanciful father seemed to be saying— But that **couldn't** be it, after all these years he'd spent pining for his late wife.

Could it?

"Her name is Pauline," Jim went on, as excited as a teenager recalling the prom date of a lifetime. "She's retired. Used to teach high school math—"

"Whoa," Tripp interrupted. "Slow down, Dad."

Jim laughed, and the sound rang with a joy Tripp hadn't heard since before his mother had died. He felt delighted and wary at the same time.

"Pauline and I are in love," Jim continued. "It's the real thing, Tripp, and I'm sure hoping you'll be happy for us."

Pauline. A math teacher. And probably not a predatory psychopath like so many of the folks featured in ID Channel "docudramas," but still... How well could Jim possibly know this woman after less than a week? "Hold on a second, Dad—"

But Jim had the proverbial bit in his teeth, and there was no reining him in.

"Pauline has an RV," he rushed on, practically bubbling over with happy enthusiasm. "We'll eventually want to settle on the ranch, I suppose, but in the meantime, we want to hit the road and see as much of the country as we can."

Tripp released a long breath, and if his head didn't quite stop reeling, at least it had slowed down. "All right," he said cautiously, drawing the words out like a short length of rope. Wasn't this what he'd wanted all along? For Jim to stop marking time and start living again?

Jim must have read Tripp's mind, because he sighed and said hoarsely, "I know this seems real sudden, son—I reckon because it **is** pretty sudden—but I've only felt like this once before in my life, when I met your mother. Love happens in its own time, for its own reasons—and I am **definitely** in love with Pauline." His voice took on a sober, uncertain tone. "What I need to know, Tripp, is that you're—well, you're okay with this."

Tripp stood with his eyes closed and his shoulders hunched. He consciously relaxed the muscles in his back. "I want you to be happy, Dad," he said. "If I seem a little...thrown, it's only because things seem to be moving really fast."

Jim chuckled, but that faintly solemn note remained. "Soon as the cruise is over, Pauline and I will head for the ranch and you can meet her for yourself. Once you do, you'll feel a whole lot better about the situation—I promise."

"Dad," Tripp put in, "you don't need my permission or my approval. It's just—"

"It's just that you've read too many of those true-crime books between flights, Captain Galloway," Jim teased. "Pauline isn't a nutcase with a trail of dead or missing husbands behind her. She's a schoolteacher, Tripp, widowed for almost twenty years. She has four kids, all happily married professionals and upstanding citizens." He paused to take a breath, evidently just getting started. "God knows, Pauline's not after my money, because I don't have a hell of a lot, and that's okay, because she doesn't either."

"What's her last name?" Tripp asked

lightly. He'd have demanded a social-security number and a credit score, too, if he could have gotten away with it.

Jim wasn't fooled by the attempted subtlety of Tripp's question, but he didn't take offense, either. He replied, with a smile in his voice, "Norbrand. Pauline Norbrand. Shall I spell it?"

Tripp laughed, feeling mildly guilty but equally determined to make sure the lady was on the level. Some things, he thought, were too important to be left to chance, and his Dad's happiness and well-being were among them.

He'd run a background check on Oakley Smyth once upon a time, with admittedly mixed results, since he still wasn't convinced Hadleigh would ever forgive him for it, and he was about to do the same thing all over again. This round, Pauline Norbrand would be the object of the investigation.

This is none of your business, lobbied the still small voice in Tripp's head.

The voice was probably right, Tripp concluded, with a twinge of his conscience.

Just the same, the truth was the truth, wasn't it? Even when tough or downright painful discoveries came to light in the process?

"Nope," he said, in belated answer to Jim's question. "You don't need to spell it."

After that, the conversation swung off in an easier direction. Jim reported that he was enjoying the cruise, seeing the sights, and the food was a revelation, after years of rustling up his own grub every day. He was putting on weight, which ought to be good news, he figured. On top of that, he'd won five hundred dollars playing bingo and, yes, he was feeling just fine and getting enough rest, and, yes, he was taking his medicine as prescribed.

"You need to quit worrying so much, son," Jim lectured affably in closing. "It'll wear you down if you don't put the brakes on."

"Okay," Tripp agreed, his smartphone already in his free hand, thumb busy scrolling for the number of his old air-force buddy's private investigation firm up in

Denver. Was the company still in business? After all, using the major search engines on the internet, most people could easily find all the information they wanted on their own.

Goodbyes were said, Jim's humorously resigned, Tripp's distracted, and the call ended.

Tripp decided to think a while before calling his friend and tossed his cell phone aside.

He didn't much care for this suspicious, skeptical side of himself, but he was also a realist. Furthermore, if he'd bothered to check out his ex-wife, Danielle, in advance, he'd have saved them **both** a lot of trouble and wasted time.

Ridley, standing with his muzzle pressed to the pet door and whining softly, seemed to be back in helpless-critter mode. Most likely, he wanted to get outside and beg scraps from the plumbers and electricians and carpenters hanging around in the yard, finishing their lunches.

"If you want to go out," Tripp told the dog flatly, "go out."

Ridley tossed him an accusing look, then low-bellied through the swinging door.

Tripp, grinning a little, immediately booted up his laptop.

"I'm throwing a party Saturday night," Bex announced at the next gathering, an impromptu tea party held in Melody's studio nearly a week after the bracelet presentation and renewal of the marriage pact. Since then, they'd all been busy, and they'd spent most of this visit just catching up on day-to-day stuff.

Now, when Bex finally voiced her plan for the following weekend, she and Hadleigh were getting ready to leave, putting on their coats, while Melody stacked the tea paraphernalia back on the tray.

"A party?" Melody echoed with a twinkle.

"Yes," Bex said, shoving her hands in the pockets of her puffy coat and jutting out her chin, although the expression in her eyes was one of lively humor. "It's not every day a person reaches a major life goal."

"Oh—you mean the franchise thing," Melody said, with a brief glance at Hadleigh. The two of them fretted, tacitly and in silence, that they might have given Bex's well-earned success short shrift, glossed over the accomplishment.

"The franchise thing," Bex confirmed, a smile flickering at the edges of her mouth. "It's a big deal, you know. People all over the country are already signing up to take the training and open All Jazzed Up clubs of their own."

"Of **course** it's a big deal," Hadleigh cried, turning to her friend, searching her face. She was mortified that she hadn't been more congratulatory, more openly excited about such a major coup. "Oh, Bex—we're so proud of you, both of us—"

She fell silent.

"I know that," Bex said gently, filling the gap.

Melody, too, was deeply chagrined. "We **are** proud, Bex. Hadleigh and I are so happy for you. We could have done a better job of showing it, though." She sighed. "Are we forgiven?"

Bex raised one shoulder slightly, her version of a shrug. She'd always been the easygoing one, the peacemaker and—on many occasions—the referee. "There's nothing to forgive," she said, letting them off the hook.

"What can we do to help you get things ready for the party?" Hadleigh asked. It worried her sometimes, Bex's long-standing habit of overlooking slights, however unintended, never allowing herself to be the squeaky wheel. Not even when she should have.

"Just show up," Bex said. "No need to fuss about what you'll wear, either, because I've reserved the Moose Jaw Tavern for this shindig, so jeans and T-shirts will be just fine."

"The Moose Jaw Tavern?" Hadleigh echoed, surprised. She'd been expecting a different location—Bex's small house, perhaps, or All Jazzed Up.

"We used to hang out at the Moose Jaw," Melody reflected, obviously warming to the idea. "Remember? There were all those pool tournaments, dancing to the jukebox, cheap beer to drink and all the free popcorn we could eat? And **what** about those red-hot rodeo cowboys who passed through town now and then?"

Bex laughed. "How could any of us forget?"

Hadleigh chuckled ruefully. "I've tried," she said. "To forget, I mean. Those were some wild nights."

Melody rolled her eyes, grinning. "Oh, yeah, right, Miss Priss," she teased. "We were real renegades, about as wild as three escapees from the nearest Girl Scout Jamboree."

"Okay," Bex interceded, taking Hadleigh by the elbow and edging her toward the door. "We're getting out of here before you two get into it again."

Melody started for the kitchen, tea tray in hand. "Good," she called over one shoulder. "Because it just so happens that I have work to do."

Bex and Hadleigh heard the remark, but neither of them responded, since they were outside by then. Bex pulled the door shut behind them, while Hadleigh retrieved her car keys from her coat pocket and made her way toward her station wagon, still parked at the curb. Melody's gift, the bracelet, sparkled on her wrist as she reached for the door handle, and her spirits rose even further.

"I'm really glad you ironed things out the other day," Bex confided, pausing on the sidewalk.

Hadleigh smiled. "Me, too," she said. "I don't know what got into me, acting the way I did."

"You're allowed to lose your cool once in a while," Bex told her. "You're only human, after all."

Hadleigh grinned. "All **too** human sometimes." She looked around, saw no sign of her friend's modest but sporty compact car. "Need a ride home? Or back to the club?"

Bex shook her head. "I'll walk," she said. "I didn't get in a workout today, and I need the exercise."

Hadleigh nodded, opened her car door and got behind the wheel. "See you," she said.

"See you," Bex chimed in happily and headed in the opposite direction, her strides long and purposeful.

With another smile and a shake of her head, Hadleigh fired up the station wagon—the woody, as Will had called it—and drove home again.

Once there she greeted Muggles and hung up her coat. Then she pushed up her sleeves and turned to the mountains of pots and pans lining the countertop. When suppertime rolled around, she'd not only cleared the surface; she'd scrubbed out the inside of the cupboard, replaced the few kettles, pots and skillets she'd decided to keep, boxed up the rest and neatly stacked the cartons on the back porch, to be taken to the drop-off station behind the thrift store.

Hadleigh made herself a grilled cheese sandwich and heated a can of soup for her evening meal, mentally reviewing the events of the day while she ate. She'd visited Earl at the hospital, put in several hours at the shop, working on her newest online class and waiting on the occasional live and in-person customer, and gone to the tea party after that. Reflecting on Bex's parting words about last week's rift with Melody, Hadleigh felt another wave of relief that she'd gone straight back to apologize and make amends. She'd **had** to.

The trouble with flying into a grand snit and stomping off when something or someone makes us angry, she recalled Gram saying long ago, after a similar incident when Hadleigh was in junior high, **is that, most of the time, people come to their senses and have to swallow their pride, turn themselves right around and apologize for throwing a tantrum.** Gram had smiled gently then, no doubt to soften the message, and finished up with, **It's much easier and much less humiliating, in the long run, just to keep one's temper in check from the beginning.**

As usual, her grandmother had been right.

Hadleigh sighed. It would have been

nice, she reflected, if that particular memory had popped into her head **before** the clash with Melody, but in her experience at least, things seldom worked out so conveniently.

She carried her soup bowl, sandwich plate and silverware to the sink, rinsed them under the faucet and placed them in the dishwasher, all under Muggles's steady surveillance.

"What?" Hadleigh finally asked, smiling at the dog.

Muggles gave a single tentative woof.

And in the next moment someone knocked at the front door, the sound muffled by distance but brisk and matter-of-fact.

Hadleigh dried her hands, and there was a strange little leap in the hollow of her throat, as brief as a heartbeat and yet leaving a silent echo reverberating in its wake. Fear? Certainly not—this was Mustang Creek, Wyoming, her hometown, a predominantly safe and peaceful place. Excitement, then? No, it wasn't that, either.

She headed through the house, Muggles

at her side, still trying to identify the sensation as she went. In the end, she settled on a combination of alertness and expectancy.

Peering out one of the long windows on either side of the front door, Hadleigh was both surprised and **not** surprised to see Tripp standing on the porch. Awash in the golden glow of the outside light, he looked mythically handsome to her, with his wheat-colored hair, his chiseled features and that sculpted physique—as if he'd been born and raised on Mount Olympus instead of the Galloway ranch, disguised himself as a mortal by replacing his toga with jeans, boots, a Western-cut shirt and a denim jacket.

A silly thought, Hadleigh chided herself, but even as she released the dead bolt, turned the knob and pulled, the magic lingered in the air, like a pulse hovering just below the level of detection.

As she gazed at Tripp through the mesh of the screen door, several things she might have said came to mind: **You should have called. Come on in. Can you stay**

awhile—say, forever?

None of these possibilities actually made the leap from her brain to her tongue, which was probably good, because she was still reeling from the sudden realization that Melody had been right all along. She **did** love Tripp Galloway, with all her heart, mind and body, and, furthermore, it was nothing new.

The knowledge slammed into her like a city bus moving at top speed.

While Hadleigh was recovering from the impact, Tripp's mouth flicked up on one side, almost imperceptibly, and she saw the brief yet lethal flash of the dimple in his right cheek. By then, she had gathered enough of her scattered wits to notice the bouquet of red rosebuds he'd brought along.

Although she still didn't speak—she wasn't even sure she **could** speak, not coherently, anyway—Hadleigh worked the small hook holding the screen door shut and stepped back, nearly falling over Muggles in the process, so Tripp could come in.

Once inside, he studied her with curious amusement, his head tilted ever so slightly to one side, his eyes alight with—what? Mischief? Amusement?

He'd been wearing a hat earlier, Hadleigh decided distractedly, still mute. She could see the faint indentation it had left in his hair.

"I should have called," Tripp said.

"But you didn't." Hadleigh heard her own words as if from a vast distance, and there was no accusation in her tone, only bemusement.

He grinned, all but vaporizing Hadleigh's knees with no more effort than that. "I figured you'd tell me to take a hike if I did," he said. With one hand, he gave the door a light backward push, closing it. With the other, he held out the bouquet. "They're from the supermarket," he told her amiably. "Somebody ought to open a flower shop in this town."

Hadleigh's own hand trembled visibly as she reached for the long-stemmed roses. Although she didn't actually count, her brain too muddled for that, she knew there were either eighteen or twenty-four of the velvety, rich-crimson buds, and their subtle fragrance made her feel slightly dizzy. "Thank you," she managed, blushing when her voice came out croaky, like a frog's. "But what—"

"I was hoping we could talk," Tripp said, the grin now gone and the glint in his eyes fading to a sort of wary tenderness.

"Why not?" Hadleigh said, more to herself than Tripp. **Why not?** her inner critic mimicked. **That's the best you can do—"why not"?** Bravely, she tried again. "You didn't bring Ridley?"

Not much better, you conversational whiz, you.

Tripp nodded but his eyes were solemn. Whatever was going on here, he wasn't playing games; his tone and his expression and his manner were too earnest for that, too open. "He's in the truck," he replied.

Hadleigh, bent on, one, getting control over the whirlwind of emotions she'd been caught up in, and, two, putting the roses in a vase full of water as soon as possible, turned without a word and practically sprinted for the kitchen.

Tripp paused to greet Muggles—the silly dog whimpered with delight—but Hadleigh kept right on going. **Don't look back.** Maybe, by some miracle, she'd regain a smidgeon of perspective by the time the trek to the kitchen was over.

She would have known Tripp was following even if she hadn't heard the soft thump of his boot heels against the floor, the eager scrabble of Muggles's claws as she hurried to keep up.

Not surprisingly, the hike to the kitchen was much too short to afford Hadleigh any miracles; her thoughts and feelings were just as jumbled as before—if not more so.

She kept her back to Tripp while she rummaged through several cupboards, looking for a vase large enough to accommodate the roses, then rifled one of the drawers for Gram's old gardening scissors.

"Hadleigh," Tripp said. His voice was low, husky, gentle.

She couldn't pretend she hadn't heard

him speak her name—she'd tensed at the sound of it—but she didn't turn around to face him, either. She simply said, "These are so beautiful. Thanks again." Meanwhile, Hadleigh rode the crest of her wild emotions like a surfer on a wave, and despite her pounding heart and racing thoughts, she moved slowly and methodically, filling the tall, cut-glass vase she'd chosen to the three-quarters mark at the sink. She removed the tissue wrapping and the pointy cellophane bag that had kept the stems damp, cutting away the rubber band holding the bouquet together and finally trimming the base of each and every thorny stalk before placing it carefully in the water.

When Tripp's hands came to rest lightly on Hadleigh's shoulders, she flinched reflexively, not because she was startled, but because the man's touch electrified her. He said her name again, hoarsely, and turned her around, taking the shears from her grasp, and then the single rose she'd been holding, setting them both aside.

Looking up at him, Hadleigh was both confused and thrilled. She blinked, opened her mouth to say something—anything—closed it again and bit down on her lower lip.

Tripp smiled, and his eyes were the tender blue of a spring sky, and yet warm. His breath tingled on her mouth—they were that close—when he spoke. "The roses will keep for a few minutes," he said. "Do you think you could maybe...**relax** a little?"

Easy for **him** to say, Hadleigh thought, joyously frantic. He was cool, calm, in charge, while she felt like one of those cartoon characters undergoing an electrical shock ferocious enough, intense enough to light up her skeleton so brightly that it might be visible through her skin.

"Okay," she said nervously, sucking in a breath and releasing it slowly.

Tripp chuckled again—the sound gruff and thoroughly masculine and, somehow, soothing, too—and cupped his hands lightly on either side of Hadleigh's face. At that point, she couldn't be sure if she'd gone pale or her cheeks were blazing, and it seemed to her that the floor shifted under her feet.

"Nothing is going to happen against your will," Tripp assured her.

Hadleigh's head spun. Was it possible to get drunk on another person's nearness, on the warmth of his flesh, the timbre of his voice? It seemed so.

"I know," she said in a near whisper. And she **did** know—her heart might not be safe with Tripp Galloway, but her body definitely was.

Tripp ran the pad of one thumb—wonderfully calloused—across Hadleigh's lower lip. "I'd like to kiss you," he said. "If that's okay, I mean."

By that point, Hadleigh thought she might die if Tripp **didn't** kiss her. She gave one jerky nod, and her arms moved easily, naturally, around his neck.

Slowly, so slowly, Tripp bent his head and touched his mouth to hers, the pressure so light that it couldn't really be called pressure. It weighed no more than a breath or a splash of moonlight.

Hadleigh groaned and rose onto her toes, seeking the fullness of what was, so far, only a promise. She felt the hard yet yielding power of Tripp, his substance and his heat, as he held her closer and then closer still.

When he finally kissed her for real, Hadleigh knew there would be no going back, not if it was up to her. Miniature fireworks flared in every nerve ending, every cell.

She heard herself whimper, and when Tripp might have withdrawn, torn his mouth from hers, she tightened her arms around his neck, held on.

And, impossibly, Tripp **deepened** the kiss.

Inside Hadleigh, a battle raged. **This is wrong,** argued her common sense. **No, this is heaven,** her body declared.

Common sense: **It's too sudden.**

Body: **I've waited so long. Too long.**

At last, Tripp broke off the kiss, rested his forehead against Hadleigh's and sighed. "Oops," he muttered, with a marked lack of regret. "Believe it or not, I wasn't planning to do that."

Hadleigh laughed, although her throat was thick with a conglomeration of complicated emotions and her eyes burned with tears she was too proud to shed. "You planned," she murmured, "if I remember correctly, on **talking.**"

Another sigh, another grin. "Yeah."

She let her fingers slide into his hair, as she'd always wanted to do. It felt silky and warm as sunlight. "It's possible," Hadleigh went on lightly, "that we've already done too **much** talking."

Tripp made a sound that was part groan, part growl, part chortle. "Hadleigh, if you're saying what I **think** you're saying—and, God, I hope you are—well, you still need to step back, take a breath and make sure you really want this to happen."

Hadleigh drew her brows together, just briefly, in a pensive frown. "I'm **saying,**" she reflected solemnly, "that you ought to go out to your truck, get Ridley and bring him inside, because you're going to be here for a while, Cowboy."

Tripp rested his chin on top of her head

and sighed again. "If we let this happen, it will change things," he reminded her gently. "And if I'm going to live with myself afterward, I have to know you're sure—that this isn't some whim—"

Hadleigh placed her palms against his chest and pushed him back an inch or two so she could look directly up into his eyes. "Some whim?" she repeated reasonably and with a twinkle of humor. "I'm a grown-up now, Tripp, not somebody's kid sister—and I know my own mind, thank you very much."

Tripp looked mildly skeptical at this, and Hadleigh supposed there was some justification for that reaction.

"Maybe I didn't always," Hadleigh hastened to clarify. "Know what I thought and felt about things, I mean. But be fair, Tripp—who does?" She paused for a beat. "You? Have **you** always been perfectly certain of your thoughts and feelings about everything and everybody, every moment of your life?"

He laughed and shook his head. "No, babe," he answered. "I haven't."

"Then why do you think **I** should be?"

"You've got me there," Tripp conceded, and the timbre of his voice was at once sandpaper-rough and incredibly tender.

For a few moments, they just stood where they were, close but not close enough, touching each other and yet achingly aware of the distance between them.

At last, Hadleigh placed the tip of one index finger against his warm, pliable lips and broke the silence. "Just bring the dog inside," she said. "If I change my mind somewhere along the way, I'll be sure to let you know."

Tripp's chuckle was so raspy it sounded almost painful. "Yeah," he said. "If you say no, Hadleigh, I'll hear you, and I'll stop—I promise you that. But I'm only human, and politically incorrect as it may be to say this, there **is** such a thing as a point of no return."

Hadleigh cocked her head slightly to one side, watching the play of emotions on his face as one gave way to the next, each distinct yet shifting quickly, like brilliantly colored patterns inside a kaleidoscope. She recognized desire, reluctance, fierce passion, hope, wary amusement, then desire again.

She finally replied, musingly, almost wistfully, to his gentle warning. "Ah, yes," she said, with a little smile, "the famous point of no return. Didn't that already happen—right around the time you kissed me?"

Tripp sighed again and thrust the splayed fingers of one hand through his Hadleigh-rumpled hair. "And you kissed me right back," he was quick to mention.

"Sure did," Hadleigh said impishly. She arched one eyebrow. "Are you going to bring that poor dog inside, or do I have to do it?"

Tripp wasn't entirely sure his feet even touched the ground, between the time he left Hadleigh standing, kiss-flushed and glowing, in her kitchen and when he got to his truck, parked out front. He unlocked the rig, released a delighted Ridley from captivity and, while the dog cavorted on the sidewalk, opened the glove compartment and rummaged for the small, battered carton he'd brought from home. Thrusting the box in his jacket pocket, he tilted his head back, looked up at the star-strewn sky and hoped to God he was doing the right thing.

No question about it—kissing Hadleigh Stevens **felt** right, 1,000 percent right—and making love to her would be even better.

Still, the night would inevitably turn into the morning after, wouldn't it, and he'd wind up standing in front of some mirror, face-to-face with himself, an obviously unavoidable confrontation, since he'd have to shave and brush his teeth and at least finger-comb his hair to feel presentable.

And Tripp Galloway wanted to be able to meet his own gaze, straight on and steady, when the time came.

Ridley, tail wagging, lifted a hind leg and sprayed the gatepost, untroubled by such dilemmas.

"You're no help at all," Tripp told the

critter. "You know that, don't you?"

Ridley stood on all fours now, the deed done, and went right on swinging his tail back and forth, sublimely secure in Tripp's good intentions, content to be just what he was—an ordinary, none-too-bright, fence-post-sprinkling dog.

He looked up at Tripp, full of trust, awaiting the next development.

And Tripp felt a sudden, seismic shift. He'd loved the dog all along, but now, suddenly, the sensation was strong enough to splinter his heart.

"Come on," he told the animal gruffly. "The lady is waiting."

The lady **was** waiting, standing on the threshold now, with both the screen door and its heavier counterpart wide-open, watching.

Tripp couldn't make out Hadleigh's expression, since she was backlit by the porch light and the glow from the entry behind her, but he wondered if she'd expected him to bolt behind the wheel of his truck, fire up the engine and fishtail it out of there.

And, if so, would she have been disappointed to see him go—or relieved?

He had no idea, didn't figure it mattered.

He walked as far as the porch steps, Ridley prancing at his side like some pony dolled up for a parade. Then Tripp paused, staring up at Hadleigh, astounded by the very fact of her existence, the miracle of such a glorious, confounding creation as a woman, as **this** woman, this beautiful, beautiful woman.

Ridley gamboled up the steps, overjoyed just to be in her presence.

Tripp understood the feeling.

Hadleigh laughed softly and bent to ruffle the dog's ears in greeting. Then, holding both doors ajar with one shapely hip, she turned her attention to the man standing spellbound at the foot of the porch steps.

Tripp silently reminded himself that he'd known Hadleigh forever.

He and Will had been about to start second grade when she was born, after all. He'd seen her take her first steps, watched her awaken to the mysteries of the world around her, looked on with his heart in his throat as she grew, as she took more and more risks, skinning her knees and elbows. He and Will had taught her to swim, to ride bikes and horses. They'd allowed her to tag along when it was a safe enough bet that they wouldn't be setting a bad example, and they'd protected her when the need arose.

And then, each in his own way, they'd broken Hadleigh's heart. Will by getting himself killed in a faraway war, Tripp by wrecking her storybook wedding and promptly announcing that—oh, yeah, hadn't he mentioned it before?—he was married.

Now, years later, Hadleigh had done what he'd been waiting for her to do all along, he suddenly realized—she'd grown into the woman he'd known she would be, and more.

Hadleigh propped her free hand on the hip that wasn't holding open the doors. "Are you just going to stand there?" she demanded, Ridley having already weaseled his way past her into the house.

"It's freezing out here, you know."

Whatever spell had turned Tripp to stone was suddenly broken; he could move again. He laughed, mounted the steps, crossed the porch and followed Hadleigh inside, where it was warm and the lights were dim and, for the time being anyway, they might have been the only man and woman on the planet.

Hadleigh wasn't a virgin, having cleared that ungainly hurdle during an awkward and mercifully brief college romance, but she wasn't exactly a sexual sophisticate, either. She'd been intimate with one, the college boyfriend, two, **another** college boyfriend, who'd looked, she could admit it now, a little like Tripp, from a distance, anyway, and if she squinted, and three, a guy she met at an out-of-town business dinner and had barely thought about since. That had been the classic one-night stand, an experience she was neither ashamed nor proud of, but a rite of passage nonetheless. According to Melody, everybody got one free pass, regarding sex with a stranger—and that once had definitely been enough for Hadleigh.

Prior to all that, of course, as an eighteen-year-old potential bride with stars in her eyes and a remarkable capacity for self-deception, she'd nearly married Oakley Smyth, a fact that could still send a shudder down her spine whenever it came to mind.

The truth about Hadleigh's relationship with Oakley would probably have surprised a lot of people—Tripp included—because she and Oakley had never progressed beyond some hand-holding and a little light necking. It hadn't seemed all that strange at the time and, looking back, Hadleigh could see why.

Oakley, inveterate cheater that he was, might have been feeling just a bit guilty about what he was doing to the other woman in his life, **and** to the two children she'd had with him. Hadleigh, on the other hand, had been playing a game, acting a part in a one-woman show she expected to be cut short well before the final curtain.

Privately, Bex and Melody had dubbed her the Virtual Virgin; even after the college romances and the one-night stand, Hadleigh didn't really get why people in books and movies made such a big deal out of sex. Sure, it could be pleasant, like a back rub or a foot massage or skinny-dipping in a cool mountain lake on a sultry summer night—and fade from memory just as quickly.

Now, teetering on the edge of a precipice, about to fling herself over the edge, not to fall but to fly, Hadleigh, unlike her eighteen-year-old self, or any of the selves that evolved later, knew **exactly** what she was doing. She knew there were emotional risks, all manner of them, knew she might well wind up getting her heart broken all over again.

If that happened, she'd just have to woman up and deal, she concluded. Broken hearts weren't fun, but they usually weren't fatal, either.

Tripp, with the cool, clean scent of a fall evening still around him, smiled quizzically and pulled Hadleigh into a loose embrace, and she was startled to realize they'd gotten all the way from the front door to the kitchen without her even noticing.

"Want to tell me about those thoughts you seem to get lost in every once in a while?" he asked. "Or is that private territory?"

Hadleigh stepped closer, slid her arms around Tripp's lean middle, allowed herself to lean into his strength and revel in it. "I spend too much time in my head," she confided in an indirect reply to his questions. "There's this little room up there, where I watch my very own movies— all about the past, or what might have happened, or should have happened, or **could** happen in the future." She paused, and her shoulders rose and fell with the force of her sigh. "Right now, I just want to occupy my whole body—every part of it—and be as fully and completely present as I possibly can."

All Tripp said was, "Oh, lady." And then he kissed her again.

It wasn't the first time, of course—but it might as well have been, because the universe, as Hadleigh knew it anyway, darkened, shrank to a pinpoint and then exploded with light and color, expanding in all directions and at breathtaking speed.

Her fingers intertwined at Tripp's nape, lest she come unmoored from the very earth and soar away into an invisible forever, like a vanishing star shooting toward oblivion. Hadleigh moaned, craving more of the kiss, more of Tripp, more of the strange magic they were creating together.

Even when he swept her up into his arms, the kiss went on, unbroken, and Hadleigh would have wept for joy if she'd had the breath to utter a single sob, but she hadn't so much as a gasp or a sigh to spare. Everything she had, everything she **was** or would ever be, was wrapped up in the fiery charge arcing between Tripp's mouth and her own.

He broke the contact only when he'd carried her out of the kitchen and into the dim corridor beyond, dragging in a breath. "Where—"

Hadleigh nearly laughed. Her childhood

room had been upstairs, tucked at a slant under the eaves, across the hall from Will's, as Tripp might recall, but some months after her grandmother had passed away, feeling cramped and needing a change, she'd redone the main-floor bedroom, by far the largest of the three, and moved in.

"There," she said in a whisper, inclining her head toward the set of double doors just beyond the entrance to the bathroom.

Tripp gave a small sigh—possibly of relief—and strode in that direction.

The room was spacious and sparely furnished. There was the antique brass bed she'd bought at an estate sale, sporting one of her favorite quilts, the sturdy dresser and long, low bureau, both old, whitewashed and artfully distressed in a combination of shabby-chic and Country French. Colorful hooked rugs graced the gleaming hardwood floors, and Hadleigh's greatest indulgence, a working fireplace constructed of old brick worn to a distinctly Tuscan shade of yellow ochre, loomed between two tall windows.

A faint spill of moonlight illuminated the space.

Tripp, still holding her in both arms, looked around, seeming a little disoriented, as though he'd suddenly found himself not merely in another room, but in another house entirely. Whatever he'd expected to see, Hadleigh deduced hazily, this wasn't it.

He shook his head once, like a man trying to get his bearings, then crossed to the bed and sat Hadleigh down on the edge of the mattress. A moment later, he was crouching in front of her, gently removing her shoes and then her socks. Instead of standing up again, or joining her on the bed, Tripp remained where he was and began to massage her right foot, pressing into the arch with both thumbs.

Hadleigh made a crooning sound, closing her eyes and pressing her palms deep into the bedding. "Now **that**," she whispered, "feels **way** too good—"

Tripp's chuckle was hoarse. "That's the general idea."

"Who would have thought a person's

feet—" Hadleigh leaned farther back, keeping her eyes closed, gasping with startled ecstasy when Tripp took hold of her other foot and proceeded to rub both the right and the left simultaneously. "Oh—Tripp—"

"Let go, Cinderella," he said quietly, a smile in his voice.

With a comical cry of resignation, Hadleigh stopped trying to sit upright and flopped down on the bed, landing with a bounce. "What," she half whispered, half purred, "does it **look** like I'm doing?"

Tripp laughed. "Now that you mention it," he replied, pausing the massage magic long enough to take off his jacket, rummage briefly in a pocket and set something on the bedside table, "it does look a lot like you're letting go."

Hadleigh's arms flew out from her sides, spread-eagle, and she wadded handfuls of quilt in her fingers so she could remain anchored in the everyday world and because if she didn't, she might start tearing off her clothes.

She was fully dressed, except for her

shoes and socks, of course, and she was **burning,** aching everywhere. The danger that she might climax, and violently, before Tripp even got through fondling her toes and arches was deliciously real.

If that happened, there could be no lingering doubts—she, Hadleigh Stevens, was a weirdo, someone with a **foot fetish,** for heaven's sake, and God only knew what else. It stood to reason, after all, that if Tripp Galloway could make her feel like this just by rubbing her feet... Well, what would it be like when he really got down to business?

Some part of Hadleigh wanted to scramble for that tiny room in her head, once again take refuge there. Yes, she would be lonely and wistful, full of sad yearning, like a fairy-tale princess imprisoned in a tower—but she knew **how** to feel lonely and wistful. Sad yearning? No problem. What Hadleigh **didn't** know how to feel, what she wanted to pull back from almost as much as she wanted to fling herself, body and soul, into the very heart of the fire, was this wild, reckless passion. It was divine.

It was terrifying.

Tripp finally released his grasp on her feet, having reduced them to the consistency, it seemed to Hadleigh, of wafting smoke. He worked the snaps on his shirt, shrugged out of the garment, consigned it easily to the same oblivion that had swallowed his jacket.

The room was lit only by moonlight, but that was enough to see Tripp's magnificent upper body, his powerful shoulders, well-sculpted chest and the distinct musculature of his midsection. A faint, wheat-gold shimmer dusted his flesh, narrowed to a V at his navel and disappeared into the low-riding waistband of his jeans.

Hadleigh marveled, shocked into silence by the sheer beauty of this man's form, his bearing, the simple fact of his presence. Of course she'd seen Tripp without a shirt on many times. He'd been her brother's best friend, after all—and he and Will had often stripped to the waist to shoot hoops out in the driveway on hot summer afternoons, and certainly at the community-center pool or one of the local swimming holes. Not to mention the legendary water fights in Gram's yard, which invariably drew kids from all over town and finally morphed into epic battles involving buckets and hoses and squirt guns.

Oh, but **this** was very different. Hadleigh was no longer an adolescent girl, awkward and never quite sure how to stand or sit, what to do with her too-long legs or her bony-elbowed arms, for that matter, and Tripp was unquestionably a **man,** not a mischievous youth.

And here they were, alone, in her bedroom.

Yikes, Hadleigh thought, and then, **Hallelujah!**

Tripp reached out, without a word, and Hadleigh gave him her hands.

He pulled her gently to her feet, still the consistency of jelly, thanks to him, and Hadleigh's knees buckled instantly.

Tripp caught her with ease, held her up. His eyes glinted, and one corner of his mouth tilted slightly upward. "Okay,

Cinderella," he said gruffly. "Decision time. We make love. We don't make love. Check one."

Hadleigh answered by hauling her T-shirt off over her head.

With an audible catch in his breath, Tripp let his gaze stray from Hadleigh's eyes, pause briefly and tantalizingly on her mouth, and finally rest on the rounding of her breasts above the delicate lace of her bra. A low, taut exclamation escaped him, and he ran the tip of one index finger over the contours of her breasts, leaving tiny trails of invisible fire leaping along her nerves.

Hadleigh, admittedly under a spell and yet never more sure of who she was and what she wanted, boldly unhooked the front catch on her bra, letting her firm breasts spill into Tripp's view.

That time, he actually groaned.

Then he caressed Hadleigh and chafed her nipples with the pads of his thumbs until **she** was the one doing the groaning.

When Tripp bent his head to suck lightly at one of the nipples he'd so deftly prepared, Hadleigh gave a little shout and leaned back in pure surrender.

The sensations Tripp wrought in her, with skillful flicks of his tongue, with the warm, loving greed of his lips, made her feverish with need, frantic and impatient, even desperate.

When he'd finished enjoying her breasts—temporarily, she hoped—Tripp kissed Hadleigh, and something broke inside her, some reservoir of passion and femininity and glorious joy, too long contained.

Tripp, seeming to sense the torrent he'd released in Hadleigh, a primal flood of physical and emotional power that could not be stopped, managed, between hungry kisses, to get rid of the rest of her clothes as well as his own. Somewhere in this process, which was as elegantly graceful as a waltz, he put on a condom.

Although neither Hadleigh nor Tripp spoke, they tacitly agreed that this first time together, they would simply give in to the demands and directives of their bodies, separate and yet somehow already one. They'd simply surrender and ride the torrents and whirlpools, eddies and undertows, wherever they took them.

Tripp lifted Hadleigh off the floor, and she instinctively clasped her long legs around his hips, tipping her head back and closing her eyes, giving herself up to him, trusting him in a way she would never have trusted any other man.

He supported her easily, his arms strong around her, nuzzling her breasts, reaching the nearest wall in a couple of strides, bracing Hadleigh against it, cupping her buttocks in the palms of his hands and kissing her long and hard and deep, kissing her breathless. She whimpered, crazed with the need for him, all of him.

"Last chance," Tripp whispered after suckling at her earlobe and then the corresponding breast.

Hadleigh writhed against him, searching with her hips, with her softest and most vulnerable place, her breath coming in swift, shallow pants. "Now, Tripp," she pleaded. **"Now."**

With a long groan and a powerful thrust,

Tripp took Hadleigh, claiming her, conquering her and being conquered himself.

The first climax seized her instantly, a long, ceaseless clenching in the depths of her femininity, perhaps even her soul. She responded without reservation, without shame, without thought, a wild creature, her body flexing against Tripp's, over and over again,.her cries throaty and primitive and tremulous with a triumph that was at once new in that moment and older than the stars.

She sobbed his name, and he soothed her, murmuring to her, kissing her neck, her eyelids, the corners of her mouth. But even as Tripp consoled Hadleigh with tender words, with caresses, with more kisses, he gave her no quarter physically. Instead, he drove deeper into her, and harder, and the pleasure grew keener and then keener still, with every movement of their bodies. As soon as one orgasm began to ebb, and Hadleigh thought she might catch her breath, another fiercer one took its place.

By the time Tripp's control finally broke, and he surrendered at last, shouting her name, Hadleigh was spent. Her fingers buried deep in his hair, she let her softness and warmth encompass him, and wring the last measure of release from him.

CHAPTER TWELVE

Hadleigh awakened from a sated sleep, in the darkest hour of the night, aware that Tripp had left her bed. He was a shadow, groping for the clothes he'd discarded earlier, doing his best to be quiet.

She felt a brief and poignant pang that might have been sorrow or joy, she couldn't tell which; Hadleigh felt no need to identify and catalog it. "Leaving?" she asked, very softly.

Tripp turned, looked down at her, still shirtless, zipping his jeans. "I have horses to feed," he said.

Hadleigh was amused—at herself. What had she expected him to say? **It's been real—see you around. Don't call me— I'll call you?** "Need any help?" she asked.

Tripp, standing near the bedside table, leaned over slightly and switched on a lamp. In the glow, she saw a grin spread across his all-too-sensual mouth. He'd worked wonders with that mouth earlier in the evening, in the frenzy of their lovemaking. "I wouldn't mind some company," he said mildly.

Hadleigh, naked and tender in certain places, tossed back the covers, had second thoughts and covered herself again, blushing. "Give me fifteen minutes to shower and dress."

He smiled again. "I'll make coffee," he said. With that, he left the bedroom.

Hadleigh was grateful—she'd been anything but shy during the night, that was for sure, and while she didn't regret a single thing she and Tripp had done together, which was plenty, she needed a little solitude, time to put herself back together.

The moment Tripp was gone, she bolted from the bed, grabbed underwear and socks from the appropriate bureau drawers, chose a comfortable pair of jeans and a faded T-shirt from the shelves in her closet, then made a dash for the master bath. Like her bedroom, this space was her own creation, boasting a garden tub, two-sink marble countertop and an oversize shower equipped with a number of strategically placed sprayers.

Juxtaposed with the other rooms in that modest house, she supposed the spiffy bed-and-bath suite would seem a little incongruent to the casual observer. She'd needed a change after her grandmother— her last remaining blood relation—had died, and, when the will was read, Hadleigh had been stunned to learn just how much she'd inherited.

Okay, Gram had been the frugal type, a dedicated saver, but Hadleigh hadn't expected to have much left over after the final expenses were paid. She'd known that the quilt shop and the house were both mortgage-free—had been for years—but as it turned out, Gram had been tucking money away for decades. She'd not only banked most of the settlement she'd received when her son and his wife, Hadleigh and Will's parents, were killed in the car accident, she'd invested both her grandchildren's monthly social security checks in mutual funds. When Will was killed in action, his military life insurance policy had bolstered the family coffers even more; Hadleigh had assumed the bulk of that had gone toward her own college tuition, plus books, her dorm room and food.

She hadn't had a clue what was really going on.

For all those years, without a word of complaint, Gram had supported both Will and Hadleigh out of the often-skimpy profits the shop brought in, diligently selling fabric and notions, pattern books and a good many of her own creations, plus teaching quilting classes whenever possible. Just as Gram had taught her.

Remembering always choked Hadleigh up, sometimes a little, sometimes a lot, and that bright, cold morning after was no exception. While she'd never know precisely how many sacrifices Gram had made to see her grandchildren through to adulthood, she could make a pretty good guess.

When Alice Stevens's friends, mostly middle-aged women like herself, widows or divorcées, had gone on trips together, pooling their funds to charter buses and heading out to destinations like Branson, Missouri, or Reno, or the Grand Canyon, or even Disneyland, she'd always stayed behind. The others would plead and cajole, but Gram refused every time, albeit with a pleasant smile. She had no business gallivanting around the country, she'd tell anybody who asked, because she had a store and two mischief-prone kids to look after, in case they'd forgotten.

There were plenty of other economies, too, both large and small. Gram, a fine seamstress, had sewn all her own clothes and many of Hadleigh's. She'd diligently clipped coupons out of the newspaper and kept a hawk's eye out for sales, worn the same two or three pairs of shoes, the "sensible" kind, of course, for years, raised a bumper crop of backyard vegetables every summer, canning plenty for winter, and never, as far as Hadleigh could recall, splurging on so much as an extra tube of lipstick or the red-hot bestseller everybody in her garden club was raving about.

Oh, no—not Gram. She owned one lipstick, purchased at the discount store, and used it up completely. All the books she read came from the public library, stacks of them. She'd declared that it wouldn't kill her to wait her turn for the potboiler du jour. She'd probably gone to a grand total of three movies since the day Will and Hadleigh moved in with her, and if anyone asked, she'd surely have said it was foolish to pay good money when there was popcorn in the pantry and plenty of programs on TV.

Except that Gram had **loved** movies.

With a sigh, Hadleigh stepped into her fancy shower. **All of that's over and done with,** her grandmother would have said. **There's no changing anything now.**

Besides, even if she and Will **had** understood how much Gram was denying herself back then and lodged a protest, that stubborn old woman would've gone right ahead and done things her way anyhow.

The insight made Hadleigh smile, and her thoughts shifted to Tripp and the night just past. Even over the running water, she could hear him in the kitchen, talking to the dogs, opening and shutting the back door, taking crockery from the cupboard.

She'd been living alone for quite a while now, and it was just plain nice to have somebody else around. All the better if that somebody was Tripp Galloway.

Damn, but the man's good in bed.

Good out **of bed, too.**

That reflection brought on a kind of visceral instant replay, and delicious tingles raced under Hadleigh's flesh from one nerve ending to the next.

Whoa! Back, girl, she silently told her wanton self, enjoying another rush of tiny thrills. **You heard the man. There are horses to feed.**

She finished her shower, wrapped herself in a towel, stepped over to the sink and brushed her teeth. She hadn't shampooed her hair because then she would've had to blow-dry it, too, and that would have taken more time than she wanted to spend. So she just combed out the tangles, twisted it into a knot on top of her head and secured it with a clip.

After dressing quickly, Hadleigh applied a light coat of mascara and some pink lip gloss—heavy makeup, for her—and walked to the kitchen at what she hoped was a sedate and dignified pace.

Knowing Tripp would be there, love-rumpled and sexy, she could hardly keep herself from breaking into a sprint. Mustn't seem too eager, though!

Except she **was** eager—way, **way** beyond eager, in fact.

She froze in the doorway, stricken by the sight of him, even though she should have been prepared. He seemed to fill the room with his presence.

She noticed that his beard was growing in, a golden stubble, impossibly sexy.

Honestly, if he'd made a move toward her—any move at all—Hadleigh would have gone hurtling into his arms. It was a memorable moment, the kind that freezes time, stops the universe in its tracks, starts it going again with a wild lurch. And yet, conversely, everything seemed so...well, **normal.**

On the counter, the coffeemaker chugged away and two mugs waited to be filled. The dogs, back inside, coats dewy from their backyard foray, stood side by side, chowing down on separate bowls of kibble. Looking at them, a person would think they'd been together from puppyhood on.

Tripp grinned that crooked little grin that always made Hadleigh's stomach flutter as though it had just sprouted wings and might take flight a heartbeat later. "You're beautiful," he told her, husky-voiced.

Hadleigh was ridiculously flattered—she knew she was attractive enough, but beautiful? Not quite.

Melody was beautiful.

So was Bex.

She, however, fell somewhere between presentable and pretty.

"Is that a line?" Hadleigh asked, with a mischievous rise of one eyebrow and a crooked grin of her own, before making a production of gesturing down at her well-worn jeans, grubby sneakers and old T-shirt.

Tripp laughed. "No," he replied. "I don't use lines. They're too cheesy—the sort of thing you'd expect from a paunchy guy wearing a slew of gold chains and a two-tone hairpiece."

"Well," Hadleigh mused, after pretending to consider the situation from every angle, "you're definitely not paunchy, and I can't image you in any kind of jewelry, let alone a toupee."

"That's good," Tripp said. "Because if you **could** imagine those things, I wouldn't give two hoots in hell for our chances."

She was still hovering in the doorway, like a damn fool, pretty much unable to move in either direction and damned if she'd let Tripp Galloway know it.

"What happens now?" she asked.

"We head out to the ranch, feed the horses and then I make you some breakfast?" Tripp suggested, with a twinkle.

"That isn't what I meant." Why couldn't

she move?

"What **did** you mean, then?" Tripp responded. He was enjoying this, the wretch.

Suddenly, Hadleigh felt thirteen again, gawky and awkward, with knobby knees, pointed elbows and a mouth full of braces. She felt heat surge into her face and locked her back molars together, refusing—**refusing**—to answer.

Tripp crossed to her, took hold of her shoulder with one hand, raised her chin with the other. "This is important, Hadleigh," he said, sounding grave now, his eyes tender and a little wary. "I don't want to screw it up by moving too fast."

She stiffened. Maybe she wasn't experienced at these things, a hot-to-trot hoochie-coochie mama, like the women Tripp was probably used to dating—hell, sleeping with—but she knew a brush-off when she heard one.

At her expression, Tripp narrowed his eyes. **"What?"** he asked, sounding beleaguered.

What, indeed? she thought. She and

Tripp were consenting adults; they'd spent half the night having seriously incendiary sex. And while that might have meant happily-ever-after in Hadleigh-world, or some fairy tale, this was **reality.**

Tripp looked pained, instead of angry, as Hadleigh had half expected him to be, and he was still holding her chin. "I said I didn't want to screw things up between us," he reminded her reasonably. "But I'm guessing you heard something else entirely."

"You think we're moving too fast?" Hadleigh practically choked on those words, words she'd had no intention whatsoever of saying at any point in time.

Tripp sighed heavily, shook his head. "No," he answered. "It's been a long and winding road to get here, though—to get to right now, this moment, I mean—and if I have any say in it, we're not going back to square one."

"Okay," Hadleigh said, confused and unable to hide the fact. "So is there a plan?"

He grinned again, and it was like seeing

the sun suddenly come out on an otherwise cloudy day. "Does there always have to be a plan?"

"I just like to know what to expect, that's all," Hadleigh told him.

Tripp inclined his head, and his mouth was very close to hers, so close that the faintest pulse rose to her lips. "Fair enough," he said. "You can expect a lot of kissing. Like this." He kissed her softly, but in a way that sent a charge of anticipatory energy surging through her like diffused lightning, and drew back long before she was ready. "And you can expect me to make love to you every chance I get," Tripp went on, his voice barely above a murmur, his eyes dancing. "Shall I tell you more? Maybe run down the list of all the places I plan on having you?"

Hadleigh went hot all over, so hot she thought she might actually faint from the rush. "Umm, no," she managed, cheeks blazing. "I'd rather be surprised."

At that, he threw back his head and gave a shout of delighted laughter. When he'd recovered, he kissed her again, lightly and briefly, like before. "We need to get going," he told her.

"Because the horses are hungry?" she asked, slipping her arms around Tripp's neck.

Tripp groaned as their bodies pressed together. "That and one other thing."

"What?" Hadleigh teased in a sultry whisper.

"We're out of condoms," Tripp replied with another groan.

This time, it was Hadleigh who laughed.

Tripp liked having Hadleigh with him, watching her gamely schlepping flakes of hay to various feeders in the barn, speaking gently to each and every horse, scratching behind their ears when they acquiesced to lower their big heads over the door of their stalls so she could reach them.

The construction crews hadn't arrived yet—it was still early—but the place would be swarming with them soon enough. He tried not to think about the plumbers and the roofers and the electricians and the painters. For now, it was just him and Hadleigh, the two dogs and the horses, and he liked it that way.

He could imagine Hadleigh living here, sitting across the table from him at meals, sharing his bed at night.

No need to imagine that, he reflected silently, wryly amused. After last night, he'd never have to wonder about that particular experience again, because he **knew** how it would be, making love to Hadleigh. It would be like nothing he'd ever felt before; it would turn him inside out, send him soaring, drive him right out of his mind—**and** make him want her all over again, practically the instant she'd called out his name, dug her fingernails into the muscles of his back and thrust her hips upward, the better to take him in. She sighed when she reached that last climax—Hadleigh was a multiple-orgasm kind of woman—and her whole body quivered. A moment later, she'd make a long, sweet crooning sound, and her body would tremble again as she descended, ever so slowly, from the heights.

And that little cry, and the way she tightened around him, would be his undoing. He'd drive deep, unable to hold back the primal response of his body or the hoarse shout she'd wrung from him, before he finally collapsed beside her, satisfied and exhausted.

Oh, yeah. He'd been satisfied, all right, down to the very core of his being—except for his awareness of the condom. It wasn't that the thing lessened his pleasure; these days, prophylactics were thinner than skin and engineered to do the job. No, it was the **efficiency** of space-age protection that bothered Tripp.

Why? Because for the first time in his life, he **wanted** to make a baby—with Hadleigh.

Fat chance of that, Cowboy, he told himself, as he brushed down the mare he'd bought at the auction, along with the two geldings, the chestnut and his favorite, the paint called Apache.

"What's her name?" Hadleigh's question startled him. Turned out she was standing just on the other side of the door to the buckskin's stall, smiling as she admired the mare.

Tripp, oddly distracted, mused for a moment or two. "I guess I don't know," he finally admitted. "Nobody mentioned a name, and there was nothing on the bill of sale, either."

Come to think of it, the same was true of the chestnut. He'd had a formal introduction to Apache, but the mare and the other gelding could have been called just about anything.

Hadleigh made a face, a cross between a wince and a grin. "Men," she said. "Animals need **names,** Tripp—just like people do. It gives them…well, an **identity,** so they can feel as though they belong."

Tripp ventured a grin, thinking he'd love this woman three week beyond forever. Why had it taken him so damn long to realize it?

"If that's so," he drawled, setting the grooming brush aside, "then I guess you'd better decide what we're going to call this little buckskin." He frowned thoughtfully. "And the chestnut could use a handle, too, if you're feeling creative."

Hadleigh smiled. "Of **course** I feel creative," she said. "I'm an artist. I design quilts for a living."

Tripp stood just on the other side of the stall door from Hadleigh, so close he could have kissed her. "Okay." He capitulated affably, although his voice came out sounding scratchy, because he was thinking about the way she'd moaned and called his name when she'd first started to climax. He'd have liked to carry her straight into the house to his bed—or, better yet, have her right there in the breezeway, standing up. Or on the pile of fresh, wood-scented shavings he'd had delivered a few days before. He had to pause, clear his throat—and his head, which proved to be a little more difficult. "Have at it."

Hadleigh looked past Tripp to the buckskin mare, evidently pondering the possibilities. After a moment or so, her face lit up. "Sugarplum," she said, clearly pleased with the choice.

Tripp sighed, even as he grinned at

Hadleigh's expression. "Can't do it," he said with cheerful regret.

"Why not?"

"Because no self-respecting Wyoming cowboy is going to walk out into the pasture on a summer morning and yell, 'Hey, Sugarplum,' that's why."

Hadleigh looked benignly exasperated. "That's silly."

"Maybe so," Tripp replied with a shrug, "but that's the way of it. I call a horse by that sissy-assed name, and I'll be laughed out of the county."

"Fine," Hadleigh said, hands on her hips. "**You** name her, then. Something suitably macho, like 'Killer' or 'Spike'— and never mind that she's a girl."

Tripp chuckled. "She's your horse," he said. "You can call her whatever you want."

"Except Sugarplum," Hadleigh retorted.

"Except Sugarplum," Tripp confirmed.

"Oh, for Pete's sake."

"The chores are done," Tripp said. "Let's go inside and have some breakfast. That'll give you time to think up a name we can both live with."

The realization struck Hadleigh visibly, if belatedly. "Did you say she's **my** horse?"

Tripp nodded. "That's what I said."

"You bought this horse for me?"

"Let's just say I could picture you riding her, right from the beginning. Giving her to you was...an impulse."

"Fairy Dust," Hadleigh almost crowed. It took Tripp a second or two to register the awful truth—impossible as it seemed, Hadleigh had just come up with an even worse name for the critter than Sugarplum.

"Ah, no," he said.

"Tinkerbell?" She was ribbing him now; he knew that by the twinkle in those amber-gold eyes.

"Oh, come on," Tripp protested, opening the stall door and stepping out to join Hadleigh in the breezeway.

Half an hour later, in the messed-up ranch house kitchen, over bacon and scrambled eggs, they finally settled on a name for the mare. Sunset.

"Because she's golden," Hadleigh had said, beaming. "Like the first evening light on a summer day."

"Sunset it is," Tripp had agreed. **I love you, Hadleigh Stevens. I want to wake up beside you every morning of my life, and go to sleep next to you every night. I want to make a baby with you. Hell, I want to make a** dozen **babies with you.**

Of course he couldn't say any of those things—not yet, anyway.

"How long since you've been in the saddle?" he asked instead, when they'd cleared the table and rinsed their plates and utensils and coffee mugs under the kitchen faucet, a combined effort that involved some hip and elbow bumping. The new dishwasher was still in its box.

"It's been a while," Hadleigh said. An impish grin curled the corners of her mouth and made her eyes sparkle. "**Or** we could drive into town and pick up a fresh supply of condoms."

Tripp laughed, then made a show of looking at the watch he wasn't wearing. Since the advent of smartphones, he rarely bothered to buckle on the only one he owned, a college graduation gift from Jim. "The crews will be here any minute," he said, turning her toward the door and giving her curvaceous backside a little swat. Then, carefully, with the condom suggestion lingering in his brain, he added, "You're using some kind of birth control, right? Taking the pill?"

"Why would I do that?" Hadleigh asked, looking back at him over her shoulder and nearly tripping over one of the dogs as Ridley and Muggles squeezed past them, zipping out onto the side porch. "I'm not sleeping with anybody."

It was, of course, good news, though Tripp had no illusions that one night of over-the-top lovemaking indicated immediate or lifelong monogamy.

"Well," Hadleigh clarified, stepping out onto the side porch, "not with anybody besides you, anyhow."

Tripp took her hand, his grip a little tenuous at first, but when she didn't pull away, he gave her fingers a light squeeze. "That's good," he said. **Let's keep it that way.**

The dogs frolicked on either side of the couple as they walked toward the barn, eager for an outing. With that distinctive canine attitude they probably didn't care about the destination **or** the process, provided they got to go along.

The sun was barely up, spilling pinkish-apricot light over the craggy peaks of the mountains, and the air, though chilly, was pure in the way only country air can be. The sky, still a dark lavender, eased toward that heartbreaking shade of pale blue Tripp would always associate with Wyoming.

"Bex is throwing a party on Saturday night," Hadleigh announced, and then looked away, evidently overtaken by shyness. Tripp saw her exquisite throat move as she swallowed.

"Yeah," he said, wanting to help her over this awkward moment. "I know."

Hadleigh stopped as they reached the entrance to the barn and looked up at him. "She invited you?"

"Yep," Tripp acknowledged. "Is that a problem?"

Hadleigh pondered the question. "No," she said. "It's just that Bex didn't mention it."

Tripp grinned, interlaced his fingers with hers. "In other words, she didn't warn you that I might be there?" he prompted.

Hadleigh hesitated, biting her lower lip.

"Could be," Tripp suggested gently, "that she was afraid you wouldn't show up, if you knew you'd probably run into me."

"I wouldn't miss this party for **any** reason," Hadleigh insisted with a touch of indignation. "Bex has accomplished something incredible, turning one little fitness club into a **national** franchise operation. That's worth celebrating. What bothers me is...well, I'm feeling a bit **ambushed**."

Tripp raised her hand to his mouth, ran his lips lightly over the backs of her knuckles and enjoyed the shiver of electricity that zipped through Hadleigh and then arced over to sizzle in his flesh, as well. "If you'd rather I didn't go to Bex's party," he told her, "I'll stay away."

"No," Hadleigh immediately protested, her eyes troubled. "Don't skip the party, please."

Tripp grinned again. "So it's a date?" he asked, and though she couldn't have known it, he held his breath while he waited for her answer. "We'll go together?"

Hadleigh's laugh was a bright, lovely sound. "**That** was slick," she said.

Tripp simply waited, watching her face, feeling much like he had the day he'd made his first solo flight—as though he'd sprouted wings of his own, as though he owned the sky. The sensation was so intense that the backs of his eyes scalded and his throat tightened.

Good thing it was Hadleigh's turn to speak, because Tripp wasn't sure he could.

"Okay," she finally conceded. "Okay, we'll do it." She blushed. "I mean, we'll go to the party together." Another pause, another hard swallow that made Tripp want to kiss the pulsing hollow in her throat. "This time, it'll be a real date."

Tripp only nodded.

An hour later, when they'd finished the barn chores and he'd saddled both

Apache and Sunset, Tripp and Hadleigh led their horses out into the late September morning. By then, they'd agreed to name the chestnut gelding "Skit," which was short for skitter, since the critter was so fidgety.

Hadleigh gamely stuck one foot into the stirrup, gripped the saddle horn and hauled herself up onto Sunset's back, and while the effort was awkward, and there were a couple of brief hitches along the way, Tripp knew he'd been right to stand back and let her do this on her own.

All he did was hold the reins—Hadleigh was an independent woman, after all, and she had her pride. He loved her for those qualities, among many others, although he had no doubt they'd lead the two of them into some head-butting matches in the years ahead.

"I guess I'm a little rusty," she confessed once she was settled squarely in the saddle, looking down at Tripp.

"You're doing just fine," he told her, separating the reins, passing the first one beneath Sunset's neck for Hadleigh to take, then handing up the second.

She immediately looped both of them around her left hand.

Tripp, about to turn away and swing up onto Apache, paused to tug the reins free of Hadleigh's white-knuckled and slightly sweaty grasp. "One in each palm," he said easily and, he hoped, diplomatically. Respecting Hadleigh's dignity was important, but so was her safety. "Hold them firmly but loosely—and **never** wrap them around your hands. If you got thrown for any reason, and you were all tangled up in the reins, you'd be dragged."

Hadleigh nodded and held the leather straps correctly. "Like this?"

"Like that," Tripp replied. "You want a firm grip, for sure, but an easy one, too. Horses are mighty perceptive, and they pick up on even the subtlest signals from anybody riding or handling them. If you're spooked, **they'll** be spooked. If you're in control, they'll know it right away, and most of them will respect that."

"Most of them?" Hadleigh echoed, a bit nervously, once Tripp was in the saddle.

Apache, a born Pegasus, was sidestepping a little in his eagerness to fly.

Tripp grinned over at Hadleigh, leaned to pat Apache's neck in a way that conveyed his message. **Not today, boy.**

"Sunset there is real gentle," he reassured Hadleigh. "I wouldn't have let you get within a city block of her if I thought otherwise."

For a fraction of a moment, she looked puzzled by this last statement, and Tripp wondered if she was thinking the same thing he was: that, as a woman, she'd been on her own from the get-go. As a little girl, she'd had her parents, of course, and then, after the accident, her grandmother and Will had definitely been there for her. It went without saying that Melody Nolan and Bex Stuart were true friends with Hadleigh's best interests at heart.

But for Hadleigh, it wasn't enough.

Tripp had an old-fashioned streak, and he would have been the first to admit it, but he wasn't so behind the times that he thought a woman needed a man to be whole and happy—or vice versa, for that matter. What he **did** believe was that, for some people, life wasn't quite complete without a partner, someone to laugh with, to console and be consoled by, someone who didn't necessarily agree and wasn't afraid to argue a point, but still treated the other person's ideas with respect.

Without respect, love wouldn't last, and trust was the other vital component.

Tripp was fairly certain Hadleigh respected him, even loved him. But did she **trust** him?

A little, he supposed; otherwise, she wouldn't have let him make love to her, wouldn't have responded so fully and so freely.

Wouldn't have made love to **him,** as she most certainly had.

Tripp had had sex with plenty of women, but he knew now that he'd never **made love** with any of them—until Hadleigh.

The thing was, "a little" trust wouldn't, to use one of Jim's favorite phrases, cut the mustard—not this time. The stakes were too high.

And the insights didn't stop there. In previous sexual encounters, even during his brief and tempestuous marriage, Tripp realized, he'd thought mostly in terms of **tonight** or even just **for the moment.**

With Hadleigh, though, he was thinking in terms of **forever.**

All these things reverberated between Tripp's brain and his heart for the next couple of hours, while he and Hadleigh rode, following the creek for a ways, splashing across at a shallow place, cutting through tall but rapidly dying grass to check out the new hayshed.

Recently finished, the structure was sturdy, filled to the rafters with prickly, fresh-smelling bales. Hadleigh was beside him on Sunset, easy in the saddle now that she'd had a chance to reacquaint herself with the nuances of riding. Tripp adjusted his hat, admiring the workmanship, knowing the shed was built to hold up against fierce rainstorms, heavy snows, muddy springs and tinder-dry summers, standing the test of time.

He wanted the life he meant to share

with Hadleigh to be that strong, or even stronger, and he wouldn't settle for less.

Slow and easy, Cowboy, Tripp reminded himself, watching his woman out of the corner of his eye and thinking heaven itself couldn't have been any more beautiful than she was. **You've got to get this right.**

CHAPTER THIRTEEN

Two things happened the following Saturday morning—Tripp bought 150 head of Hereford cattle from a neighbor and old friend, and Jim showed up, riding shotgun in his lady-love Pauline's long, shiny RV. Pauline had flaming red hair and a smile Tripp could see even through the windshield.

When the RV horn bleated cheerfully, Ridley low-bellied it under Tripp's truck, and every horse in the pasture spooked, kicking and sidestepping and whinnying like crazy. There was a comical, circuslike aspect to the scene.

Tripp, working with the still unnamed chestnut gelding in the corral—the animal was a mite skittish around a saddle and bridle—paused to take this all in. He'd known about Pauline, known about the

RV, too, of course, as well as the couple's plans to get married and then hit the road for an indeterminate length of time. What he **hadn't** known was exactly when he'd run smack into the reality of his stepdad's new life.

He wasn't too sure, since he hadn't kept track, but it seemed to Tripp that they must have abandoned the cruise ship early. Perhaps, in their eagerness, he thought whimsically, they'd just jumped overboard and **swum** back to Seattle.

With a grin and a shake of his head, Tripp gave up trying to saddle the gelding and left the critter to its own devices there in the corral. With the bridle draped over one shoulder, he hauled the saddle and blanket over to the fence, rested them on the top rail, along with the bridle, and climbed over. The RV, well kept but certainly not new, shut down with an audible cough and a few rattles.

The doors on either side swung open simultaneously, and Jim bounded out on the passenger side, looking twenty years younger than when he'd left for the cruise, while Pauline stepped down from the driver's side, making use of the running board along the way.

Probably in her fifties, the lady had, as Tripp had already noticed, the kind of smile that makes a man take notice. And her body wasn't bad, either, come to think of it.

Clad in jeans, fancy sandals and an oversize white shirt with the tails tied into a knot at her waist, Pauline beamed at Tripp, clearly expecting a welcome.

Jim came around the front of the RV and slid an arm around Pauline's middle. His grin was wider than the Bliss River at flood tide, and his eyes shone with merriment and well-being.

"This is Pauline," he told Tripp proudly.

Tripp nodded. "So I figured," he said. If Jim was happy, he was happy; he'd decided that a few days back, after the background check he'd hired his air force buddy-turned-investigator to run. He'd vacillated on doing it, but in the end had gone ahead and done it. As he'd expected, Pauline's reputation was squeaky-clean.

As he approached, Tripp wiped his palms on the thighs of his jeans, well aware that he was worse than grubby, since he hadn't bothered to shave and had been working with horses most of the day. He put out a hand to Pauline in greeting. Instead of taking it, she stepped up, rose onto her tiptoes and planted a smacking kiss on his cheek.

"You must be Tripp," she said, stepping back into the curve of Jim's arm.

"Even if I wasn't," he responded with a twinkle, "I'd have said I was, just to get that kiss."

Jim looked pleased and more than a little relieved, too. He gestured with his free hand, taking in all the construction rigs, the crews still swarming over both the house and the barn, and pretended to frown. "This place is like a beehive," he mock complained. "And what's up with all those cattle I spotted out there on the range?"

"The construction is almost finished," Tripp replied affably. "As for the cattle—well, I bought those from old Pete

Helgeson, next door. Made for a pretty simple delivery, since all we had to do was take down some of his fence line and drive them through."

"What's wrong with Pete?" Jim immediately wanted to know, and this time, the frown was real.

"Nothing," Tripp replied easily. "He says he's too old to go 'chasing after a bunch of knot-headed cows,' that's all. I made him an offer, and he took me up on it."

Pauline gave Jim a subtle jab with one elbow.

Jim seemed baffled for a moment, then regrouped. He took Pauline's left hand and held it up to display the wide gold band she was wearing.

"I hope you won't think we jumped the gun, or feel slighted because we got hitched without you at the ceremony, but we just couldn't wait," Jim almost crowed.

Out of the corner of his eye, Tripp saw Ridley crawl out from under the truck and move cautiously in their direction.

Tripp's grin broadened. "I've only got one thing to say about this, Dad," he told the old man. "And that's congratulations."

Jim's chest swelled, and he let go of Pauline long enough to haul Tripp into a brief and manly bear hug. "I'm one lucky man," Jim said, grinning from ear to ear as his eyes misted over. He cleared his throat and said, "Now, if the two of you wouldn't mind my neglecting you for a few minutes, I think I'll have myself a look around, see what you've done to the old place while my back was turned."

Pauline slipped her arm through Tripp's and ushered him away from her bridegroom. "Jim's told me how much he loved your mother," she confided in a warm whisper. "She must have been a wonderful woman."

"She was," Tripp agreed, his voice going husky. "But she's been gone a long time, and Jim's been real lonely, going it alone. Mom would be glad he's finally found somebody to love, Pauline."

Pauline stopped, her arm still linked with Tripp's, and looked up at him, her green eyes shining behind unshed tears, her lower lip wobbling slightly. "Ellie meant the world to him," she said, "just like my Herb meant the world to me. And so do you, Tripp. No man ever loved a son more than Jim Galloway loves you."

Tripp's throat tightened, and he had to glance away briefly, get a grip on his emotions. "Well," he said huskily, watching as his dad stood a dozen yards away, with his back to them, checking out the barn with its new roof and paint job in progress, "it's mutual."

Ridley inched closer and shyly sniffled at Pauline's right knee, not just wagging his tail, but his whole back end.

She laughed and leaned down to muss the dog's ears, saying gently, "Hello, there, you handsome little critter. Does this mean we can be friends?"

As far as Tripp was concerned, Pauline's response to Ridley's tentative overture was far more telling than any background check. While he definitely believed good folks came in all varieties, including some who preferred not to keep pets for one reason or another, he didn't have much in common with that sort. They were usually a shade too worried about getting dirty to make for easy company, in his opinion.

Jim, apparently okay with the changes being made to the barn, turned and headed toward them, gesturing at the corral. "I don't recognize that gelding," he said, in his plainspoken way.

"Just bought him," Tripp explained. "Along with a paint called Apache and a little mare named Sunset."

"You've been busy," Jim remarked drily.

"Winter's not far off," Tripp reminded him. "Makes sense to be ready."

Jim chuckled. "That's my boy," he said. Taking Pauline's hand again, he led her toward the house. "I believe I'll show my bride through the house—that is, if I can still find my way around the place, given all the changes you've probably made."

Tripp nodded, slapped his dad lightly on the back. "I think you'll do fine."

"The man bought two dishwashing machines," Jim told Pauline. "Can you believe that?"

She laughed. "Sure, I can, you old fool," she teased with obvious affection. "This is the twenty-first century, you know. Two dishwashers would come in mighty handy when there's been a party, and at Thanksgiving and Christmas, too."

"We don't do much entertaining around here," Jim mused, looking in Tripp's direction, holding back a grin and yet obviously a little puzzled. "Leastways, not recently."

Tripp hung back, thinking he might be intruding if he joined his dad and Pauline in the house. "If you're still going on about the twin dishwashers," he called after Jim, "you're in for a hell of a shock when you see the main bathroom."

Pauline turned without pulling away from Jim's side and gestured to both Tripp and, ostensibly, the dog. "Come on inside," she urged cheerfully. "It's too early in the day for us to be doing any honeymooning."

"That's what **you** say," Jim joked, poking his nose into all that dark red hair for a moment.

Pauline laughed again and swatted at him. "You behave," she said in an undertone that carried.

Tripp was supposed to pick Hadleigh up for Bex's party in a few hours, and he still had chores to do before he could shower and shave and put on clean clothes, so he waved them off. "I'll be in after a while," he said.

Ridley, that turncoat of a dog, left him behind without a backward glance, trotting alongside Pauline as if he'd known her forever.

Tripp shook his head, smiling, and went back to the corral to put the chestnut gelding away for the day. After that, he saddled Apache and took a quick ride out onto the range to check on the new cattle.

They were making themselves right at home, it turned out, grazing on the last of the summer grass, drinking noisily from the creek. He and old Pete had already put the fence line back in place, though, like so many things, it would need replacing.

After that, Tripp rode back, put Apache away and brought the other horses in from the nearby pasture, leading them one by one into their stalls. He made sure the newly installed electric waterers were clear of debris and working properly, then added hay to the feeders.

All the while, Tripp had been thinking about Hadleigh. He hadn't seen her, except from a distance, since the morning after they made love, and her absence surrounded him, like some kind of void, a silence that pounded at him. Maybe she'd benefited from the separation, but it hadn't worked that way for Tripp. Sure, he missed the sex—**more** than missed it—thought he'd go crazy, sometimes, if he couldn't hold her, breathe in the scent of her hair and her skin, please her so thoroughly that she cried out his name, clutched at his back and shoulders, raised her body to meet his, seeking more and still more.

The sun was lowering by the time he started for the house, and it lifted his spirits to see lights glowing in the windows and to know he'd have somebody besides Ridley to talk to—for a while, at least. The construction guys had long since called it a day, taking their tools and their rigs with them, and the lumber stacked around the yard was almost gone, along with the paint cans that had crowded the side porch. At least now he could walk between the house and the barn without feeling as though he'd run an obstacle course.

Inside, he found Jim sitting in his customary chair at the kitchen table, going through the mail that had accumulated while he was away. Probably because he didn't shop online, or even own a computer in the first place, he still got a few regular letters, along with plenty of magazines and catalogs and, of course, junk.

Ridley lay contentedly at his feet, greeting Tripp with a roll of his eyes before shutting them again, but there was no sign of Pauline.

"Where's the wife?" Tripp asked, rolling up his sleeves and flipping on the water at the sink with a motion of one elbow, reaching for the familiar bar of yellow soap and scrubbing his hands and forearms, prior to the planned hot shower and careful shave.

Jim smiled and removed his reading

glasses, the rimless kind sold in drugstores and supermarkets. "She's plumb worn-out from driving all day," he replied. "She had a sandwich, took a bath and went to bed." Jim paused, looking solemnly at Tripp. "Something's different about you, son," he said. "What's going on?"

Tripp sighed contentedly, dried his hands on a wad of paper towels and faced his dad. "It would take me half the night to tell you," he replied, "and I'm due in town in a little more than an hour. Suppose we talk tomorrow?"

A sly grin broke over Jim's face. "Fine by me," he said. "But don't be surprised if I jump to a few conclusions in the meantime."

Tripp tossed away the used paper towels and laughed. "Such as?"

"Such as, you're in such an all-fired hurry to get to town because Hadleigh will be waiting for you," Jim answered, looking a mite smug. "Do I dare hope the two of you have finally woken up to the fact that you were meant for each other?"

Tripp cleared his throat diplomatically.

"Hope away," he teased. Mentally, he was already rehearsing the evening to come. He'd make a quick stop at the supermarket for another bouquet of flowers, along with a new box of condoms, which, considering that everybody in Mustang Creek knew everybody else—and way too well at that—would require some subtlety.

In her one communiqué, a text Tripp had received the night before, Hadleigh had asked him to pick her up at the shop, claiming she'd been neglecting her business and had some catching up to do.

"You have yourself a fine time tonight," Jim interjected, putting on his reading glasses again, pushing them up his nose and focusing on the letter he'd just opened. "I'll expect to hear about it over breakfast—provided you're back here by then."

Tripp gave a wry laugh and headed for his room.

Hadleigh had put in a busy day—**several** busy days, in fact—filming parts of the new how-to video she planned to offer, for a small fee, on her website. She'd helped customers, taught a beginner's class and done a sort of mock-up of her next project—a quilt so special, so personal, that even thinking about it made her heart beat a little faster.

When she glanced at the old-fashioned regulator clock on the wall behind the sales counter, a little gasp escaped her. Tripp would probably walk through the door in a few minutes, and she wasn't ready—not appearance-wise anyway. She hadn't seen Tripp in several days, although they'd spoken on the phone a couple of times, and she was **definitely** ready for an encounter of the face-to-face kind.

She hurried into the shop's tiny bathroom, stripped off her day-job clothes—a flannel shirt, the tank top beneath it, her sneakers, socks and jeans. That done, she stood at the sink in her bra and panties, splashing water onto her face. Her hair, caught on top of her head in a squeeze-comb, didn't qualify as a disaster, but it wasn't party-ready, either.

Hastily, Hadleigh dried her face on one

of the rough brown paper towels from the wall dispenser, smoothed on a layer of tinted moisturizer from her makeup bag and swiped some mascara onto her lashes. She decided to hold off on the lip gloss until she'd put on the outfit she'd brought from home that morning.

Any other night, Muggles would have been a concern, but a neighbor, who also volunteered at the animal shelter, was taking her over to Shady Pines Nursing Home for a visit with Earl. It was all part of an outreach program, designed to cheer up the residents of both the shelter and the nursing home, and Hadleigh thought it was a wonderful idea. Once visiting hours were over at Shady Pines, that same neighbor would bring Muggles back to Hadleigh's place and let her inside, using the key from under the doormat.

When Bex's party was over, Hadleigh would go straight home, where Muggles would be waiting for her.

She reddened slightly, realizing she might not be alone at that point, and shimmied into her new getup, a pair of sleek black palazzo pants and a long, slinky red shirt with a sexy slanted hem. The garments emphasized her curves without hugging them too tightly, and Hadleigh loved the way they felt against her skin, all gossamer and soft. She sat on the closed lid of the toilet to pull on some knee-high nylons before poking her feet into a pair of black velvet flats.

A distant knock distracted her, quickening her heartbeat and turning her breath shallow.

Tripp. He was here, and she wasn't ready. Her hair was still a mess, and she hadn't put on any lip gloss.

Hadleigh debated briefly, concluded that she couldn't have the man thinking she'd changed her mind about going to the party with him, or even that she was hiding out somewhere in the shop, hoping he'd go away.

After a moment of muttering, she called out, "Just a second! Be right there!" and dashed for the shop door.

There was a man on the other side, for sure, peering in through the glass, his hands cupped on either side of his face, a foolish grin wreathing his mouth—but it wasn't Tripp.

Of all nights, of all times, Oakley Smyth had decided to pay her a visit.

Hadleigh probably wouldn't have let him in, but he'd seen her, of course, and small-town etiquette demanded a more polite reception. She didn't hate Oakley, and she certainly wasn't afraid of him, but they didn't pal around, either. In fact, she'd seen him no more than half a dozen times since their almost-wedding.

Oakley was still handsome, if somewhat dissipated, in the way of the privileged and not particularly responsible—a rare commodity in Mustang Creek, where people were accustomed to taking life as it came, whether good or bad, pretty much without comment. Now the near-miss bridegroom let his eyes drift over her before stepping over the threshold, though Hadleigh hadn't actually invited him.

"Still beautiful," he said, putting almost no breath behind the words.

"This isn't a good time," Hadleigh

blurted. "I'm going out and—"

Just then, headlights swept across the shop windows.

Tripp.

Although he didn't turn his head to look back, Oakley seemed to know who was about to walk in.

"Are you afraid of him, Hadleigh?" he asked. "The pilot cowboy, I mean?"

"Afraid of him?" Hadleigh echoed, indignant. "Of course not." Impatience overcame her effort at good manners. "What do you want, Oakley?"

"Why are you so nervous if you're not scared of Galloway?" Oakley asked, causing Hadleigh to wonder if he was on pills or something; he didn't smell of alcohol but that didn't mean he was sober.

She was **nervous** because any encounter—or even the anticipation of an encounter—with Tripp made her nerves dance under her skin. And she was damned if she'd explain that or anything else to Oakley Smyth, her personal life being none of his business.

Tripp came in, slanted a quizzical glance

at Hadleigh, as if to make sure she was okay and finally turned to face Oakley.

In that instant, Hadleigh understood what was at stake. Everything—every-thing—depended on what happened next. If Tripp got violent with Oakley, or if he showed any sign that he didn't trust her, their relationship would be over before it had really gotten started.

Hadleigh held her breath, wide-eyed with alarm.

For a long moment, the two men watched each other, reminding Hadleigh of two rams fixing to lock horns any second.

Then Tripp's attention swung back to Hadleigh. He smiled one of his tilted smiles and asked, "Are you ready to go, or do you need a few minutes?"

Hadleigh gulped, so relieved she thought she might actually faint from the rush in her head. "I'm **almost** ready," she said.

"Good." Tripp's blue eyes were as peaceful as a cloudless sky. Then he handed her the bouquet of bright yellow, orange and white zinnias he'd been holding behind his back. "It was these or more roses," he told her. "And that seemed redundant."

Hadleigh's hands shook as she reached for the flowers, and a smile trembled on her mouth. Oakley might as well have vanished into thin air, like the proverbial puff of smoke. "Thank you," she said shakily. And then she raced for the bathroom.

When she came out, perhaps ten minutes later, Oakley was gone and Tripp wasn't immediately visible, either.

"Tripp?" Hadleigh called. She might have wondered if her Saturday-night date had ditched her, but his truck was parked in front of the shop and the faint soap-and-sunshine scent of his skin lingered in the still air.

"In here," Tripp replied from the back room where she taught classes, worked out designs and recorded the videos for her website.

She stepped over the threshold, carrying the bouquet, which she'd dutifully trimmed and put into a canning jar full of sink water.

She set the whole thing aside, feeling strangely, **sweetly** stricken.

Tripp stood with his back to her, studying the mock-up pinned to her huge design board—the sketch of the special quilt she hadn't shown anyone, not even Melody and Bex, because it might as well have been a map of her heart, it revealed so much.

Carefully, he raised one hand, traced the face of one of the figures she'd sketched on the oversize sheet of paper, torn from the roll she kept above her cutting table. The face he touched so gently was her own—in the sketch she was smiling, wearing jeans and a long-sleeved shirt and holding a blonde toddler, a little girl, on one hip. The other figure was clearly Tripp, and he, too, was holding a child, a boy, slightly older than the plump-cheeked girl. In the background, green rangeland unfurled, meeting a pale blue and cloudless sky at the distant horizon.

Although he had to know she was there, frozen in the doorway, Tripp didn't say anything. Instead he went on looking at the design.

When he finally turned around, Hadleigh's heart had wedged itself in her throat and her cheeks burned.

"Is this how you see us?" Tripp asked, so quietly she had to strain to hear him over the pounding in her ears.

Hadleigh bit her lower lip, found herself unable to speak and simply nodded.

That was when he smiled, and she knew she hadn't scared him off by putting her deepest dreams on paper in such an obvious way.

Tripp glanced back at the happy-family sketch, then crossed to Hadleigh and placed his hands tenderly on either side of her face. He gazed into her eyes for a long time before he spoke. "I love you," he told her solemnly. The grin flashed again, practically dazzling her with its summer-sun brightness. "But you might as well know right up front that I'm going to want more than two kids."

Hadleigh didn't know whether to laugh or cry, so she did both, and then Tripp kissed her, and kissed her again.

And they almost missed the party entirely.

The parking lot at the Moose Jaw Tavern had been cordoned off with red-and-blue crepe paper streamers, and the portable reader board, which usually listed the lunch special and the date of the next pool tournament, stood close to the unpaved street. Haphazard stick-on letters proclaimed **Private Party.**

There was even an attendant on duty, clipboard in hand, evidently checking names off a list.

The Moose Jaw was jumping, jukebox music pouring into the night at top volume, and cars, trucks and motorcycles were parked close together, like sardines in a tin. In Mustang Creek, the term **private party** meant everybody in the county was welcome. Furthermore, if some hapless soul crashed the shindig, he'd be handed a plate and told to get in line for the buffet.

Hadleigh glanced over at Tripp. A moment later, he knew she'd read his mind. "Bex gets a little carried away sometimes," she said.

Tripp drew up alongside the lot attendant, a local kid sporting an orange reflector vest and a self-important attitude. "Name, sir?" he asked.

The whippersnapper's father owned the local feed store, having inherited the business from his father, who had, of course, inherited it from **his** father, and so on. Everybody who worked there was a blood relative to everybody else, and the two families, Tripp's and the boy's, went way back. "I was Tripp Galloway yesterday afternoon, when you loaded all those bags of horse feed in the back of this same truck, **Darrell,** and according to my driver's license, I'm **still** Tripp Galloway."

Darrell looked up from his clipboard and then over at Hadleigh, who greeted him with a smile and a slight motion of one hand. He blushed, but his eyes narrowed slightly when he turned his attention back to Tripp. "Jeez," he muttered. "I'm just trying to do a good job."

Tripp grinned. "If you're grilling people

you've known since you could walk, boy, you must be mighty tough on strangers."

Darrell made a resolute check mark on his paperwork and, finally, grinned back. "So far," he admitted, "there haven't been any." With that, he got serious again, stepped away from Tripp's truck and waved him into the parking lot, impatient to deal with the next vehicle in line.

Tripp parked behind the tavern, not in the lot but in the alley. That way, he figured, there was a fighting chance that he and Hadleigh wouldn't find themselves blocked in if they decided to leave the party early.

"It's dark back here," Hadleigh observed, without apparent concern.

Tripp smiled. "Yeah," he agreed. "But I'll protect you."

He shut off the engine, got out of the truck, came around to Hadleigh's side and opened the door for her. For a few seconds, as she stood there on the running board looking down at him, her face aglow with moonlight, Tripp flashed back to the day he'd hoisted her over one shoulder and carried her out of the redbrick church.

"What did you say to Oakley after I left the two of you alone tonight?" she asked.

Tripp had expected the question; he'd just thought a little more time would pass first. Hadleigh waited calmly for his reply, still on the running board, a cowgirl goddess with stars catching in her hair.

Tripp sighed. "I asked him if he'd decided to take up quilting," he said.

Hadleigh made a soft sound that might have been a stifled laugh—or not. "And?" she prompted.

"He said he'd come by to say hello to you, that was all, but if it seemed there was a glimmer of hope you'd give him a second chance, he'd jump at it."

Remembering the brief conversation now, Tripp found himself respecting Oakley's honest answer, if not Oakley himself. "I said he'd have to ask you about second chances, because it wasn't my call." He paused, cleared his throat, went on. "I also told him I plan on marrying you, when and if you'll have me, that is. He said in that case, he might just show up right before we said our **I dos,** because that would settle a score."

It was hard to tell how all of this was going over with Hadleigh, because she didn't speak or move, and he couldn't make out her expression since the light from the moon and the stars and the back windows of the Moose Jaw Tavern was behind her. If he hadn't seen that sketch on the wall at her shop, he might have panicked.

Tripp sighed. Might as well bring this on home and be done with it. "I answered that if he did a damn fool thing like that, he'd better be ready for a fight, because I'd give him one then and there, church or no church."

Hadleigh rested her hands on Tripp's shoulders and he took hold of her waist, lifted her down. His heartbeat felt like blows from a sledgehammer, hard enough to bust right through his rib cage.

Looking up at him, she asked, "You want to marry me?"

He could only nod. His throat was dry

as sawdust and all his innards felt as if they were trying to shinny up into it at once.

"And you'd fight for me?"

Tripp forced himself to speak. "Lady," he ground out, "I'd do **anything** for you."

Her arms slid around his neck, and he could feel her luscious breasts pressing against his chest. "So did you just propose?" she asked in a sultry purr.

Tripp considered the matter, then gave a gruff burst of laughter. "Yeah," he answered. "I think I did. Since I don't have a ring handy, and I'm standing up instead of down on one knee, I guess it was a pretty back-asswards way of asking you to be my wife, so I wouldn't blame you if you wanted a do-over." A pause. "Just say yes," he added, and he wasn't laughing now; he wasn't even grinning.

Hadleigh tipped her head to one side, and he saw her lush lips curve into a little smile. Her fingers slid into his hair.

"All right, Tripp Galloway," she said. "Yes. Yes now, yes tomorrow, yes forever."

CHAPTER FOURTEEN

The following June

Hadleigh, Melody and Bex sat side by side on Bex's old-fashioned side porch on chairs they'd dragged out from the kitchen. They all wore shorts and tank tops of varying colors, and their feet, propped comfortably on the whitewashed railing, were bare. Their toenails were all painted the same naughty shade of pink—a throwback to the slumber parties of yesteryear.

The sun had just gone down, and the first stars were popping out, like the lights of some distant celestial city, winking on a few at a time. The summer air was cool, a blessing after an unusually hot day, and smelled of freshly cut grass, Bex's English roses and concrete sidewalks slowly drying now that most of the neighbors had shut off their sprinklers for the night. Kids played in nearby yards, their voices breathless and high-pitched as they rushed, in happy desperation, to have all the fun they possibly could before mothers or fathers called them inside for supper.

Muggles, lying on a time-tattered hooked rug next to Hadleigh's chair, lifted her head, perked up her ears and made a soft, whining sound, as though she longed to join in the end-of-the-day games.

Hadleigh smiled and reached down to pat the dog's gleaming golden head. "No worries, my friend," she told the animal. "One day soon, you'll have all the playmates you could want."

Simultaneously, Melody and Bex both took their feet from the railing and plunked them down hard on the painted floor of the porch.

"Is there something you aren't telling us?" Melody demanded good-naturedly.

"Like, for instance, that you're **pregnant?**" Bex clarified, as if Melody's meaning hadn't been perfectly obvious in the first place.

Hadleigh laughed, kept her feet propped up—she'd been on them for days, it seemed, tying up loose ends at the shop so she could take a few months off, having hired a temporary manager—and wriggled her toes. "Not yet," she said mischievously.

"You **know** all the old biddies will be checking off the months on their calendars," Melody said, "starting tomorrow. The truth **will** come out."

Hadleigh allowed herself a dreamy sigh. Tomorrow. The day she and Tripp were getting married. "So you two want to beat the 'old biddies' to the punch?" she teased. "Get the inside scoop?"

"Of course we do," Bex said, in all seriousness. She **did** have a sense of humor, but lately she'd been so busy traveling all over the country on franchise business that she practically met herself coming and going.

Melody elbowed Bex, but gently, though her entire focus was on Hadleigh. "You'd tell us if you were having a baby, wouldn't you? Your very best friends? The only two women in the world who love you enough to wear daffodil-yellow bridesmaids' dresses?"

"Organdy," Bex added darkly. **"With ruffles."**

"**Silk** organdy," Hadleigh pointed out cheerfully.

The aforementioned gowns, though bright yellow with, yes, the merest hint of a ruffle slanting across the skirt, were not the horrors Bex and Melody had scoffed at after seeing them online and in just about every bridal shop within five hundred miles of Mustang Creek. In fact, they were elegant, floor-length sheaths, with a sexy slit on one side, starting at the hem and ending at the knee, affording the occasional glimpse of leg.

When, months ago, after an exhaustive search, Hadleigh had finally settled on the graceful garments now hanging on the doors of both Bex and Melody's closets, carefully shrouded in cellophane, they'd given the choice a rousing thumbs-up.

And, being Bex and Melody, they hadn't missed a chance to razz Hadleigh about the dresses ever since.

"After Tripp," she said, "you'd be the first to know."

It was clear that Hadleigh's friends believed her. It was also clear that they were disappointed.

Melody sighed, then leaned over to rummage through her oversize handbag. She brought out three small red velvet boxes, letting one rest in her lap and holding out the other two to Hadleigh and Bex.

"I was going to wait until just before the wedding to give you these," Melody told them both before focusing on Hadleigh again, "but, much as I believe in girlfriend power, tomorrow should be about you and Tripp and your future together."

Hadleigh held the box, unopened, in one palm. Suddenly, she was choked up, and her vision blurred slightly.

Melody laughed, though she was tearful, too, then wrapped one arm around Bex and the other around Hadleigh and pulled them close for a moment.

"Remember the marriage pact?" she

asked.

Hadleigh looked down at the empty charm bracelet Melody had given her months before. It was the one piece of jewelry, besides her engagement ring, that she never took off.

Bex, as bewildered as Hadleigh, nodded slowly and held up one arm to show that she was wearing her bracelet, too.

"Open the boxes," Melody urged in a quiet voice. Her eyes, though dry now, remained luminous. Then she sniffled and added, "We have something to celebrate, and this is it. One of us is finally getting married."

Hadleigh lifted the hinged lid, peered into the box, and caught her breath, pressing the splayed fingers of her free hand against her heart. The charm, a tiny golden horse, running free, its exquisitely detailed mane and tail flying in an invisible wind, was perfect right down to its eyes, ears, nostrils and hooves.

"Oh, Melody," Hadleigh whispered. "It's so beautiful…"

Bex had the same charm in her box, as

did Melody.

Melody sucked in a breath, expelled it and sat up a little straighter in her chair. "Since you're the first of us to get married," she told Hadleigh, "you get the first charm. The horse is supposed to look like Sunset, but it also represents the freedom you found when you opened your heart and let all that dammed-up love loose, once and for all. That was a very brave thing to do, my friend."

"It was," Bex agreed, beaming. At the same time, tears trickled down her cheeks. "Is there anything scarier than being in love?"

Knowing the question was rhetorical, neither Melody nor Hadleigh offered a reply. In fact, Hadleigh was fumbling with the charm, eager to put it on her bracelet, but her fingers weren't working properly.

Melody finally did it for her.

A few minutes later, they were all wearing them.

"One for all," Melody said, "and all for one. I'll make matching charms for the three of us—unique ones, of course, representing each individual in some way. Then, wherever we wind up, together or apart, we'll have something to remind us that dreams come true."

"Just promise mine won't be a workout shoe," Bex said with a grin. "Or, worse, a teeny-tiny dumbbell—I might take that personally."

Both Hadleigh and Melody laughed.

"Seriously, Bex?" Hadleigh chided. "You actually think anyone in their right mind could ever consider you **stupid?**"

"Yeah, Ms. Not-even-thirty-and-set-for-life," Melody added. "You're brilliant, Bex. All the time we were growing up, you said you were going to be rich someday, and here you are. **You did it, girl.** And we are **so** proud of you."

Hadleigh nodded in sincere agreement.

But Bex looked wistful as she gazed down at her bracelet, fondled the dangling charm and asked softly, "Did you ever get something you thought you wanted more than anything else in the world, only to find out that it didn't really change anything? Not inside, where it counts."

"Group hug!" Melody cried, and the three women stood up, flung their arms around each other and clung. In a way, this evening was the end of an era.

And while Hadleigh knew they would always be best friends, she and Bex and Melody, there was no denying that, after tomorrow, things would be different, too.

Presently, they broke the huddle and retreated into the house, hauling the chairs as they went, because it was getting chilly and the mosquitoes were out.

Muggles dutifully followed.

Tripp opened his eyes to a bedroom full of blinding light and Jim standing over him, grinning like a damn fool and already dressed for the wedding.

In a nanosecond, panic replaced irritation.

"What time is it?" Tripp flung back the covers.

Jim chuckled. He'd filled out since he'd married Pauline and they'd taken to roaming the country like a pair of gypsies, sending a postcard from every national or state park west of the Mississippi, along with intermittent camera-phone pictures showing the two of them in front of geysers and on roller coasters or admiring the world's largest ball of string—and, once, memorably, standing next to a colorful sign that read, "See the Amazing Eighteen-Foot Reptile!"

"Relax," Jim said. "It's not even eight o'clock, and the wedding isn't until two this afternoon."

Tripp let out his breath, partly in relief, partly in frustration, and shoved his fingers through his hair. He worked as hard as anybody else, but since he'd hired a crew of reliable ranch hands, he didn't get up at the crack of dawn anymore.

He reached for yesterday's jeans, hauled them on and stood, letting his gaze run over Jim's spiffy three-piece suit. "Aren't you jumping the gun just a little?" he asked, but his mood was already improving now that he knew he hadn't overslept, missed the biggest event of his life and permanently pissed off the only woman he'd ever love.

Jim fiddled with his clip-on tie. "I thought I'd try this getup on, that's all," he replied affably. "Get your opinion."

"My opinion," Tripp said, unable to hold back the grin twitching at one side of his mouth, "is that you're a crazy man. The suit looked fine when Pauline picked it out for you, and it looks fine now."

Jim frowned, but his eyes sparkled with mischief. "I don't know," he said, musing. "Pauline's been baking a lot of cakes and pies since we got back here. The oven in the RV is about the size of a cereal box, so we don't eat near as many sweets when we're on the road, but I've been chowing down like there's no tomorrow, and that's a fact."

Tripp finally laughed, tugging a T-shirt over his head. "Did you wake me up to tell me you're worried about your weight, old man?"

"I woke you up because this is a special day," Jim said, and the humor in his eyes was gone, replaced by a solemn expression. "I thought maybe we should—well, have ourselves a talk, man to man."

"You're not planning to tell me about the birds and the bees, are you?" Tripp joked.

Jim shook his head, but the serious look in his eyes didn't change. "**That** horse got out of the barn a long time ago," he replied. Then he slapped Tripp on the shoulder and asked, "What do you say I swap out these stylish duds for some regular clothes and we saddle up a couple of horses and ride for a while, just you and me?"

Tripp was moved by the invitation—and a little worried. "Answer one question," he said. "Are you sick again?"

Jim's eyes widened. "No," he said, clearly surprised at the inquiry. "I'm healthy as—well, a horse."

Relief swept over Tripp like a tidal wave. "That's good," he said, thick-voiced and gruff. "I'll meet you by the corral in fifteen minutes."

Jim smiled, nodded once, as though he'd asked a question and gotten an answer he liked.

A quarter of an hour later, Tripp left the house, with Ridley beside him, and saw the Jim he knew, the one he remembered from as far back as his recollection went—the tough, able rancher with quiet ways and a soul generous enough to take in not only a spirited, stubborn woman, used to fighting her own battles, but her little boy, too. There had always been plenty of room in Jim Galloway's heart for the both of them, and even in Tripp's teens, difficult years when he'd been rebellious, moody and apt to run off at the mouth more often than not, when he'd needed to test the borders of his stepfather's acceptance, Jim's commitment to another man's child had never wavered.

He'd just gone right on loving Tripp, quietly, insistently.

In that moment, Tripp knew that if he could be as good a husband as Jim had been to his mom, and was now, to Pauline, if he could be the kind of father to his and Hadleigh's children as this man had been to him, he'd be getting the important stuff right.

He rustled up a grin as he walked toward Jim, who'd saddled both Apache and Skit, the chestnut gelding. What he liked best about the name was that Hadleigh smiled every time she said it.

"This Skit yahoo here," Jim said, "could use some work. I'm not even in the saddle yet, and he's already dancing around like a tenderfoot on a gravel road."

"Feel free," Tripp replied, swinging up onto Apache's back. "I've tried, but he's a hard case, old Skit. So far, he hasn't taken a liking to anybody except Hadleigh."

Jim mounted with the ease of a much younger man and adjusted his beat-up old hat. "Well, then," he boomed out, "there's hope for him yet. If he's cottoned to our Hadleigh, he's got excellent taste."

Tripp laughed, and they rode, passing through a couple of gates before they reached the range. The cattle had wintered well, and there'd been a healthy crop of calves in the spring.

"You've done a lot with this place," Jim said, when they'd covered some ground and the herd came into view. "Does my heart good to see it."

Tripp didn't answer, didn't figure he'd done anything more than he should have.

After all, he'd had plenty of capital from the start, the means to buy cattle and horses and make necessary improvements to the place. Jim, on the other hand, had held on to that ranch through good times and bad, year after year, often with nothing much to depend on besides his own grit, gumption and common sense.

They'd stopped to water Apache and Skit at the creek when Jim finally got around to speaking his mind.

"Pauline and me," he said, watching Tripp from beneath the brim of his hat, "we're fixing to sell the RV and settle down."

As far as Tripp was concerned, this was good news. He worried about the two of them, out there on the road, although he had too much respect for Jim's pride to say so. "Okay," he said, in a tone that encouraged elaboration.

Jim shifted in the saddle, stood up briefly in the stirrups as if to stretch his legs. "Thing is, we figure we'd rather be in town. 'Specially when winter comes on. Pauline's the sociable type, and she likes going to church and belonging to book clubs and the like. She's real taken with Mustang Creek, so I reckon we'll get ourselves a little house on a quiet street and live like city folks."

"What about you?" Tripp asked carefully. At least they hadn't decided to set up housekeeping in some faraway place. "You've lived on this ranch your whole life, Jim. It's your home—"

Jim interrupted with a sigh and a shake of the head. "Son, I've got a **new** life now, with Pauline. And I meant it, a while back, when I told you I've had my fill of bad winters and sick cattle and all the rest of it. If you don't want this place, that's one thing, but I think you do, hard as you've worked. And if I'm right, well, the best thing I can imagine would be to see you and Hadleigh turning this old spread into the kind of home it once was and ought to be again." The old man paused, brooded for a while and then grinned. "You'll see to that? Make sure I get some grandchildren out of the deal?"

Tripp **did** love the ranch; it was home,

pure and simple. Still, he couldn't see letting Jim just hand it over, especially when he could well afford to pay a fair price. He was about to say that, or something like it, when Jim frowned for real and held up a hand in a familiar bid for silence.

"I may not be rich," he said, his tone as stern and unyieldingly earnest as his manner, "but I've got all I need and then some. **Damn** it, Tripp, a man wants to pass something on to his son—you'll understand that one day. And I would've done the same for a daughter. I'm just hoping you'll respect my decision, because it isn't going to change."

Tripp was silent for a long time, absorbing what his dad had said. He'd heard a version of the speech before, soon after his return to Mustang Creek, but now realized he must not have registered how important this whole living legacy thing really was to Jim.

Sure, there was probably some cussed male pride in the equation, but there was a much deeper meaning beneath that, solid as bedrock. Handing down a ranch that had been in the family for generations, a place he'd worked and prayed and fought to keep, was a declaration on Jim's part: **You are my son.**

He'd said that often, right from the first. And he'd walked his talk, with never a misstep.

Tripp knew in that moment—in fact, he was downright thunderstruck by the insight—that he'd always held something back from Jim, that he'd been afraid to trust so profound a gift, believing it was what it seemed, too good to be true. Just beneath the surface of awareness, he'd considered himself an outsider, well treated but an outsider all the same, somebody who wouldn't have been there if he wasn't part of a package deal. He'd been a kid and he'd reasoned like one, concluding that if Jim loved Ellie and wanted to make her his wife, then, like it or not, that meant taking in her boy, too.

Well, damn it, Tripp thought, he wasn't a kid anymore, so there went that excuse. He was a man now, and he loved a woman,

Hadleigh, with his whole being, every breath, every heartbeat. And he knew for sure that if **she'd** already had a child when they decided to get married—hell, if she'd had a **dozen**—he'd have made room in his heart, just as Jim had done for him.

Because that was what a good man did when he loved a woman. He loved who she was now, and who she would become as the years passed—and he loved the person she'd been before he entered the picture in the first place, if only because being **there** had inevitably led to being **here.** If he'd found himself with a ready-made family, so much the better.

Jim spoke up, interrupting Tripp's ruminations. "You gonna give me an answer, son, or you gonna sit there staring at the creek for the rest of the day?"

Tripp had to look away for a moment, though he did manage a hoarse laugh that barely made it past his throat. When he met Jim's gaze, he was grinning. "All right, old man," he said. "You win. I'll take this ranch, and see that it thrives and be damn grateful to you for the rest of my days." He paused, swallowed. "And not just because you're handing the place over, either. I'll make you proud, Dad. I promise."

Jim pointed an index finger at him and said, poker-faced, "It so happens that I'm already proud—have been since the first time I laid eyes on you—but you see that it stays that way. You know I think mighty highly of Hadleigh. She's the daughter I never had, till now. You'd better be good to her, because you'll have me to deal with if you aren't."

Tripp turned his horse and rode alongside Jim, so they were facing each other, though pointed in different directions. He put out a hand. "I love that woman way too much to be anything **but** good to her," he said, his voice catching. "You have my word."

Jim took the offered hand, and they shook on it. Then Jim reached out, put his arm around Tripp's neck, and hauled him close enough that their heads knocked together. They both laughed and drew apart, but the old bond between them, formed long ago, still held, stronger than ever.

Different dress.
Different man.
Same church and, for the most part, same guests packing the pews, lining the walls and filling the choir loft. Same preacher, too.

Peeking out of the little room just off the sanctuary, Hadleigh wondered if Mr. Deever was wearing overalls under his ministerial robes, in anticipation of the chores awaiting him on his farm. But a second later, her attention was riveted on the man she was about to marry, standing straight and tall next to the altar, with Spence Hogan as his best man.

For the merest fraction of a moment, Hadleigh thought she saw Will, alive and whole and handsome in his dress uniform, in Spence's place, and she had to swallow back tears. Though she hadn't seen her, she knew Gram was there, too, sharing in the celebration.

Bex, looking seriously good in her much-maligned bridesmaid's dress, as Melody did in hers, tugged at the lacy sleeve of Hadleigh's bridal gown and whispered, "For Pete's sake, somebody will see you if you aren't careful!"

"Horrors," Melody said, with a smile and a roll of the eyes.

"It's bad luck," Bex insisted. "Nobody is supposed to see the bride before the ceremony—what if **Tripp** had glanced over here?"

"**We** see the bride," Melody reasoned. She slipped one arm around Bex's shoulders and the other around Hadleigh's. "And she's beautiful."

"**Don't,**" Hadleigh pleaded, blinking furiously. "If I cry, my mascara will run."

"Now that," Melody teased, "would qualify as bad luck."

They stepped apart, and Hadleigh lifted her right hand into a shaft of sunlight. The horse charm dangled, glowing, from her bracelet.

"The marriage pact forever," she said.

Bex and Melody both reached up, bracelets shining, and they all clasped each other's hands.

"Forever," Melody confirmed.

"Or until we're all married," Bex said. "Whichever comes first and, sometimes, I think it'll be 'forever.'"

Hadleigh leaned in, letting her forehead rest against Bex's. "Have faith," she whispered with a smile.

"Yeah," Melody agreed. "What good is a sacred pact if you don't believe in it?"

Before Bex could answer, there was a light rap at the door, beyond which was a short corridor that led to the church's small entryway. At Hadleigh's "come in," Jim Galloway stuck his still-handsome head into the room and winked at his future daughter-in-law.

"You ready, beautiful lady?" he asked.

Hadleigh smiled back at him. "I'm ready," she replied, as Melody and Bex moved in to fuss with her veil and fluff out her copious skirts.

Bex took the bouquets out of their boxes and handed Hadleigh the spill of yellow roses and ribbon and Queen Anne's lace, assembled by a local woman. She and

Melody would carry white carnations, accented with ribbons that matched their dresses.

Jim crooked an arm for Hadleigh, and she took it, feeling a swell of warmth for this man who already regarded her as a daughter. They followed Melody and Bex through the hall, Hadleigh's dress barely fitting between the walls and making a lovely rustling sound as she moved.

Once they'd gathered in the entry, alongside racks of pamphlets, carefully folded newsletters and collection envelopes, Melody stepped into the wide doorway and, that being the organist's cue, the music started.

For Hadleigh, everything and everyone seemed surrounded by a warm, golden haze. If this was a dream, she thought, she definitely did not want to wake up—ever.

Melody proceeded up the aisle, with Bex a few paces behind.

Then the first notes of the wedding march sounded, and, leaning on Jim's arm, Hadleigh stepped onto the threshold of forever.

When the congregation stood, Hadleigh wasn't looking at them, but **beyond** them, to the place where Tripp stood, waiting for her, that slight grin curving his lips.

Most brides probably remember their weddings in great detail, but that day, Hadleigh was the exception. All she could see was Tripp; even Mr. Deever had become a blur of robe and man and Bible.

Still, she managed to respond when it was her turn.

Did she take this man to be her lawful wedded husband?

She did. Oh, yes, she definitely did!

"Hadleigh?" Mr. Deever prompted, in a whisper.

"I do!" she cried exuberantly, causing a ripple of affectionate laughter to move through the congregation. They'd been a tense group, though Hadleigh wouldn't realize that until much later, when she watched the recording. They'd relaxed with a collective sigh and a slackening of shoulders only after Mr. Deever got past the does-anyone-object part of the ceremony.

No one did, of course, because everybody in Bliss County believed Tripp and Hadleigh were meant for each other, with the possible exception of Oakley Smyth, who was gracious enough to stay away. Or, in any case, smarter than most people would have given him credit for.

After the minister pronounced the happy couple husband and wife, and Tripp had raised Hadleigh's veils and kissed her with a thoroughness that would stir up gossip for months to come, the organist struck a triumphant chord.

Tripp, never a slave to tradition, swept his bride right off her feet and carried her down the aisle for the second time in a decade, a man in a hurry.

This time, though, she was in his arms, not slung over his shoulder.

And she was smiling, eyes brimming with joyous tears, mascara be darned, instead of kicking and yelling in protest.

The reception, held in the meeting room of the public library, directly across the street from the church, seemed endless to Tripp. He wanted to be alone with his wife, and that was pretty much all he could think about, which made him wary of standing anywhere but behind a table or any other waist-high object he could find.

He smiled for the pictures.

He and Hadleigh fed each other cake, and they were both feeling so rambunctious that the ritual nearly turned into a food fight.

The first dance was a combination of ecstasy and torment. At least, Tripp was holding Hadleigh in his arms. There was all that dress between them, but he still felt her soft, warm curves as surely as if they'd both been naked.

Finally, it was time to leave, and Tripp didn't waste a second. He grabbed Hadleigh's hand and headed straight for the nearest exit, much to the amusement of the guests, who probably planned on dancing till dawn.

Let them eat, drink and be merry.

Tripp had other plans, and they didn't involve a crowd.

Hadleigh laughed when her new husband bundled her, billowing dress and all, into the passenger seat of his truck, groped around until he'd located both ends of her seat belt and fastened it.

"This all seems strangely familiar," she teased. "Are we going to Bad Billy's?"

Tripp bent his head and nipped playfully at Hadleigh's lace-covered breast. "Not unless you want to stir up the mother of all scandals," he drawled, his eyes blazing blue as he looked into her face.

Hadleigh's decorum, none too sturdy in the first place, completely deserted her. She groaned softly. "I'm all for the stirring up part," she murmured, flushed, "but let's keep the scandal to ourselves."

"Good idea," Tripp said.

A moment later, he was behind the wheel and they were moving.

They hadn't planned a honeymoon trip, for the simple reason that they both wanted to spend their wedding night in their bedroom at the ranch house, not in some hotel. Home, after all, was where their story would begin.

Tripp drove like a crazy man, but they didn't quite make it to the ranch.

Instead, he pulled off onto a side road, parked the truck in a copse of trees and looked over at Hadleigh. "Well, Mrs. Galloway, if you're willing, I'm about to have you."

Heat surged through Hadleigh. "I'm ready, Mr. Galloway," she said.

Tripp got out of the truck, came around to her side, found the snap on her seat belt with some difficulty and lifted her down. They stood facing each other, in cool shadows and pine needles and sweet silence.

Hadleigh turned so her back was to Tripp, and he unfastened what seemed like nine million buttons, which took forever. Finally, though, Hadleigh stepped out of the magnificent dress and faced Tripp again, wearing only her silk petticoat, a delicate camisole with a built-in bra, stockings and garters. She'd slipped out of her shoes the moment she'd gotten into the truck.

Tripp made a strangled sound that thrilled Hadleigh, and, finally, he kissed her.

"My dress," she reminded him when she could breathe again. She wanted their daughters to wear that gown at **their** weddings, and maybe their daughters' daughters, too.

He bent, gathered up the mound of lace and silk and netting and seed pearls in both arms and shoved the whole works into the front seat of the truck. If Hadleigh hadn't already been half out of her mind with wanting him, she might have been puzzled by that. Instead, she watched, amused, as Tripp battled yards of fabric, which seemed bent on escape.

At last, though, he managed to get every scrap of skirt and bodice and sleeve into the truck and close the door.

"Wouldn't it have been easier to put it in the backseat?" Hadleigh asked, as Tripp returned to her.

"I have other plans for the backseat," he replied. With that, he opened the rear door, hoisted Hadleigh onto the seat, sideways, and slowly relieved her of both stockings and her garter.

By the time he'd bared her legs, she knew what he was going to do, and she lay down on her back, moaning as he slid the petticoat down over her hips and thighs, which were already parting for him. She'd delighted in teasing Tripp over the past couple of weeks, telling him she wasn't planning to wear panties under her wedding finery, and she hadn't.

It was payback time.

Tripp eased her legs apart, trailing whispering kisses along the tender flesh on the insides of her thighs, first one, then the other.

Frantically, Hadleigh undid the hook that fastened her camisole together, between her breasts, and shimmied out of it. She needed to be naked for Tripp **now,** and for herself, too.

She wriggled free of the last shred of clothing, and then she felt his breath on the most intimate, most sensitive part of her body. When he caressed her with his mouth, she arched her back and cried out with all the lust of the wild creature she became whenever Tripp made love to her.

She buried her hands in his hair, feverish as the pleasure mounted, already begging, wanting him inside her, deep inside her.

Instead, Tripp went right on savoring her, teasing her, driving her to a shattering climax, and then another. By the time he'd finished, Hadleigh was spent, so thoroughly satisfied that she could hardly move or speak. Soon enough, though, he would arouse her again, have her writhing and moaning beneath him or straddling him, or both. That was how it went on the rare nights when they hadn't already exhausted each other.

Right now, it was the latter.

Tripp got into the truck, arranged a crooning Hadleigh on his lap, alternately suckling and fondling her bare breasts until she bucked with need. Only then did he enter her, in a smooth, powerful thrust that brought her to instant orgasm.

She collapsed against Tripp when the climax subsided, resting her forehead against his shoulder while, gently gripping her hips, he raised and lowered her, murmuring soothing words, letting the tension build for both of them.

Soon enough, Hadleigh was rocking and groaning again, and Tripp drove deeper, moving faster and faster. When he came, it was with a throaty cry—her name—and that was when she reached the final orgasm, the most powerful one of all.

For a long time afterward, neither of them moved.

Tripp's hands moved idly up and down Hadleigh's back. "Somehow," he said, on a ragged breath, "it never crossed my mind that we'd end up consummating our marriage in the backseat of a pickup."

Hadleigh grinned impishly. He was still inside her and, if she had her way, there would be at least one more go-round before they went home. "Good thing you made an honest woman out of me today," she said, making slow revolutions with her hips, delighting in Tripp's groan. "Otherwise, I would definitely be compromised."

He moaned.

The revolutions continued.

"Damn it, woman," Tripp gasped, surging inside her. "Have a little mercy on a man."

Hadleigh bent to nibble at his neck, then his earlobe. "Not a chance, Cowboy," she replied, as he began to move beneath her. "This is going to be one long, **long** rodeo."

* * * * *